Praise f
The Alex Light

"I had a hard time putting it down last night and fell asleep
with my iPhone in hand. I really enjoyed the twist at the
end."
(Glen Lemert, Mystery Author)

"Funny and cute. Relatable characters. Interesting
photography aspects. Very real dialogue. I loved it!"
(Tennille Gilreath, Cozy Author)

"Well-written"
"Loved the witty banter"
"I look forward to reading more from [Kari Ganske] in the
future"
(Goodreads reviews)

Also by Kari Ganske

Alex Lightwood Series

Secrets in a Still Life

One Click in the Grave (*available Fall 2021*)

Bait and Click *(available Fall 2021)*

Lenses Leather and Lies
(aFREE for subscribing to Kari's Cozy Newsletter)

SECRETS
in a
STILL LIFE
An Alex Lightwood Mystery
Book 1

By
Kari Ganske

Blue Heron Press

Publisher's Note: This is a work of fiction. Names, characters, places, and incidents are the product of the author's imagination. Locales and public names are sometimes used for atmospheric purposes. Any resemblance to actual people, living or dead, or to businesses, companies, events, institutions, or locales is completely coincidental.

If you want more cozy mysteries, photography tips, and Alex Lightwood adventures, join Kari's VIP Readers Club
https://dl.bookfunnel.com/ssn3i8nmeh

To my beautiful daughters:

Camden and Avery

Chapter 1

In the middle of Rural Route 97, I sat pouting in my idling car, vacillating between forging ahead to my childhood hometown or crawling under a rock and hiding.

Forever.

This was not the triumphant return I'd imagined. No, this was the adult equivalent of a walk of shame. Riding back into town, not the successful one-who-got-out but, instead, with my tail between my three-weeks-overdue, unshaven legs.

I had left Piney Ridge, a teeny-tiny town in a teeny-tiny county in teeny-tiny Maryland, right after high school graduation. I crossed the stage, hung a left, and headed north to New York with no plans of looking back. Despite pleas from my family to stay, Piney Ridge was not the place to kick off what I hoped would be a successful photojournalism career. The biggest news headline to hit town during my childhood—"Escaped Cow Pins Mail Carrier Against Truck."

Well, except for my big brother Harrison who went missing at nine years old, but I tried not to think about that at all.

Sure, I'd been back to Piney Ridge several times in the intervening years. But those were just visits—with an end date. I'd been passing through on my way to the next great adventure. This time, however, I had an open ticket.

If I continued on my current trajectory, toward Piney Ridge, Harrison's disappearance wouldn't be the only ghost threatening to creep back into my life. Not that I cared to admit it, but I'd burned a few bridges when I left so quickly after graduation. And small towns weren't quick to forget past indiscretions. They thrived on gossip, absorbed the secrets of their inhabitants, cradled memories for generations. The more painful and salacious, the more power the small town seemed to have. And Piney Ridge proved the cliché. One of the many reasons I had chosen New York City—for its perfect, blissful anonymity.

On the other hand, finding a rock big enough to store my camera gear and my precious crowntail betta fish, Lashatelle Lady Gretchen, under would be near impossible.

I was still in a war with my right foot when two things happened in quick succession. First, my cell phone rang, startling me out of the solo pity party. Second, as I reached to silence it, a horn honked loudly behind me, scaring me into fumbling the phone and simultaneously floorboarding the gas pedal.

Right into the Welcome to Piney Ridge sign.

After impact, I batted the airbag out of my face and coughed from the dust. I checked on Lash—pronounced Lah-sh, not lash because she wasn't part of an eye—still sloshing around in her bowl and mean-mugging me, but otherwise fine. I opened the door to get out of the stench from the airbag, but my seat belt locked me in place. A cracking sound paused my efforts to unbuckle. I leaned forward in my seat to peer out the windshield. The large wooden Welcome sign above me tipped precariously backward.

Perhaps "sign" is a bit misleading. The town calls it a sign—specifically the Welcome sign—but size-wise it's somewhere between a billboard and the drive-in movie screen. It had stood for generations as a guidepost and landmark for giving directions, as a photo opportunity for proud mayors and out-of-town visitors, and as a reminder of the beautiful landscape from which Piney Ridge took its name. This was no metal highway sign. Oh no. This sign was carved from locally sourced wood and featured a once colorful, beautifully detailed depiction of the local reservoir and surrounding pine forest.

With a final crack and a sad, resigned, little shudder, the sign gave in to its injury and hit the ground with an echoing boom. A dust cloud formed around it and enveloped my car.

"Great. So much for sneaking back in quietly," I said into the dust.

"Holy Christmas! Are you okay?" a voice asked from beside me.

I jolted in my seat and turned to see the freckled face of a curly redhead staring back at me. Despite my less than triumphant return, I smiled. Those flaming red curls and emerald eyes could only belong to one person this side of the Mason-Dixon—my childhood best friend, Colleen McMurphy. Probably the one person, except my parents, genuinely glad to see me.

"Alex? Is that you?" she asked, waving her hand to try to clear the air.

"What gave me away? My exceptional grace and poise?" I managed to unbuckle, finally, and stepped out of the car onto wobbly legs.

9

Before I could move to the front of the vehicle to assess the damage, Colleen threw her arms around me in an exuberant embrace. "Girl! It's been too long since I last saw you!"

I hugged Colleen back. "Well, you'll be seeing a lot more of me now."

Colleen held my shoulders at arm's length, eyes wide with surprise and excitement. "You're really staying? Your mom hinted as much when I saw her at our book club, but I didn't really believe her. Especially since my best friend didn't say anything to me about it."

I winced. "Sorry. It happened kind of fast. I wanted to simply sneak back in. I would've called you when I got settled."

"Eh, I forgive you." She leaned back even more to look me over. "Besides a small cut on your forehead, you seem to be okay. Are you okay? That was quite a hit."

"I'm fine. A little shaky, but fine." I reached up to touch the cut. My fingers came away sticky. I wiped them unceremoniously on my leggings. Must have been from the airbag smashing my sunglasses against my face.

At least I hoped that was the crunch I heard and not my nose. I gently pinched the bridge between my fingers, but it didn't feel overly tender. Hopefully I wouldn't have two black eyes.

"What were you doing just sitting in the middle of the road?" Colleen asked. "I almost ran right into the back of you."

I shrugged. How to sum up all those feelings. "I—"

"Never mind," Colleen cut me off. "I know exactly why, Miss City Slicker. But you'll see that Piney Ridge isn't all that bad. Some of us are actually happy making our life here." She gave me a pointed look.

She still knew me so well. We could go months without talking, especially if I was on location for a shoot, but when we did reconnect, it was like no time passed at all.

"I know. My hesitation has more to do with a crippling sense of failure and less to do with the town. I'll get over it. I just need to wallow a little longer."

I moved away from Colleen to walk around the car and assess the damage. The front fender wrapped neatly around the sign pole. It didn't look terribly bad, but what I knew about cars could fit comfortably inside a change purse. I couldn't tell if the smoke came from the airbag, the lingering dust storm, or my poor, crumpled car.

Colleen joined me. "Not drivable. But probably not totaled."

"Goody. I guess I should call my parents for a ride." I gave another glance at the sign on the ground. "And the police."

"Funny you should mention the police," Colleen mumbled.

Chapter 2

That's when I heard the sirens. Yes, plural. A pang of homesickness for New York blew through me at the sound. Add the smell of exhaust and hot dogs, and I'd be home. The homesickness was quickly replaced by a different kind of queasiness.

Many sirens in New York? Totally normal.

Many sirens in Piney Ridge? Juicy gossip. Every busybody and their brother had a police scanner going nonstop in their kitchens. My grandmother, Nana Klafkeniewski—known lovingly as Nana K by everyone who can't pronounce her very Polish surname—included.

"Who exactly did you call?" I asked Colleen.

"Listen, I wasn't sure how hurt you were," Colleen said defensively. "So I asked for paramedics. And then I saw the sign wobble, so I suggested they also send a fire truck. And, of course, the police always respond to a roadside accident..." She trailed off as a shiny red fire truck screeched to a halt on the shoulder. Compared to the battered and dented New York City trucks, this one looked barely used. In fact, the only time I remembered seeing fire trucks were for the biyearly parades—Fourth of July and Christmas.

Colleen rushed to add, "To be fair, I didn't know it was you when I called."

The flashing lights from the truck illuminated the still settling dust from the sign's demise, creating a retro dance club vibe on the side of Rural Route 97. I squinted my eyes as the first firefighter emerged from the truck. He came into focus slowly through the dust and lights, one glorious muscle after another taking shape as he neared. His station-issued T-shirt fit snug across broad shoulders and sculpted abs. He might be the only man who looked good in suspenders. Maybe Piney Ridge did have something to offer after all.

"Is it too late to fake a more serious injury?" I asked Colleen, smoothing out my rumpled T-shirt. Even though I swore off men after my last experience, I wasn't dead.

She laughed. "Just wait."

"Wait for wha—" I started to ask. Then Mr. Bulging Bicep's face came into full focus through the dust. The sexy club music playing in my head scratched to a halt, replaced immediately with the Darth Vader theme. How fitting that one of my burned bridges grew up to be a firefighter.

Lincoln Livestrong—childhood nemesis-slash-best friend-slash-silly crush-slash-broken heart-slash-biggest regret. We'd been thrown together all throughout our school years due to the alphabetical proximity of our last names. A fact that at first annoyed me and then pleased me and then annoyed me again as we aged.

"Sexy Lexi. I should have guessed," he said, using the old nickname I hated. His eyes lit with amusement; one corner of his mouth hitched into the annoyingly adorable smirk I wrote embarrassing poems about in high school.

"Lincoln Towncar," I returned. Two could play the nickname game. "Who else is gonna show up? We might as well make it a high school reunion."

"What did you do?" His deep, rich voice was equal parts amused and astonished.

"I'm redecorating." I crossed my arms over my chest and popped a hip defiantly.

He moved his steel-gray eyes from the sign back to me. He gave me a quick once-over—no doubt clocking the ketchup-stained shirt, worn-out leggings, mismatched flip-flops, and road hair—then zeroed in on my forehead.

"You're bleeding." He encircled my wrist in his large hand.

"I can wait for the paramedics, thanks," I said, trying to pull out of his grasp. He held on tighter, dragged me over to the fire truck, and deposited me firmly on the back fender.

He smirked again. "You're looking at the paramedic. It's a small town. We all fill many roles," he added with a chuckle. "Sit. I'll get the first-aid kit."

I was about to tell him where *he* could sit when a fluff ball that might be a dog—or maybe a Muppet—laid a head on my lap and snuffled my hand. The tension and snark that filled me so completely a moment ago vanished, and I melted into a big pile of goo.

"Hello, there," I cooed in a voice all women reserved for babies and puppies. "Where did you come from?"

"That's Fang," Linc said as he walked away.

"Aren't you a sweetie?" I buried my hands in his soft fur. He drooled on my leg. The dog was so furry, I couldn't even tell if it had eyes.

I was pushing the massive amount of black and white fur out of the way to inspect when the rest of the uniformed calvary arrived. Chief Duncan, who had been chief since I was in high school, rolled out of his car. After adjusting his pants over his rotund belly, he surveyed the scene until his sleepy brown eyes landed on me. I gave him a small finger wave and what I hoped passed for a sheepish smile. He lumbered over, hands on hips.

"When I heard the call come over the radio, I didn't believe it," he said instead of a greeting. "Do you know how long that sign has stood at the town's edge?"

I shook my head forlornly. I'm sure I learned that tidbit in school at some point, but I absolutely had not cared enough to retain it.

Linc came back with the first-aid kit. Chief Duncan gave him a grunt and a nod, then turned his attention back to me. "Since 1947."

"It was an accident," I mumbled stupidly. Linc snorted beside me but covered it by coughing. He pulled an alcohol pad and butterfly Band-Aid from the kit.

"Your mother is going to kill you, Alex, so I'll spare you the lecture. But I am going to have to write you a ticket. And you'll have to appear in court," the chief continued. "Probably pay to have the sign fixed."

Just what an unemployed thirtysomething wanted to hear. I groaned and tried to put my head in my hands. Linc grabbed my chin and lifted it back up.

"Hold still," he commanded in a deep tenor.

As he dabbed at my cut with an alcohol swab, he kept his fingers on my jaw, a lighter touch than I would have expected from someone so muscular. Since his focus was on my forehead, I took a moment to take in his features. Same gray eyes framed by the enviably long lashes that I remembered. But his face was more angular, his jaw more pronounced. And covered in stubble. Somewhere in the intervening years, this annoying teenager had turned into a man. I sat on my hands to keep them from reaching out to touch his arm muscles through his shirt. Man, I was a sucker for arm muscles. And, of course, Linc would have them to spare. So far, karma was not on my side. I'd taken comfort in

15

imagining him as a hunchback with a hooknose and acne one could see from space.

"Alex, are you listening?" Chief Duncan asked.

"She might have a concussion, you know," Colleen said from somewhere beside me. "The airbag did deploy."

"I'll call a tow truck," the chief said.

"I feel fine. Thank you all so much for asking," I mumbled. I was having a hard time forming words. Totally because Linc still held my jaw, not because of his nearness.

Totally.

"Do you really feel okay?" he asked, backing up a little. I could finally breathe. "You don't feel nauseous or dizzy?"

"Nope. I honestly wasn't going that fast when I collided with the sign. I was actually at a dead stop. Colleen honked behind me and scared me into pressing the gas. That's when I hit the sign," I explained, absently rubbing Fang's head. "I swear those poles were dry-rotted for that thing to topple with barely a tap."

Linc and the chief both looked at my fender hugging the remaining stump of the post, then back at me with eyebrows raised. The look was so identical, I swallowed a laugh. They must teach incredulity in first-responder class or something.

"Okay, fine," I conceded. "Maybe it was a little more than a tap."

"Uh-oh," Colleen said, looking at the road.

"What?" I peeked around Lincoln's broad chest.

"I swear I didn't call her," Colleen said with a wince. The way Colleen said "her" coupled with a "please don't blame me" expression meant only one thing—my mother had arrived.

I grabbed Linc's shirt. "Hide me. Or better yet, stage me to look like I'm unconscious. Or even better yet, that I vaporized."

Mercilessly, he pried my fingers off his clothing and clucked his tongue. "Alex, Alex, Alex. Look at you. In your thirties and still scared of your mother."

"Alexandretta Harriet Lightwood!" my mother bellowed. I cringed. Heck, half of Maryland cringed. Linc tried to step aside, but I scooted over so he still blocked me. That worked for all of two seconds.

My mother, Constance Lightwood, was a five-foot-five whirling dervish of strong emotions and fierce convictions. Her morals were as strong as her bowling arm and her voice as loud as her clothing. Currently, she wore a bright yellow housedress with large green and purple flowers. Her hair was in rollers under a babushka. Matching bright yellow Crocs slap-slap-slapped the pavement as she barreled toward us.

"Mom," I whined when we made eye contact. "I'm so glad you're here. I always need my mama when I'm hurt." I pointed to the Band-Aid on my head and tried to drum up some tears.

"Oh no you don't," my mother scolded, wagging her pointer finger at me. "Look what you did!" She turned that finger toward the sign.

I hung my head, wishing Linc hadn't whistled for Fang and disappeared around the truck. I could use a buffer. Even Colleen skedaddled, the chicken.

"I didn't mean it."

"I'm going to forever be the mother of the Sign Killer. I better not get kicked out of our book club for this," she said, arms gesticulating wildly as she spoke. "It's all over the police scanner already. And now I'm on the side of the road in my curlers and housecoat."

She grabbed my face in her hands and lifted it so our eyes met again. The hard edges of my mother's expression softened; she kissed my forehead.

"Ah, *po ptakach*," she said, using the Polish for *it's all over now*. "I am glad you're here, Peanut. But next time, a simple phone call will suffice."

"I think my car is undrivable," I said, wrapping my arms around my mother's middle. As indiscreetly as I could, I savored her smell like an addict. No matter the circumstance, she always smelled the same—a little bit of lemon, a dash of vanilla, a pinch of dough, and all of home. Every time I was even in the vicinity of a lemon danish, images of my mother in the kitchen with Nana K, making pierogis from scratch or homemade cookies for one of her many clubs, popped immediately into my mind.

"Undrivable isn't a word, Peanut," Mom said absently, stroking my hair. "We'll transfer all your stuff into my car. Doesn't look like it'll take too long."

Leave it to my mother to notice my lack of belongings. And point it out to everyone.

"Tow truck is on the way, Connie," Chief Duncan said. He ripped a ticket from his pad and handed it to me. "Don't miss your court date."

I jumped off the fender and walked with my mom toward my car to begin unloading my stuff. Linc stuck his head out the window of the fire truck.

"Hey, Alex," he called. I glanced up at him. "Welcome back to Piney Ridge. You know, in case you didn't see the sign."

Chapter 3

My mother kept a running commentary as we drove through town toward my childhood home. No going back now, I thought, sighing heavily through my nose. It made a little fog print on the window glass. I adjusted Lash's bowl in my lap so I could wipe it away with my sleeve.

Piney Ridge rolled by as we drove, pretty much the same as I remembered it. Some of the storefronts on Main Street had changed ownership over the years as businesses came and went, but overall, the façades remained the same. Same color palette, same light posts, same crack in the sidewalk in front of the cigar shop.

We turned off Main and onto Brightview, where the dogwoods lining the streets had grown exponentially since I'd been here last. In the waning spring, the once burgeoning flowers were beginning to lose their petals, creating a mosaic of pink and white polka dots on the sidewalk and parked cars. The small petals fluttered about the air in the slight breeze. My fingers itched to photograph the flower shower.

But I'd never squeeze a word in edgewise with my mom in time to ask her to stop. Anyway, my camera gear bag was stowed somewhere in the back of the car. I glanced into the rearview mirror at the meager pile of belongings in the back seat. What was once a source of pride—living sparse with a small footprint—was now another reminder of my current pathetic life. What other thirty-two-year-old could pack all of their worldly belongings into the back seat of a Fiat?

I tried to shake myself out of my funk. I'd had more possessions a few weeks ago, I told myself. I'd sold a bunch of furniture before leaving the city. And by a bunch, I meant the bed frame and the couch—two things I knew my conniving ex-boyfriend, Rick, would miss the most. Picturing him entering the apartment to an empty living room brought a hint of color to my otherwise drab life of late. Just wait until he noticed the hot sauce in his mouthwash. I was almost sorry I wouldn't be there to see the smug smile drop from his serpentine face.

Almost.

Despite my best efforts to the contrary, Wreck-it Rick kept creeping back into my thoughts. To be expected, I supposed, after living and working together for almost a year, but frustrating nonetheless, since I absolutely promised myself I would never waste another brain cell on him. He may have caused my life to take a swift turn south, but I wasn't going to give him the satisfaction of dwelling on it. I'd worked too hard to overcome the inherent prejudice people had against my gender and age in the photojournalism community to let a man ruin it.

When I first broke into the scene, I felt like Peter Parker, sans Spiderman, peddling human interest stories to the *Daily Prophet* as a freelancer. Sometimes newspapers or magazines would commission me to do a specific shoot, but I realized quickly these tended to be light and fluffy events— high-society weddings, gala openings, candids of the dog park. All of which I could have easily photographed back in

Piney Ridge. The male photographers were sent to riots and political events and even overseas on location.

So, I did what any other self-respecting young woman would do in a patriarchal profession—I lied. No, not lied exactly, but blurred the truth. I took advantage of my gender-neutral nickname, Alex, on résumés and job applications to get my foot in the door. By the time magazines and news outlets realized I was actually a young, petite woman, my photographs had already spoken for themselves. It wasn't my fault people jumped to conclusions. When I became the go-to photographer for *Nature* magazine, the ends absolutely justified the means.

Then Rick had wrecked it all out of spite. And now I was back at square one—unemployed and alone.

Well, not entirely alone; I had Lashatelle on my lap. And anyone who claimed fish didn't have personalities were full of bologna Traveling on location to photograph news and nature didn't allow for pets of the furry or feathered varieties, so a fish was the perfect companion. Low maintenance, quiet, and a little judgy—kinda like me.

"Alex, are you listening to me?" my mother's shrill voice cut into my sulk, reminding me that I had her and my father on my side as well.

"Yes, Mom," I said. I had been half listening. I grasped at the last thing I heard clearly. "I think I should get settled in first before joining your clubs, okay?"

"Sure, Peanut. I understand. We need to let this sign debacle blow over first anyway."

I would have chuckled at the double meaning of the sign blowing over, but I knew she didn't say the pun on purpose. I turned my attention out the window as she rambled through choices for dinner.

Ms. Granger, my fourth-grade teacher, sat on her porch in her rocker, waving at all the cars driving by. I lifted my hand in return, as I did every time I passed her house since she retired a few decades ago.

A little way down the street, Ms. Walker struggled with a large golden retriever who bounded after a squirrel. The dog's name, I knew, was Rocket. They'd had a Rocket since I was in middle school. Their first Rocket, a beautiful, docile golden had been the fabric of the family. When she got sick, we all thought Robbie Walker would die right along with the dog, they were so devoted. But when Rocket made a full recovery a few weeks later, the whole town rejoiced in Robbie's joy. In fact, her recovery was so complete, she seemed like a totally different dog.

Come to find out later, it *was* a different dog. The original Rocket sadly passed away from her illness, but instead of telling Robbie, they'd simply replaced her with a new Rocket and led Robbie to believe she'd made a complete recovery. The cycle had repeated until Robbie went to college and found out the truth. Now, no matter what they tried to name their dogs, everyone called them Rocket. The Walkers finally stopped trying to fight it.

I smiled—part rueful, part amused—as memories rolled through me as swiftly as we rolled through the streets. The old pear tree, perfect for climbing, in the lot beside the elementary school that Linc and I fought over for ownership during recess. The community book drop on the corner where Colleen and I snatched bodice-rippers left by anonymous housewives. The duck pond, aptly named because of all the wild ducks and geese that made their homes there, where all three of us had grown up—first riding our bikes along the paths, then picnicking under the pavilion, finally talking for hours while we threw bread to the fowl.

I'd left all of this and more when I hightailed it to New York. Before I could let the emotions wash over me completely, I shut the floodgates of my memories. I didn't regret my choice then; my career and my mental health needed the move. But I did wish I would've thought about these small, happy moments more often instead of focusing on all the reasons why I left.

My father, George Lightwood, stood on the front porch of my childhood home as we pulled into the driveway. Without even looking too closely, I knew he'd be wearing a pair of brown pants, a button-down shirt, and a sweater vest in some ridiculous pattern my mother had picked out. He'd have today's paper tucked under one arm with his hand in his pocket and the other resting on his belly. I had an exact picture like this hanging in the New York apartment.

I swear the only thing that really changed in Piney Ridge was the level of the reservoir during a heavy rain.

I got out of the car with Lash in my hands.

"Hey, Princess," my father called, raising his hand. Of the two nicknames from my parents, Princess was by far my favorite. My mother only called me Peanut because I was so short as a child. Truthfully, I was still short, but a thirty-two-year-old Peanut wasn't quite as cute. Or womanly.

"Hi, Dad," I said. I paused beside him so he could kiss my cheek. I'd have hugged him if I wasn't holding Lash's bowl.

"I heard you had a little run-in on the way here." He tried to hide his smile, unsuccessfully.

"I see the dad jokes are still going strong," I quipped lightly.

"The phone has already started ringing with concerned neighbors," he said. And as if on cue, I heard the shrill ring of the house phone reminding me that everyone in Piney Ridge likely already knew the entire story.

Chapter 4

My picture was front page news. Above the fold. And not even a recent picture, like the professional headshot I use for my byline. Nope. My high school senior picture graced the page with the headline: "Local Woman Returns With a Bang." The main reason I left Piney Ridge was because I didn't want my pictures confined to the local paper. At least it was a picture *of* me, not one I had taken. Which actually made me feel a little better in a twisted sort of way. I still retained integrity in my art.

For now, anyway. I may need to amend my convictions depending on how much my car and the sign cost to fix.

My mother would rather I not be part of the news in any way. She'd been fielding phone calls for days from concerned friends and citizens. She'd dutifully supported me out loud to whomever would listen—that old, decrepit sign needed to be fixed anyway; Alex was forced off the road; we are so thankful she's okay—all the while giving me death stares and sharp head shakes.

"Concerned, my big Polish *dupa*," Mom muttered after a particularly long string of calls one afternoon. "They just want to gossip."

"Sorry, Mom," I said for the bazillionth time. I focused on the soggy Cheerios floating around my bowl to avoid the evil eye.

The phone rang again. Mom huffed and took it off the receiver. Yes, my parents still had a house phone. The same yellow landline with the same long, yellow cord that I used to stretch from the kitchen to my bedroom in high school. Cell phones, apparently, were for emergencies only. And heaven forbid Mom would actually text someone. Nana K, on the other hand, had a substantial following on several social media platforms. Go figure.

"This is ridiculous," Mom exclaimed. "You haven't been out of the house since you've been home."

She narrowed her eyes at me—a clear sign she was about to make an outrageous suggestion. I narrowed my eyes right back at her. I had learned from the best after all.

"What is going through that meddling mind of yours?" I asked.

"We are going out," Mom said definitively. "No more hiding."

"I'm not hiding!" I lied. I was totally hiding. I hadn't even seen Colleen since that first disastrous moment.

"I'm making you an appointment at Missy K's Hair Salon," Mom said.

I rolled my eyes. Mom ignored me and snapped the phone back on the hook long enough for a dial tone, then punched in numbers.

"There is no more public place than the hair salon to show we are holding our heads high. Plus, Kelly will be able to make you look more like an adult and less like you spent months in the desert."

"I *did* spend months in the desert!"

My mother knew this; I always provided my travel itinerary and sent plenty of pictures when I was on location. Before returning to Piney Ridge, I'd traveled to the Sahara for a spread in *Nature* magazine with my douche-canoe, journalist ex-boyfriend, Wreck-it Rick. It was after that trip that he ran out on me faster than our camels on hot sand. And took my career, and my pride, with him.

But there was no reminding my mother that hair salons were hard to come by in the middle of the actual, literal desert.

I looked at my father for support. He sat at the table with the local paper and a half-empty cup of coffee he'd let go cold on him. Same as he did every morning. Harrison made him that mug for Father's Day one year, the childish Sharpie drawings were almost worn away from age and use. He glanced at me over the top of the paper and shrugged.

"'You're meddling with powers you cannot possibly comprehend,'" he said with a smirk, quoting *Indiana Jones and the Last Crusade*.

I furrowed my brow at him. I'd come to terms with my father's obsession with the *Indiana Jones* movies—how could I not with a name like Alexandretta—but I didn't have to like it. Still, I knew arguing was futile: once my mother made up her mind about something, not even a hurricane could budge her. A fact my father had learned long ago, so he chose to exert his efforts elsewhere.

Two hours later, I sat begrudgingly in a salon chair getting my head massaged by a girl that looked young enough to be my offspring. Truth be told, it actually felt kinda good to have someone else wash my mess of long, brownish-blonde hair.

At one point, I thought I heard the girl ask, "Is that sand?"

"Yes. Yes, it is," I muttered. I'd be finding sand everywhere forever. Yet another lovely, long-lasting reminder of my final trip as a respected member of the photojournalism community.

"Okay. We're almost done here. Then Kelly is going to see to you personally," the shampoo girl said in monotone. Clearly, she'd rather be anywhere but at work. "Kelly is one of the owners."

I transitioned to the salon chair and waited for co-owner Kelly. A shadow appeared behind me as I scrolled through my phone. I looked up to see Kelly Kirkwood, a girl I knew in high school. A girl I didn't especially like in high school.

"Alex. Long time no see," Kelly said cheerfully.

"I didn't realize you were the Kelly that worked here."

I tried to get up, but Kelly planted her hand heavily on my shoulder. My mother gave me a fierce "you'd better not cause another scene" glare from where she sat getting her nails done. I stayed put but couldn't quite fix the scowl on my face. I missed the anonymity of New York where I didn't run into someone I knew every time I blinked.

"What did you have in mind today?" Kelly asked, running her fingers through my long, thin hair.

"I guess a trim. Nothing fancy," I said. The sooner I left this chair, the better. This was the problem with small towns—everyone knew everyone and had a history with each other. So even though Kelly graduated a few years ahead of me, we crossed paths enough to make an impact. Not a good one. I willed Kelly not to bring up anything from high school.

"No color?"

I shook my head.

Kelly tsked and frowned. "Okay. It's your head."

She started combing, being none too gentle, in my opinion. The bell jingled over the door as more patrons entered.

"She just ran right into the sign! Can you imagine? Hasn't been back in *years,* and this is how she announces her return. So typical. One time in high school she knocked over an entire cart of beakers in science. Glass everywhere. Can you imagine?" I heard a female voice say.

"Oh, shhhh. There's her mother right there," another voice commented. I squeezed my eyes shut hoping it made me invisible.

Kelly said, "Alex is right here too, ladies. I'm sure she already heard you. We all heard you."

I peeked an eye open to give her one of Mom's death stares in the mirror, but Kelly kept her attention focused on my hair.

"Oh, hi, Alex!" the voice singsonged, coming closer.

In the mirror I caught the reflection of the face attached to the sugary-sweet voice and cringed before I could fix my face. I was looking into the face of the high school mean girl, Missy Poledark. Missy, the self-appointed leader of the "Snob Blob," as my small but close-knit group of misfit friends called them, was to Piney Ridge as Regina George was to North Shore High School in *Mean Girls.* Not only did Missy make my introverted, artistic life a living horror show, but she also dated Linc and pulled him even further away from me. Then subsequently rubbed it in my face every chance she got. My once close friendship with Linc didn't quite come out the other side of the "Missy months" as strong as it went in—another lesser-known reason I left Piney Ridge as soon as humanly possible.

"I heard you were back in town," Missy said with a plaster smile. Then her mean, snake eyes glinted, her lips curled into a smirk. "Actually, I read it in the paper. Front page, impressive. I guess you'll have to pay to replace that monumental sign. Are you still taking those little pictures?"

I snorted. Little did Missy know that one of those little pictures could earn me a few thousand dollars if someone bought the rights to it.

"Yes. I am," I said proudly. Using my photography career against me was the wrong move; it was one of the only things I was proud of.

Operative word being *was*.

I left my face blank to hide my discomfort and said, "Maybe you saw my spread in *Nature* magazine last month? The one about the ecosystem in the rain forests of Brazil?"

Missy's smug smile faltered, but only a little. "Can't say that I did. I'm too busy with my children and husband. Do you have kids?"

"Not unless you count my fish." I thought Rick and I were headed that way—marriage, kids, the white-picket fence—but he apparently had other plans.

Plans that didn't involve me.

Plans that did involve a big-breasted, toothy-grinned, barely legal journalist at his office.

Missy gave me a fake sympathetic look and made sure to flash her huge diamond ring in my eyeline. "That's too bad. Children really are life's greatest gift. Just look at my two precious angels."

Missy opened a gold, heart-shaped locket that hung around her neck, shoving it in my face. Since Kelly's scissors were still snip-snipping around my head, I couldn't even move away. The photo on the left, small and grainy, seemed to show two smiling children—a girl and a boy. Missy's thumb covered the other side which I assumed held a picture of her husband.

"Yup. Those are kids," I said, unable to help my snark. Thank goodness my mother was out of earshot.

Missy snapped the locket closed and harrumphed. "Better hurry and snag a husband quick. You're not getting any younger, you know."

"We're the same age, Missy," I reminded her, but she'd already moved away.

"Did I tell you Michael Junior is the starting pitcher for his little league team this year?" she asked her companion, her voice loud enough to carry through the entire salon. I thought I saw the girl beside Missy roll her eyes but couldn't be sure from the angle. I'd absolutely be rolling my eyes if I had to listen to Missy blather on all day.

"Easy to do when your father is the coach," Kelly murmured. "I don't often speak ill of children, but Missy's are as snobby and spoiled as she is. No fault of theirs; they only know what they're taught. Poor things. I can't believe I was friends with her once."

"Not anymore?" I asked, my opinion of adult Kelly improving some.

Kelly looked around to make sure Missy moved out of earshot. She dropped her voice as she said, "She and I co-own this salon. It was a mistake from day one, but she had the capital I needed to buy it from the previous owner. Unfortunately, she still thinks that makes her the boss. It's been five years, and I've more than made up for that initial contribution. But you know Missy. She works as little as possible and takes all the credit. Even tricked me into naming the salon after her."

"Sounds about Missy," I said. "Zero work, full credit. I remember her doing the same thing with group projects in high school."

"Yeah, not all of us matured after that milestone. I've tried to buy her out numerous times, but she won't budge. My stupid fault for trusting her back in the day," Kelly said as she snipped away at my hair. I hoped her anger didn't manifest on my head.

Kelly continued her rant. "The stupid part is she doesn't even have to work. Her husband has enough money for both of them."

"Who'd she end up marrying?" I asked.

If Missy still lived in this small town, chances were she'd met her husband here. Which meant I knew him too. I chanced a glance in Missy's direction. The shampoo girl had joined Missy and her friend behind the counter. Who'd want to marry her?

"Mike Vandenburg," Kelly answered. "He graduated my year."

"Oh, I remember him. Wasn't he the one Missy dated right before she went to study abroad?" I asked. Rumor had it she cheated on Linc with Mike. Among others.

"Study abroad, my butt. I have it on good authority that she went to fat camp. Remember how she packed on the pounds sophomore year?" Kelly asked with a chuckle.

"I honestly didn't pay that much attention to her. I tried to avoid your group as much as possible."

"Can't blame you. We were awful. Missy hasn't changed. In fact, it's gotten worse since Mike became acting mayor. She struts around like the first lady. But between you, me, and this hair dryer, he's as worthless as she is. He has a job at Daddy Vandenburg's seafood distribution company, but it's only an excuse for an allowance."

"Sounds like a great family," I scoffed.

We lapsed into silence as Kelly blew out my hair. I observed the room in the mirror. My photographer's eye homed in on the light bouncing off the colored-product bottles, so I framed shots in my mind since I couldn't do it with my camera.

Next, I moved to the people; my real interest. My mother sat on the edge of her seat at the manicure station—poised for action, never really still. Her mouth moved as fast as her free hand. The manicurist gently took the newly polished flailing appendage and placed it back under the dryer. It stayed there for all of three seconds before my mother continued the story she told.

Behind the counter, Missy droned on about her kids, not really talking to anyone in particular, just liking the sound of her own voice. The two girls with her had given up on trying to look interested. The shampoo girl twirled a piece of hair, chomped gum, and scrolled through her phone. Occasionally, she'd give a little nod to acknowledge Missy's words, but Missy might as well have been talking to a brick wall. The epitome of the generation gap, I thought. If I were to shoot this moment, I'd use Missy's back as foreground and focus on the half-closed eyelids of the girl. I'd wait until the girl blew a bubble, or maybe just as it popped, to snap the photo.

"All done," Kelly said a few moments later. I wrenched my eyes away from the scene at the counter and ran my fingers through my newly cut and styled hair.

"Nice job!" I said, genuinely surprised. My hair actually had a little volume and some shape. No small feat given its thinness. Stupid Polish genes.

"Hope you don't mind. I added some layers. It's easy to maintain and gives you some movement and style."

"I love it," I said and meant it. "Thanks, Kelly. Hey, who's that girl with Missy? The one who shampooed my hair," I asked as Kelly removed my apron.

The girl's expression had changed slightly from dismissal to annoyance as Missy continued to talk. Something about her seemed familiar.

"That's Jodie. Missy's little sister."

"That's Jodie?" I asked in disbelief. The last time I saw the kid was when Jodie was a toddler. Nothing like a grown child to personify the passage of time. I really had been gone a long time.

"Yup. All grown-up and annoyed at the world. Like all teenage girls," Kelly said. "She works here sometimes whenever she can be bothered. Which isn't very often." She gestured with the scissors toward the counter. "As you can see."

"She must be what? Eighteen?"

"A little over twenty actually," Kelly said.

"Shoot. Time flies," I murmured. As I met Mom at the counter to pay, I gave the girl another cursory glance. I could see the resemblance now that I stood closer. Jodie looked a lot like teenaged Missy. I nodded in her direction when she caught me staring.

"Careful driving home, Alex," Missy called, sarcasm dripping from her honeyed voice as Mom and I walked out the door. "There are a couple more signs still left standing in town."

I closed the door on her laugh.

I got almost to the car before my embarrassment turned fully into anger and annoyance. Who did Missy think she was? We were supposed to be adults.

I turned on the scuffed heel of my boot and marched back toward the building.

"Alex! What are you doing?" Mom called a little desperately. I ignored her. I'd handled vipers in the Sahara and a troop of monkeys in the jungle. Surely, I could handle Missy Poledark.

When I pushed through the door, I heard Missy's loud, clear voice saying, "... never live this one down. She should just pack up and go back to the jungles of Brazil or

33

whatever. She'd fit in there better anyway. I mean, did you see her boots?"

I cleared my throat and glared. Missy looked startled for a half second, then glared right back at me like a mongoose looks at a mouse. Well, this mouse wasn't going down quietly any longer.

"If you have something to say to me, Missy, why don't you say it to my face. Like an adult. Instead of spreading gossip and rumors behind my back. I don't know if you realize it, but high school ended a long time ago."

Missy stood up. She had me beat by a few inches. I didn't back down though, simply crossed my arms and waited. The rest of the salon slipped into silence. Jodie raised an amused eyebrow.

"You're right. High school was a long time ago, but it looks like you never grew out of your awkward stage."

"And it looks like you never grew out of your mean-girl stage. I've heard that bullies put other people down because they themselves are insecure. It's a shame you have such low self-esteem," I shot back. I could feel the heat rising on my neck and prayed I didn't go totally blotchy until I made it outside. Confrontation gave me hives.

Missy gave a little laugh of surprise. "Me? Insecure? What would I have to be insecure about? My husband is the mayor, in case you haven't heard."

"So?"

"So? That's like the most important job in town!"

Now it was my turn to chuckle. "I'm sorry. Did you just say that being the *acting* mayor of Small-Town, USA is the most important job? Puh-lease."

Missy scowled for real now. "His position holds a lot of power in this town. He has the ear of the judge and the chief of police. So, someone who recently had an unfortunate run-in with the law should be careful who they are insulting."

I cocked my head. "Are you threatening me?"

She shrugged. "I'm just stating a fact."

"I swear if you use your husband's title to interfere in my life all because of a high school grudge, I'll—" I faltered. What could I possibly threaten Missy with?

"You'll what?" A look of triumph flashed in Missy's eyes.

"Just keep my name out of your mouth from now on," I said, hating to let the bully win. I gave Missy one last glare and stormed out of the salon.

At least I had the last word.

Chapter 5

"Like she has any room to judge anyone else," Mom said as she hate-scrubbed the kitchen counter later that afternoon.

"Are you still rambling about Missy?" I asked. My mother had been huffing under her breath about Missy ever since we got home. "I hardly think she's worth the time."

"You forget how small towns work," she said, pointing her rag at me for emphasis. "She'll have bad-mouthed you all over by now. And like it or not, she has clout in town because of her husband's family."

"I don't care. You shouldn't either." I waved away my mother's protest before she could form the words. "I know, I know. Easier said than done. Plus, I haven't lived here in a long time. I don't have to answer to my book club or bowling league or cooking club or the Ladies' Auxiliary."

Mom clamped her mouth shut since I indeed took the words out of her mouth. Instead, she nodded in agreement and found something else to scrub. I felt my own anxiety ratcheting up just watching her frenzied pace. I needed some quiet. I needed some alone time.

I needed to find my own place, pronto. That would be priority one tomorrow. Today, I wanted to shoot. The usual tug of my camera had failed me since I'd been back in town. I chalked that up to the stifling, claustrophobic feeling I got from being here. But now, finally, the will to pick up my trusty, old friend had returned.

"I'm going to the reservoir. Don't wait for me for dinner," I said and scooted out of the room before my mother could protest. I grabbed my gear bag from the bedroom where it had been sitting, neglected, since my return earlier that week. Quickly, I checked the battery, memory card, and lenses before stuffing my wallet and car keys into the side pocket and sneaking out the front door.

I stopped short in the empty driveway. Where the heck was my car? The crunch of metal against wood sounded in my consciousness, and I remembered the poor thing was still in the shop. For all of four seconds, I contemplated asking my mother to borrow the family car. But that would require going back into the house and potentially getting another lecture. Or worse, she might ask to come with me. I love my mother, but there would be no quiet if she came. I didn't think Connie Lightwood understood the word "quiet."

The forecast promised no chance for rain, so I could walk. I set off through the backyard path well worn by countless feet, including mine, throughout the decades. One of the first built in modern Piney Ridge, my parents' neighborhood sat on the edge of the pine forest surrounding the reservoir. The hike was harder than sticking to the sidewalks, but I really didn't want to run into anyone else in town at the moment.

The sun hung low in the sky as evening neared, creating interesting patterns through the trees and across the path. I'd almost forgotten how peaceful this little slice of wilderness was. Living in New York for the last dozen-plus years had me accustomed to horns, sirens, shouts, and sizzles. In Piney Ridge, birds chirping and leaves rustling serenaded me. As I neared the reservoir, gentle waves lapping the rocky shore joined the natural symphony.

Piney Ridge may not have as robust and diverse ecosystem as the Brazilian rain forest or the interesting ever-changing hustle and bustle of New York, but it definitely held its own charm and beauty. I set about capturing that beauty with my camera. Although I preferred to photograph people or animals—expressive eyes, emotions, energy—it couldn't hurt to expand my stock photography portfolio. Who knew when I would get picked up for another commercial shoot after Rick lied about me in all the important circles? I needed to have steady, supplemental income. Especially if I had to pay for the stupid Welcome sign.

A group of cardinals flitting about a nearby bush caught my attention. I snapped on my longer lens so I could capture them without getting any closer. The sun backlit them, creating small sunbursts in between the birds and branches. I closed the aperture to really make those sunbursts more prominent in camera. Although that would cause more of the photograph to be in focus, the light was the actual star of this shoot, so the sacrifice was worth it. The playful birds acted as supporting characters to add some movement and interest. I could always blur the background in post-processing if I felt it necessary.

When I got a few different angles, I moved my attention to a different part of the path near the water, switching my lens to a shorter length. Uncaring if anyone saw me, I lay down on my belly on the damp stones of the shore to get some eye-level shots of the water hitting the shoreline. I adjusted focal points for different perspectives—

some with the rocks in focus, some with the water, one of a lone feather left by a passing duck or goose.

On impulse, I stacked a few rocks in a tower and took pictures of that from ground level and from above. For whatever reason, these types of shots did really well in stock photography. Something about representing balance and stability—two things I knew very little about in my own life of late. Maybe I could garner some through photographic osmosis?

When I had to up the ISO to let in more light, I knew it was time to head back to my parents' house. I still had to walk all the way back, and the light was fading quickly. I replaced my expensive lens with a smaller, lighter one and hung the camera around my neck for the walk home. If it bumped into something, replacing that glass wouldn't break my depleting bank account like other lenses in my collection.

I marveled again at how less peopley this forest was from Central Park. I'd barely run into anyone while out here this evening. A young boy throwing a ball in the reservoir for a joyous golden retriever. A man about my age walking along the path with a book tucked under his arm. A teenager running along the path. I felt a twang of jealousy at the teen's energy and motivation. Maybe I should start running?

Maybe elephants would learn to tap dance. I snorted at myself. Missy may be Mistress of Mean, but she was right about one thing—I tended toward awkward, not graceful. I'd once tripped over the small kitchen rug in front of the sink, sending spaghetti flying around the room and sticking to every surface. No, running was probably out of the realm of possibilities for me; I'd likely sprain an ankle on the second step.

I realized, as the reference to Missy filled my head, I hadn't thought of her, or my obnoxious ex, for the hours I'd spent in the woods with my camera. Creating pictures never failed to lift my spirits and remind me that the world was bigger and brighter than any one person or any one moment. I'd been in stickier situations than this and managed a way out of them. Hitting a sign with my car was only a small blip in my timeline. The gossip train in Piney Ridge may be fast and sometimes vicious, but it was also hungry. Soon enough something else would happen to pull attention away from me.

Seeing a light on in the kitchen of my childhood home, I sneaked in the side door and tiptoed up toward my room. If my mother caught me, I'd get guilted into helping with dinner. I really wanted to curl up in bed with my laptop and a cup of tea to scroll through the images I took today. Tonight, the tea would have to wait. I couldn't risk a trip to the kitchen.

One of my favorite parts of photography was culling the photos after the shoot. Did my vision come to fruition through the lens? Was I able to capture a memorable or important moment? Did I make a connection with my subject?

The pictures revealed themselves in the downloading and editing process. Not quite the same thrill as the days of film, but still a thrill, nonetheless. And, bonus, I didn't lose as many nose hairs from all the darkroom chemicals. Sometimes creative editing can enhance a so-so picture and bring it to life. As a photojournalist, I usually did very little to alter the photos I created while on location. However, these personal shots for stock photography or my own portfolio allowed me to play to my heart's content.

I heard my parents' voices drifting up the steps as I set up the laptop and external hard drive: my mother's fast and almost constant; my father's a low grumble interjected in between. I'd almost forgotten their familiar cadence in my years away. As a child, I'd fallen asleep to the rhythm of my parents' conversations, their friendship and comfort with one another evident and enviable. Their unwavering devotion to each other even got us through Harrison's disappearance intact. I rubbed my chest where a bloom of pain started radiating, locking it away in the little box where it belonged.

I shook out the negative thoughts and tried to regain the calm serenity I'd felt in the woods. Sitting down to flag the pictures would help with that—take me back to the moments when I shot each one—remembering the light and the quiet and the stillness. I did a cursory, quick glance through each of them, flagging my favorites as I scrolled. I'd do another slower look later, but I'd grown to trust my first impressions. If I felt a tug for some reason as I looked through quickly, chances were others would too.

Halfway through my second run-through, my mother called up the steps, "Alex? Are you home?"

"Upstairs," I called back absently. I heard my mother's heavy tread on the steps.

"I didn't hear you come in, Peanut. Dinner's almost ready. Did you have a nice walk?" Mom asked from the doorway.

"Mmmm-hmmm," I murmured, only half listening as I focused on the photo on my screen. Something in the grass behind the cardinals pulled my attention. It was a good shot, but I wasn't sure it was worth the effort to crop the offender out. Especially since I may have another similar shot without it. I scrolled through the series.

Nope, just my luck, it was evident in the whole series. What was it, though? I originally pegged it as a bald spot in the grass. If it were some sort of bag or trash that I could have moved and didn't, I would kick myself.

I heard my mother's voice through the fog of concentration, her words registering in disjointed snippets.

"I ran naked down Main Street today, so that should take some of the spotlight off you," Mom said, testing my attention.

"Thanks, Mom," I said automatically. I opened the picture larger than the thumbnail to zoom in. Not a bag. Or bald ground. What was that in the tall grass?

"We're having cooked snake for dinner," Mom tried again.

"Cheese and crackers!" I exclaimed, finally realizing what I was seeing. I rubbed my eyes to clear my vision. It couldn't possibly be.

"No. Snake. Like I said. With a side of anchovies."

"It's a woman," I squeaked out. "I think... I think she's dead."

Chapter 6

"Maybe you were paying attention after all. Although I will say, this little tug-of-war has taken a dark turn," Mom said, clearly believing I was messing with her as she'd done to me moments ago.

My hands starting shaking. I felt a bit faint. I must have looked upset because in two quick strides Mom was by my side, peering over my shoulder.

She asked, "What's a woman?"

"There. In the brush." I pointed a trembling finger to the picture. Just visible was the leg of a woman, turned at an odd angle away from her body. Most of her body was hidden by the bush in the foreground—the main subject of the photo—but no one would just lay in the grass with their body positioned like that. And why hadn't the woman moved at all when I was there taking pictures?

"It's a joke, right? Someone saw me taking pictures and photo bombed. That's all. Right? That teenager I saw in the woods maybe. Gotta be a prank," I babbled, trying to rationalize the scene.

"I think we better call Chief Duncan," my mother said quietly beside me. "Come downstairs. Sit with your father."

What seemed like only moments later, Chief Duncan knocked on the door. He greeted my parents first. Both wore worried expressions. Mom was as pale as I felt. I sat at the kitchen table strangling a cloth napkin in my hands.

"This is getting to be a bad habit—you and I," Chief Duncan said to me.

I blinked up at him and tried to focus. Everything seemed to be happening in slow motion. Everything except my racing thoughts and even faster heartbeat. I kept trying to see the scene live. How had I missed the woman laying on the ground when I was there in person?

But I hadn't. I'd been so focused on the light and getting my settings right.

"Your mom said you found a body," the chief prompted when I remained quiet.

If the situation weren't so serious, I probably would've found his expression comical. This was likely the first unnatural dead body he'd had to deal with in his career in Piney Ridge. He had his hands folded and resting on his large middle; his face mimicked all the cops in crime dramas, but just missed the mark. He looked half constipated and half angry instead of stern and serious.

I nodded slightly. "I think so," I said in response to his question. I barely recognized my own voice, now thin and unsure.

"Tell me what happened." He pulled a notepad out of his pocket. Mainly for show, I thought as I watched him. I could see the skepticism plainly splashed across his face.

Things like murder didn't happen in Piney Ridge. And I was already a troublemaker because of the Welcome sign.

"Let me show you instead," I said, turning my laptop to face him. A picture was worth a thousand words. And would hopefully also stop a thousand denials.

He wandered over to peer at the screen. "What am I looking at? Looks like a bunch of birds," he said, squinting.

I pointed to the leg in the background of the photo. "Look here. Beyond the birds. See, in the grass there? It's a woman's leg."

He raised an eyebrow. "Could be. Could be it's a mannequin. Or a kid playing a prank. Or a trick of the light."

"I hope so," Mom said, standing behind me with comforting hands on my shoulders. "But we thought it warranted a least a look."

The chief glanced out the window at the darkness beyond. "Where was this taken? When?"

I explained my photo walk in the woods earlier that evening. "I didn't see it—her—when I was there. Like you, I focused on the birds. Focused on getting the light right in camera."

"Do you know how to use Photoshop?" he asked, one eyebrow raised.

I narrowed my eyes at him. "Yes. I'm not sure what that has to do—"

He cut me off. "It lets you add things to photos, right? Manipulate them?"

"Sure. But this is straight out of the camera. I haven't edited it at all," I said, resenting the insinuation.

"We'll see soon enough. Can you find this spot again?" he asked, cutting off further protest about my credibility. He put the unused notebook back in his pocket.

"I'm sure I could. It's down the path at the back of the house." I pointed in the general direction.

"Grab your hiking boots and a flashlight. I'm going to call Linc."

I paused halfway out of my chair. "Why Linc? Why do you have to call Linc? Why Linc?"

He gave me a curious look. As did my parents. "He's the EMT. If this woman is actually there, she may need medical attention."

"*If,*" I echoed. "You really don't believe me."

"In this day and age of Photoshop and filters, I need to see it with my own eyes. No offense." He turned away with the phone to his ear.

Mom huffed an angry breath. "Well, really, how rude. Come on, Peanut. I'll find you a flashlight. George, get your shoes on. You're going with them."

We met Linc and Fang at the head of the path. Armed with powerful flashlights, I led the men into the woods. At the risk of being ridiculous, I stuck close to my father's steady, warm frame. As a light-chaser by profession and by passion, the darkness always unnerved me. Yet another reason I loved New York—it was never fully dark, never fully still.

An owl hooted, and, startled, I stopped on the path. Linc ran right into the back of me, almost knocking me to my knees. He grabbed my arms before I pitched forward.

"Whoa there. You okay?" he asked, steadying me against his broad chest. Being there felt much too comfortable and much too dangerous at the same time. Fang danced around our legs.

"Sorry. I'm a bit spooked." I took a breath and a tentative step forward out of his grasp. I found it easier to breathe when I wasn't so close to him. "I'm not used to so much darkness."

"Ah, New York, right? The city that never sleeps."

I frowned, glad he couldn't see my face. I didn't realize he'd known where I lived. Of course, with a mother like Connie, the whole town probably knew my exact address in Manhattan.

I slowed again as we reached the spot by the reservoir. I pointed, and four light beams followed my finger.

"My girl's no liar," I heard my father mumble. This time, I wished it were true. But visible in the grass, in a perfect, albeit shadowy, replica of the photograph on my laptop, was the body of a woman.

With a "Fang, stay," Linc launched into action, carefully picking his way through the tall grasses and pricker bushes to kneel beside the woman. Chief Duncan didn't follow. I don't know why his inaction surprised me, but it did. He probably didn't want to get his shiny shoes dirty.

Linc looked toward the group. Even though I knew she was dead—she'd been lying unmoving for hours—when Linc gave a small shake of his head, my knees buckled a little.

My father's strong arms wrapped around me. "Got you, Princess," he whispered into my hair.

"I hoped I was wrong. I hoped it was a mannequin."

"It's never a mannequin," my father quipped.

Chief Duncan called it in on his radio. The Piney Ridge police force consisted of the chief and two deputies, none of which were properly equipped to handle a dead body in the woods. Hopefully, he also called in the state police. At least they would have crime scene techs.

Linc stood and walked back over to us, a dazed and pinched expression on his usually jovial face.

"I know her," he said, stunned. Fang whimpered at his tone. "I mean, it's dark and she's pretty messed up, but I'm like ninety-nine percent sure."

47

Chief Duncan took him by the arm and led him a little away. They talked in low murmurs. Despite my better judgment, despite knowing I would absolutely regret it later, I inched closer to the body, moving my flashlight beam to her face.

Missy Poledark Vandenburg.

I gasped. Except for the unnatural red bloom spreading on her chest, she could've been sleeping. Hands on my shoulders twisted me around so I faced away from the body. I leaned into my father's chest.

"Why would you do that? Why would you look?" Linc asked from behind us. I looked over Dad's shoulder to see Linc's stormy gray eyes full of concern.

"I found her. I had to know. It's Missy," I said.

"Yeah. That's what I thought too."

I saw an unnamed emotion pass across Linc's face. I didn't even like Missy, and I felt terrible. Linc had been friends with her—dated her even—he must be feeling ten times what I was.

"I'm sorry, Linc. I'm so sorry."

He waved away my sympathy. I saw him visibly put emotions aside and transform back into first-responder mode. Unfortunately, I didn't have that ability.

"She was murdered, Linc," I said, trembling in earnest now. Ice coursed through my veins and embedded in my bones. "Her chest. All that blood."

"Linc," Chief Duncan called. "Take Alex and George back to the house. Then wait at the trailhead for the others. I'll wait here."

"Wouldn't it make more sense for them to come in from the park?" Linc asked. "I can drive around and meet them there instead."

"Oh, uh, sure. That's fine. I'll radio to let them know."

Linc gave my arm a little squeeze. "We'll take care of her now."

Dad took my shoulders to guide me up the path toward the house. Linc and Fang followed close behind.

"Alex, I'm going to want to ask you some more questions," the chief said. "Don't go anywhere."

I nodded. "The only place I'm going is into a hot shower."

I wanted to wash the day away. Wash the memory of Missy's lifeless body from the inside of my eyelids. I'd seen violent death before—on location in far away war-torn cities. But never this unexpected. Never this close to home. Never someone I knew personally. And although I didn't particularly like Missy Poledark, I'd never wish this on her. I wouldn't even wish this on Wreck-it Rick.

Mom enveloped me and Dad in her arms as we arrived back on the doorstep. She fussed and fumed and fed. I ate without tasting, mechanically and only because my mother stood over me until I did so.

"I'm going to take a shower," I announced when I thought I ate enough to satisfy my mother's fretting. "Let me know when the chief comes back."

Chapter 7

Hot water, as hot as I could stand it without my skin melting off, cascaded over my head and down my back as I stood under the spray. When I closed my eyes, I saw Missy's lifeless body, the dark red stain blossoming on her chest. When I opened my eyes, I got water in them. The whole situation felt a little like my life right now—damned if you do, damned if you don't. Still, I stood there until the temperature turned cold, then forced myself to turn off the water and function as a human again.

When I emerged from the bathroom, I could hear voices downstairs—more voices than just my parents'. The police must be back. I threw on a sweatshirt and some leggings—I still couldn't seem to warm my bones—ran a brush through my wet hair and joined the group in the kitchen.

I scanned the crowd huddled there. Dad sat stoically at the table; Mom stood vibrating behind him. Chief Duncan lounged across from my father, leaning back in the chair, feet outstretched and a coffee mug in his beefy hand. A young woman in a Piney Ridge PD uniform stood in the corner of the room holding a notepad. An unfamiliar man sat next to Chief Duncan, wearing a sports jacket and a five-o'clock shadow. Unlike Chief Duncan, this man sat forward in his chair, nodding as my father spoke and taking notes on a small notepad.

When I walked farther into the room, all eyes turned to me. The man in the jacket stood to shake my hand.

"Detective James Spaulding with the Maryland State Police. I'll be working in tandem with Piney Ridge PD on this investigation. Mind if we ask you a few questions, Ms. Lightwood?" he asked.

His handshake was firm, his eyes sharp. I immediately relaxed a little. He'd clearly done this before. I trusted him a heck of a lot more than I trusted Chief Duncan, who did nothing but take another sip of coffee when I entered.

"Sure. I'm happy to help," I said. I glanced again at the woman in the corner.

"I'm Officer Martinez," the woman said when I caught her eye. She pointed at the badge pinned to her uniform. "With the Piney Ridge PD."

I gave her a nod, mustered up a small smile, then turned my focus back to Detective Spaulding, who held out a chair for me to sit. When I did, my mother came and stood behind me. She placed a hot mug of tea in my hands. I sipped automatically.

"Can you tell me how you found the body?" Detective Spaulding asked.

"I saw it in a picture I took," I explained. I told him about my photo walk. He interjected here and there to ask some clarifying questions, but mainly let me talk unimpeded. When I got to the part about downloading the pictures onto my computer, Chief Duncan sat up in his chair, suddenly interested.

"I noticed something in the back of the picture and zoomed in to see how easy it would be to edit out," I said.

"Ah-ha! So you admit to altering photographs," Chief Duncan blurted out.

"I already told you I know how to use photo manipulation software. It isn't a secret. I haven't used any on that picture yet," I explained again. My shocked stupor moved quickly into annoyance. If he questioned my integrity again, irritation would undoubtedly become full-blown anger.

"You're a photographer? Professionally?" Detective Spaulding asked, pulling my attention back to him. He was a little older than me, or maybe that was the stress of the job, but had a mollifying way about him underneath the ripples of power and confidence. Some, who were not in the middle of an interrogation, might even call him dark, brooding, and ruggedly handsome. The scar running across his chin added to his mystery. He screamed cop whereas Chief Duncan screamed Homer Simpson.

"Yes. A photojournalist mostly, so I don't manipulate those photos at all," I said pointedly, staring at Chief Duncan. "The photos from today were for my stock photography page. I put them up on a host site where advertisers, bloggers, and authors can buy the rights to use the pictures. It's a profitable side hustle. Although I can manipulate stock pictures as much as I want to, I haven't gotten to that stage in the process yet for today's shoot. I was doing an initial cull to see which ones were the most marketable," I explained.

"So, you noticed something in the back of the photograph?" Detective Spaulding prompted, easing me back into my story. He kept his alert brown eyes trained on mine.

"Yes. I thought it was a bit of trash or a bald spot in the grass. It pulled my eye away from the main subject. I zoomed in a little closer and realized it was a woman's leg."

I shuddered as the icy fingers of dread gripped my bones once again. My mother's grasp on my shoulders tightened. She leaned over me to press the hot mug into my hands once again.

"We decided to call the police," my mother said, picking up the thread. "Even if it was a mannequin or someone playing a trick, we wanted to report it just in case."

"Convenient that Alex is the one to discover a body right after being the subject of another criminal investigation," Chief Duncan remarked, one eyebrow raised.

"Now, Chief," my father cut in, his voice carrying a warning. "I'd hardly label Alex's traffic accident criminal."

"It's convenient, is all," the chief mumbled.

"Convenient, how?" I asked, that prick of annoyance returning full force. "You think I wanted to discover a body? You think I wanted someone dead? Why? To get my picture off the front page of some rinky-dink newspaper?"

"Okay, Ms. Lightwood. I'm sure that isn't what the chief was implying," Detective Spaulding said, giving the chief a pointed look. "Can you walk us through the rest of the evening? Your father already gave us his statement, but we'd like to hear your version of events."

I nodded and described walking Linc, my father, and the chief back to the spot where Missy lay. I drew from my many years on-site with journalists to remove myself from the moment and report the events factually.

"You recognized the woman?" Detective Spaulding asked when I finished.

I nodded.

"How?" Chief Duncan asked. "You haven't been in town in years, and yet you recognized someone in one glance."

That gave me pause. Should I mention the fight at the salon? It wasn't really a fight, just a few women exchanging words. And insults. Deciding it would only confuse things, I chose to keep it to myself for now.

"We went to high school together," I said lamely.

"Almost fifteen years ago!" Chief Duncan leaned forward in his chair and pointed his stubby finger at me. I recoiled backward instinctively even though the table separated us.

"Clive Duncan!" my mother exclaimed, hands on hips. "I've invited you into my house. If you can't act appropriately, you can leave this instant."

"I'm asking relevant questions," he said, huffing back in his chair once again.

"This is sounding more and more like an interrogation. Like you think Alex could possibly have something to do with Missy's murder. Which is just ridiculous," Mom spluttered.

Detective Spaulding cut in, "It's much too early in the investigation for anyone to be jumping to conclusions. We simply need the facts, and getting them right away while they are fresh in your memory is best."

"So answer the question," Chief Duncan said.

"What question?" I asked, trying and failing to keep the snippiness out of my voice.

"How did you recognize Ms. Vandenburg after fifteen years?" Detective Spaulding asked. His tone, like mine earlier, was matter of fact, not accusatory.

"I got my hair done in her salon, Missy K's, this morning," I explained, twisting the tips of a few wet strands in my fingers.

Chief Duncan snorted again, but wisely kept his mouth shut this time. With that reaction, any residual doubt I had about mentioning my small fight with Missy vanished. I willed my gossipy mother to keep the events to herself for once.

Dad cleared his throat. "I think any more questions can wait until the morning. It's already really late."

"Unfortunately, murder doesn't keep regular business hours," Detective Spaulding quipped. "But, you're right. We've got enough for now." He rose from his chair. "Is there a number where I can reach you if I have any follow-up questions?"

I gave him my cell number. My father stood up from the table to escort the trio of police to the door. I heard him say, "Chief, if you want to ask my daughter any more questions, you can direct them to our lawyer. I'll call you with the number tomorrow."

When he returned to the table, his face was grim. "I don't like Clive Duncan's tone. He has it out for you, Alex. Be careful what you tell them."

"Can you blame him, though?" I asked. "I am the anomaly in town. I've already wrecked a town landmark. And Missy and I had words at the salon in front of plenty of witnesses. If I were the murderer, it would wrap all this up in a nice pretty bow."

"Did you murder her?" my father asked, his face blank.

"Of course not!" my mother and I shouted at the same time.

"Exactly. The truth will out. Just don't help Chief Duncan along in his delusions."

"No problem there," I said and sighed, tired straight down to my bones. "I'm going to bed. It's been quite a day. Quite a week."

"I meant what I told him. We're getting you a lawyer tomorrow. Better safe than sorry. The only murder Chief Duncan has ever investigated is the one on *Law and Order*."

"Thanks, Daddy," I said. I gave him a quick kiss on his bald head. "You know, 'you are oddly attired—for a knight.'"

My father smiled at the *Last Crusade* reference. "That's my girl."

Chapter 8

As if my time so far in Piney Ridge wasn't crappy enough, karma gave me the middle finger by scheduling my court date the Monday after I found a dead body. Which was why I now stood grimacing at my meager offering of clothes. My wardrobe hit both ends of the spectrum: perfectly acceptable for traipsing around in a foreign country or going out to a night club in New York. Not much in the middle and not a lot that said "responsible adult." I finally broke down and asked my mother to borrow an outfit.

"I look like Auntie Delores," I muttered forlornly after I tried on the least loud spring dress I could find in my mother's closet—a lavender A-line with dancing flamingos wearing sunglasses. Luckily, the flamingos were small enough that from a distance they looked like geometric shapes.

At least that's what I told myself anyway.

"You aren't in a fashion show," my mother said, dismissing my dismay with a wave of a hand and throwing a cardigan at me. "And for the record, your Aunt Delores had impeccable taste."

I hid my snort behind a cough. Auntie Delores gave Mom a run for her money in terms of outlandish prints. She even liked to mix and match them in inventive ways. According to my aunt, cheetahs and zebras lived together in the same country, so they could live together on her body as well.

I checked the time. "It'll have to do. I'm running late already."

"Are you sure you don't want me to come?" Mom asked for the bajillionth time.

"Yes. I'll be fine. I'll apologize profusely, promise to pay for the damages, and be on my way," I said. Although I wouldn't have minded the moral support, I knew my mother wouldn't be able to refrain from talking. And based on my many years of true crime binge-watching, silence was golden in the courtroom.

"Call if you need anything," Mom said as I shut the door of her car. She gave a wave as I backed down the driveway and headed to the courthouse.

I sat in the back row, head lowered, and waited for my turn. Luckily, I didn't have to wait long since there were only a few minor traffic violations and a drunk-and-disorderly ahead of me. The sooner this was over, the sooner I could go crawl back under my rock.

"Now, Mr. Oliphant, this isn't your first time standing before me," the judge said. Mr. Oliphant hung his head dutifully. "Now I know a man likes to have a cold one or two after a hard day's work."

Mr. Oliphant lifted his head expectantly.

"But," the judge continued, "it isn't fair to the citizens of Piney Ridge to have drunkards wandering through town being belligerent. Especially when they aren't wearing any pants."

Mr. Oliphant hung his head again. "I 'pologized 'bout that," he mumbled. "Not my proudest moment."

"I would guess not. I'm ordering you to three hundred hours of community service to be served at the businesses along Main Street since that is where you ran amok. If I find you in front of me again, Mr. Oliphant, it will be jail time." The judge leaned forward and added, "Listen, Teddy, just stay home and drink. Lock yourself in the house if you have to. Or call your sister to babysit you."

"I know, I know," Mr. Oliphant said. "Thanks, Judge."

"Pick up your order and pay the court fine on your way out." He looked at his docket. "Alexandretta Lightwood."

I stood and walked to the front of the courtroom, avoiding eye contact with everyone else.

"Go get 'em, Lexi," a familiar voice whispered as I passed the front row. I snapped my head around, hoping I mis-recognized the voice. But no, Linc sat there with an amused smile on his handsome face. Perfect. I rolled my eyes to the heavens but didn't stop moving. Was he going to be present for all of my misfortunes from now on?

"Lightwood," the judge repeated. "Any chance you're Connie and George's girl?"

"That's me," I squeaked. A small laugh bubbled from the gallery. I cleared my throat. Off to a great start.

"You're the one who knocked over the Welcome sign," he said without even looking down. My reputation preceded me.

"Also me," I said with an apologetic smile.

"I have the police reports here. It seems pretty cut and dry. Anything you want to say for yourself before I proceed with sentencing?"

I paled. Sentencing sounded serious. Still, if Mr. Oliphant could run through town pantless and only get community service, perhaps my punishment wouldn't be so severe.

"I'm really sorry. It was totally an accident. I'm happy to pay for the damages. Although, depending on how much it will be, I might need a payment plan."

The judge smiled. "According to the estimate from our local woodsmith, the sign itself wasn't damaged. You'll be responsible for replacing the posts and the labor to remount it. Truth be told, I'm surprised a strong gust of wind didn't knock that rotted thing down sooner."

"Thank you, sir," I said. I'd thought the same thing.

"I'm also ordering one hundred hours of community service to be served with the fire department," he said.

I almost opened my mouth to protest, to ask for a few nights in jail instead. The fire department meant I'd have to see Linc. A lot. Well, at least for one hundred hours, much more than I'd planned on spending with him. I tried to avoid awkward situations as much as possible. And things between me and Linc definitely qualified as awkward.

"Ms. Lightwood? Did you hear me?" Judge Cockran asked. I refocused on him. "One hundred hours community service, and you'll surrender your driver's license for three months or until you complete a driver's safety class."

"Three months? How am I supposed to get to my community service?" I asked before my brain reconnected to my mouth. When it finally caught up, I backpedaled. "I mean, thank you, sir. That's very kind. I promise to stay out of trouble from now on."

Finding a body notwithstanding, of course. But I kept that thought to myself.

"See that you do. Pick up your order, hand over your license, and pay the court fine on your way out," he said. He moved on to the next case as I hung my head and exited the side door toward the clerk's office.

A little while later, sans license, I was trying to figure out how to get my mother's car—and myself—home as I exited the courthouse into the bright sun of the afternoon. I squinted my eyes, adjusting them from the artificial light of the inside, and ran smack into someone before they could adjust fully.

"We've got to stop meeting like this," Linc said, holding me by my elbows to steady me. "If I didn't know any better, I'd start to think you liked being pressed up against me."

I backed up abruptly. "If you weren't always in my way, I'd stop bumping into you."

"I thought you might need a ride," he said, ignoring me.

"I'm fine. I can walk."

"You are not going to walk all the way home. So, we can argue about it for another ten minutes, and then I can drive you home. Or you can just get in my truck now and save some time."

I glared at him. Part of me really wanted to push by him and walk home anyway. A bigger part, the part that included my feet which were currently drowning in the two-sizes-too-big shoes I'd borrowed from my mother, really wanted that ride.

I huffed, but said, "Fine. You can tell me all about what I'll be doing at the firehouse for one hundred hours."

He lowered his sunglasses and flashed his full megawatt smile at me. He was what my mother would call traditionally handsome—like the dashing male stars of the mid-1900s. He looked like if Gene Kelly and Chris Hemsworth had a baby. Throw in a dash of wholesome guy-next-door, and Lincoln Livestrong was every small-town mother's dream. I wondered what all those mothers would think if I told them it was Linc and I who'd let the goats loose in the high school as a senior prank.

"Are you getting in my truck or are we fighting? One or the other, because standing here with you silently staring at me is unnerving." Linc smirked again. He was perpetually amused at life. Whereas life seemed to be perpetually amused by me.

"I'm getting in the stupid truck," I said, pulling my eyes away from him. "Where are you parked?"

He gestured in the direction, then put his hand on the small of my back to escort me. I tried to ignore the wave of heat that crashed through my body at his touch.

"What were you doing here today anyway?" I asked as we walked.

"Mondays at the courthouse? Best entertainment in town!" he said with a chuckle. "Lots of craziness happens on the weekends. That bit with Mr. Oliphant—totally worth it. Not to mention the look on your face when Judge Cockran announced you'd be doing your community service at the firehouse. Priceless."

I smacked his arm. "It surprised me, that's all. And I don't believe you for a second. Don't you have imperative firehouse stuff to do? It is business hours."

Linc shrugged and stopped beside a beat-up red pickup truck. I recognized it immediately.

"Holy Moses! You still have this thing? Is it safe?"

"Perfectly safe," he said, giving the door a loving pat as he opened it for me. It squealed in protest. "Just needs a bit of grease in the hinges."

"Tell me this is a replica of the one you had in high school," I said, hesitating at the open door.

"Same frame, new trimmings under the hood. I rebuilt her a few years ago. Lots of good memories in this baby," he added, holding my gaze.

I swallowed hard and looked away, the heat from his touch now creeping up my neck in a blush. I had some memories in this rattletrap too, only I didn't know if I would consider them good or not. Good at the time, absolutely—no one would argue that a few moments alone with teenaged Linc on this bench seat wasn't good. But good, now, in hindsight, knowing the humiliation that came after? That's where the line between good and not-so-much started to blur. I'd been able to get past those memories by chalking it up to a learning experience.

Totally past it. Hardly ever thought about it.

I pushed those memories aside once again and climbed in. Linc shut the door as I settled into the all too familiar seat. It still smelled the same—leather and oil and Lincoln—and as much as I tried to squelch my memories, they persevered. I'd ridden here countless times to and from school, to and from the mall, to and from the reservoir. Of course, that was before the "teach me how to kiss" episode in our senior year. It seemed like a great idea at the time—I didn't want to go to college without having my first kiss; Linc knew how to kiss if Missy's stories were any indication. Plus, he was my best friend. My safe space. Easy peasy, no-brainer.

Except it turned into a disaster of epic proportions that ended in humility, slobber, and tears—all on my part.

When he hopped into the driver's seat, I willed the fire threatening to overtake my face to stay put in my gut where it belonged.

"What are you gonna make me do?" I asked.

He snickered, and I realized how it sounded.

"At the firehouse," I added quickly. "For my community service."

"There's lots of stuff to do. We definitely need help organizing the office. And we need someone to spearhead the calendar shoot."

I gaped at him. "You don't seriously do a Piney Ridge Firehouse calendar. How cliché. How small town."

"Whatever works. People love it. We include adoptable pets too. Think you can handle that, Ms. World Famous Photojournalist?"

I scoffed at him. "A few decrepit firemen and some cats? I think I'll be fine."

"Who are you calling decrepit?" he asked, feigning offense.

"Current company excluded. How does Piney Ridge have enough firemen to fill a calendar? This place only has three police officers."

"First of all, the correct term is fire*fighter*. We have a few women among our volunteers, I'll have you know. Between those of us who are paid, the volunteers, the support staff, and the three police officers, we have enough to get us through September. Then we double up for the rest of the year. I'm usually in two months—"

"Of course you are," I mumbled. I was actually surprised he wasn't in every month. Besides the mothers in town, half of our high school graduating class would snap that calendar up in a New York minute.

"Why do you need my help now?" I asked.

"Our usual photographer was the husband of one of the volunteers."

"Emphasis on 'was,'" I noted.

Linc nodded. "They've recently had a falling out. As in, she caught him falling out of his pants with another woman. So we can't use him any longer. I figured you'd be

64

the perfect replacement. Which is why I sneaked over to the courthouse earlier to finagle Judge Cockran into assigning you the community service at the firehouse. Win-win for both of us. We get a free photoshoot with a professional photographer, and you get to complete your court-ordered punishment doing something you love."

Well, color me surprised. "That's—that's actually really thoughtful."

"It also keeps you from having to work somewhere in town where by now everyone knows you were the one to discover Missy's body."

"Don't remind me." I sulked into my seat at the mention of it. "Chief Duncan thinks I did it. He pretty much accused me of murder last night."

"Don't listen to him. He couldn't investigate himself out of a wet paper bag."

Linc turned the wrong way down Poole Avenue, away from my house.

"Forget the way to my parents' house?" I asked.

"Nope. I thought we'd make a pit stop first. In my experience, nothing cures a case of the blues like Scoop There It Is Creamery."

Chapter 9

Linc wasn't wrong. I'd yet to visit Scoop There It Is, affectionately known as Scoops to the locals, since my return. Mainly, I'd been avoiding the crowds since my infamous road accident marking my return. And now I felt my anxiety ratchet up again. As much as I wanted the homemade ice cream, I wanted to disappear into oblivion first.

I groaned. "I'll wait in the truck."

"Nonsense. They've added new flavors in the years since you've been away. How could you possibly know what you want?"

I crossed my arms and slunk down even lower in the seat. "What I want is to avoid the crowds and gossip," I whined, sounding every bit like a disgruntled teenager and not caring.

"It's eleven o'clock on a Monday morning. Everyone is either at work or at the diner for an early lunch. The crowds don't pick up until after school lets out."

I gave him a side-eyed look. "Fine. But if there's more than, like, three cars in the parking lot, I'm staying put."

"Have it your way, but I'm not carrying two cones out the door. You want ice cream? You gotta come in."

"Meany." I pouted. My heartbeat, on overdrive since finding Missy's body, kicked up another notch the closer we got to the parking lot. I really wanted the ice cream—no place made better ice cream, and I'd literally been around the world—but my recent misadventures were making me a bit of an agoraphobic. Luckily, a virtually empty parking lot greeted us. I let out a long breath. Linc chuckled beside me.

"My panic attacks amuse you?"

"It's just ice cream, Alex," he said, pulling into a parking spot and cutting the engine. I took another deep breath and followed him into the store. Maybe I could hide behind his broad frame.

As soon as I entered the familiar shop, nostalgia and peace washed over me. I'd spent so many afternoons in this room after school with a milkshake or ice cream cone in hand. I could still taste the wooden sample spoons. The smell of cream and fruit and cold was part of my being—or at least a part of my stomach. I'd sampled every single flavor, tried every combination of topping, and used a fair share of napkins to dry tears of joy and tears of sorrow. The same colorful shelving holding stacked rows of sprinkles, candies, and chocolates lined the right wall. Underneath were bistro tables for patrons to stay inside and eat. To the left stood freezers holding the vats of homemade ice cream in every flavor from rich, creamy vanilla to more unique apple pie, and strawberry cheesecake. All made on the premises using the Huffleman family recipe handed down through the generations.

The same letter board above the glass ice cream cases listed the current flavors and reminded customers to order milkshakes first. Milkshakes so thick, you needed a spoon, and available in every flavor they offered. The prices, although a little higher than the last time I came in, were extremely reasonable when compared to what I paid for a generic soft-serve cone in New York.

Linc nudged my shoulder with his considerable bicep and flashed me an "I told you so" smile. He sauntered over to the counter and rested an arm on the top of the refrigerated case as he ordered. His T-shirt rode up a little at his waist as he leaned, and I could see the defined muscles of his abs. Forget it, I didn't want ice cream, I wanted to lick him from head to toe. And back again. If I hadn't sworn off men forever, I'd show him I'd learned to kiss in the years since the "teach me" incident. But I wanted nothing to do with his particular gender. Not that I—plain Jane—would have any possibility whatsoever of turning the eye of a man like Linc.

As Mary Huffleman scooped his ice cream, I watched him, simultaneously trying not to drool while also swimming in memories of being in this exact place with him so many times before. He used to share in my joys and sorrows, as I did his. Right up until he replaced me with popularity and the Snob Blob.

And Missy.

A vision of Missy's lifeless body flashed unbidden in my brain. I blanched and sank into one of the nearby chairs. Here I was boo-hooing over things that happened in high school when a wife and mother had lost her life.

Linc shoved an ice cream cone under my nose, bringing me out of my thoughts.

"I took the liberty of ordering for you since you didn't answer the three times I asked what you wanted. One scoop of apple pie, one scoop of cinnamon on a cake cone."

I almost cried. It was exactly what I would have ordered myself. Exactly what I always ordered. He'd remembered.

"Please don't be nice to me. I can't handle it right now," I whispered.

"I took a big lick of your cone, just to make sure it wasn't poisoned. So, I'm not that nice," he said, taking a lick of his own. And now I wanted to be an ice cream cone. Desperately.

"Thinking about high school? Or Missy?" he asked, still able to read me like a book.

"A little bit of both," I admitted. "She was definitely murdered, wasn't she? No chance it was a trail accident?"

He shook his head slowly. "Unfortunately not. Look, I'm not sure how much I'm allowed to tell you. I've never handled a murder victim before," he said.

I noticed, then, the pallor under his normal complexion, the sadness in his usually amused gray-blue eyes. This trip for ice cream was just as much for him as it was for me.

"And I've never been suspected of murder before. You aren't bound by investigative privilege, right?" I asked, taking a bite of the ice cream. The trick was to get equal amounts of cinnamon and apple pie in the same bite—an art I'd been perfecting for years before I left.

"I don't even think that's a thing."

"Then spill, Livestrong," I said. "I need to know what I'm up against. Was she shot? Could it have been a hunting accident?" I still didn't want it to be a murder.

"Not shot. I'm not a medical examiner, but I know that wasn't a bullet hole. And it was no accident." He sighed and rubbed a hand over his face. His stubble rasped under his fingers. "The state guys took her to their lab for the autopsy since Dr. Wells has never worked a murder before."

"Stabbed?" I whispered.

"That would be my guess. I only saw her briefly as I checked for a pulse and then again when I helped load her into the van. And her hands were messed up."

I shuddered. "Like she put up a fight."

"Exactly."

"Then I'm off the hook!" I said, louder than I intended. Mary, wiping down the counter, raised her eyebrow. I lowered my voice. "I don't have any wounds from being in a fight. So, it couldn't have been me."

"Were you unsure?" Linc asked with the ghost of a smile.

"No, dingbat. *I* know I didn't do it. But Chief Duncan was all over me like ants at a picnic the night we found her. I'm numero uno on his suspect list." I grabbed a napkin from the canister on the table to catch a dribble on my chin.

Linc took the napkin from me and dabbed at my nose. It was ridiculously charming, and I felt it in my gut. I gave myself a mental shake. What was wrong with me? Clearly, the emotional events of the last week were also affecting my hormones. Also, clearly high school crushes were as deeply ingrained in me as the taste of Scoop's ice cream. Nostalgia was playing havoc on my mental state lately.

"Like I said, Chief Duncan is used to public intoxication and kids stealing candy bars," Linc continued the conversation after returning my napkin. "In the last few years, he's gotten even more lackadaisical, pawning off anything substantial to Andrea Martinez, then taking credit for it. The only reason he isn't out of office is because no one ever runs against him."

I licked my ice cream as I thought. Even though Chief Duncan was acting like a bumbling idiot, there were a lot of things stacked against me—I had an argument with the victim; I found the body; Missy and I had a volatile history; I was new in town; I didn't have a solid alibi; I'd already killed a sign. Could I really blame Chief Duncan for focusing on me?

But, on my side, I didn't have defense wounds; I hadn't touched any scissors, and I didn't have a strong motive. With the way Kelly talked, Missy was far from the town sweetheart. Not to mention the fact that Missy was a few inches taller and quite a bit heavier than me.

And I didn't do it.

I took another lick and refocused on Linc. His expression knocked me back—his eyes dark, lips in a tight line. Was he mad at me? He exuded intensity. When I cocked my head in question, his usual half-amused, half-bored façade slipped back into place. Maybe I'd imagined it.

"At least Detective Spaulding seems like he knows what he's doing," I said, choosing to ignore it. "I just need to lie low and avoid Chief Duncan."

Linc winced and looked away.

"What? What is that look for?"

He remained mute.

"Lincoln Livestrong, if you don't want ice cream in your lap, tell me what you aren't telling me," I demanded. Not that I would ever waste Scoop's ice cream by spilling it in his lap, but he didn't need to know that. I held it aloft to give credence to the threat.

"Okay, okay," he said, holding up his hands in surrender. "It's nothing really. Except that the firehouse is kinda connected to the police station offices." He mumbled the last part, but I caught enough.

"Wait? What? When did that happen?" I asked. The police station had always been in the building beside the high school. The firehouse was across town.

"We renovated a few years back. The town council thought a one-stop shop for all your emergency needs would be better. The high schoolers were thrilled."

"I bet. Well, good thing I won't be—" I cut myself off with a gasp. "Oh no. Oh crap. Oh no. The community service."

"Hence the wince." He had the good grace to look sheepish again. "I didn't think of that when I offered to have you do the community service at the firehouse."

My shoulders slumped. Still, I'd rather work in the firehouse than among the town gossips. I'd have to pull up my big-girl panties and get over it. And absolutely still try to avoid Chief Duncan.

I rubbed two fingers on my forehead to stave off the tension headache threatening to overtake me.

"When do I start?" I asked, resigned to my fate. The sooner I started, the sooner I could finish.

"What are you doing tomorrow?" He raised his eyebrows and crunched into his cone.

"Absolutely nothing." Jeez, my life was pathetic.

"I get to the station around nine. Drop by any time after that." He leaned back in his chair and smirked behind his cone. "Bonus points if you wear that flamingo dress. Or maybe find one with Dalmatians."

I seriously considered dropping the rest of my ice cream in his lap.

Chapter 10

I did not wear a Dalmatian dress for my first day at the firehouse, as Linc had suggested, instead opting for cargo pants and a tank top—my usual uniform and much easier to ride a bike in. I thanked the gods of karma and awkward women that my mother had a fairly new adult bike in the garage from her brief stint in the Coastbusters, the local motorcycle club. Sure, it was banana yellow with a basket strapped to the front, but it was a thousand times better than riding through town on my rusty, purple ten-speed with banana seat and multicolored streamers blowing in the wind.

I rode past the hair salon and tried not to think about the last time I was there. Today, Kelly stood outside with a few men in hard hats. I slowed the bike to see what was going on. A new sign hung above the entrance. No longer did it say "Missy K's Hair Salon" in bright pink and lime green. Now it read "Shear-lock Combs" in a more subdued burgundy and gray. As Kelly instructed the men who were washing the old name off the windows and repainting the door, I watched in fascination, craning my neck to see what other changes Kelly had instigated.

Kelly turned, spotted me, and raised a hand to wave. Then her eyes went wide, and her mouth formed a little "o."

She said, "Alex! Watch out—" right before I ran my mother's bike into the old Missy K's sign that rested against the curb.

I managed to catch myself before completely tumbling over the handlebars. Barely. I landed with a thud and a whimper on the concrete sidewalk with the bike on top of me. Piney Ridge signs - 2. Alex Lightwood - 0.

Kelly and the construction crew ran over to help. One of the men lifted the bike, while another grabbed me under the armpits to hoist me up. Kelly wrung her hands and paced.

"Oh man. Are you okay? Do you need some ice? I have some in the staff room," she fretted. "I knew we should've put that stupid thing right in the dumpster."

"I'm okay," I said, assessing my abraded elbow. "I'm headed to the firehouse anyway, so Linc can take a look at it."

"Your next haircut is on me. The works. Whatever you want."

"That's kind but unnecessary. I seem to have a knack for running into signs," I deadpanned. I showed the sign my favorite finger.

Kelly barked a surprised laugh. The construction crew, seeing that I was alive, went back to their work.

I gestured at the front of the shop. "Doing a little redecorating?"

"I'm so excited. I've been wanting to rebrand for a while now, but Missy kept insisting consistency was key. I tried to tell her that no one came to the salon because the '90s threw up on the decor."

Now it was my turn to laugh. A more perfect description of the neon-pink and lime-green color scheme couldn't be found.

"I like the new look. Very modern and chic," I said.

And very quick after Missy's death. To hide my expression, I leaned over to pick up the bike. The basket was a little bent, but other than that, and a few minor scuffs, it seemed to be in working order. Much better than my ankle, which was now throbbing and beginning to swell. I willed it to hold out long enough to bike to the firehouse. I wanted to tell Linc about this new development in the "Alex Didn't Do It" case file.

"I guess you have sole ownership of the salon now?" I asked, hoping I sounded conversational and not accusatory.

"Mostly. Some of Missy's stock goes to her kids. But I finally get creative control."

I swore I heard the devilish "mwahaha" in Kelly's head. I waited for Kelly to tap her fingers together like the villains in the film noir movies I liked to watch before bed.

My astonishment must have shown on my face because Kelly quickly added, "I know it sounds horrible. Missy just"—she waved her hand, looking for an appropriate word—"passed away, but you have to understand, I've been waiting *years* for this to happen. Like I said the other day, Missy was a difficult business partner. And that was on a good day."

"I can see that. I was only around her for a few minutes, and I wanted to throw a kielbasa at her," I admitted.

"You and half the town," Kelly muttered. "I don't like to speak ill of the dead, but she really rubbed a lot of people the wrong way."

"Did you tell any of that to Chief Duncan?" I asked.

"No. It didn't come up. He and that hot state detective asked about business and what happened the day she died."

I bit my lip. "Did you tell them about the argument Missy and I had in the salon?"

Kelly shook her head. "Girl, if I mentioned every person Missy pissed off on a daily basis, I would still be talking to them. Trust me, your little tiff was hardly a blip on her radar."

I let out a breath. "Okay. Not that it's a secret, but the chief already has me in the crosshairs since I found her."

"Consider my silence part of payment for leaving the stupid sign in the street. I can't say the same for the rest of the salon patrons, but the cops won't hear about it from me," Kelly promised.

"Thanks." I swung my leg over the bike seat. When I tentatively put some pressure on my hurt ankle, a dull pain shot up my leg. Not great, but I could work with it, if I hurried. Still, there was one more thing I needed to know. One more thing that might help exonerate me even further. "What time did Missy leave the salon?"

"Oh. She and Jodie left about an hour after you and your mom. Didn't even tell me she was leaving. Typical," Kelly said.

I frowned. So much for that. I'd hoped Missy had either put in a full day at the salon or left immediately after us so my alibi would be a bit tighter. Not that "home with my mom" was a great alibi. Lots of moms would lie to protect their children, mine included.

"Great job on the rebrand, Kelly. I love the new name," I said as I maneuvered the bike back into the bike lane.

"Thanks. And stop by anytime for that free haircut," Kelly called after me.

A few long minutes later, I limped as gracefully as possible into the firehouse office. Linc looked up from the computer behind the desk. Noticing me, he looked pointedly at the clock hanging on the wall behind him.

"Hey sleepyhead. I expected you like an—" He stopped midsentence when he saw me limp. He squinted his eyes and gave me a once over. "What the heck happened to you? Fight another sign?"

"Ha ha. But actually, yes." I held up a hand to ward off his questions. "Don't want to talk about it. Can you put your EMT hat on and take a look at my ankle? I think it's sprained."

He walked around the desk and draped my arm over his shoulder to help support me as I hobbled to the row of chairs against the wall. Fang came in from the door between the office and the engine bay. He danced around our feet as Linc lowered me into the chair. When I was seated, Fang placed his head on my knee, much like he did that first day by the fire truck.

"Is he trained to do that?" I asked, burying my hands once again into his soft fur.

Linc nodded. "He's great for calming people down."

Kneeling in front of me, Linc placed my hurt ankle on his knee. After rolling up my pant leg, he gave my Achilles tendon a little pinch.

I yelped in pain. "Ow! Watch it, you sadist!"

"Guess that's a little tender."

"You think?" I tried to pull my foot away, but he clamped down on my knee. "Don't you have an ice pack or something?"

He ignored me. "I'm going to remove your shoe and sock to take a closer look. This may increase the swelling a little bit, but that's to be expected."

I held my breath and squeezed my eyes shut as he gingerly loosened the laces of my sneakers. Fang lapped at my hand with his tongue. Linc's fingers brushed my skin as he pulled off my sock.

"Siren red," he said. "I never would have guessed."

I peeked open an eye to see him smiling up at me with eyebrow raised. He'd noticed my toenail polish. "Yeah, well, I'm just full of surprises."

I thought I heard him mumble, "I'll bet you are," but couldn't be sure through my growing haze of pain.

"The red goes well with the blue-and-purple bruise you have forming."

"Great. Just what I need."

"Can you move your ankle?" he asked. I wiggled it back and forth with limited pain.

"It's mainly when I put pressure on it that it hurts," I explained.

"Looks and sounds like a sprain to me. You'll be fine in a few days. I have crutches in the back you can borrow. Wait here."

"But I'll be late for the marathon I'm running this afternoon," I said as he gently lowered my ankle off his knee.

A moment later, he returned with supplies. We got me set up at the desk so I could work on organizing some of the files on the computer. Fang, sensing my stress decreasing, disappeared back into the engine bay.

"I need to hear the story of your second sign attack," he said as I started moving the myriad of desktop icons into some semblance of order. I filled him in as I worked, unable to control the excitement in my voice.

78

"So that's weird, right?" I asked, forgetting about the computer and leaning my chin on my knuckles. "Missy has been gone for barely forty-eight hours, and Kelly is already renaming and redecorating? I mean, who can have a custom sign made that quickly? She definitely had that thing laying around before Sunday. Right?"

He ran his fingers over his chin. "The timing does seem a bit inappropriate. We haven't even had a funeral yet."

"Exactly! She totally had motive and opportunity." I realized my voice had taken on the pitch of a kid on Christmas morning. But the sooner I figured out the real killer, the sooner I'd stop being the prime suspect. I tried to bring my excitement down a notch. "Should we tell Chief Duncan?"

"I think that's a bit premature," Linc said.

I gaped at him. Why was he not on my side?

"Really, Alex. We don't even have the time of death. For all we know, Kelly has an airtight alibi because she was knuckle-deep in someone's hair while Missy was being murdered."

That blew the wind out of my sails. He was right, dangit. "Okay. So we sit on this until the autopsy results come back."

"Any other townspeople you want to accuse of murder today?" he asked.

"Well, it has to be somebody," I grumbled, turning my attention back to the computer.

Chapter 11

I didn't even argue when Linc offered to drive me home at the end of the day. Although I'd been icing and elevating my hurt ankle, and the swelling had gone down a bit, it still hurt when I put pressure on it. As evidenced by the fact I almost fell twice while trying to go to the bathroom earlier. Awkwardness and crutches were not a good mix.

"Keep icing that ankle. Twenty minutes on, twenty minutes off," Linc instructed as he lifted my mother's now less-than pristine bike from the bed of his truck. He wheeled it to the garage and then ran back to help me hobble to the door.

"What in blazing turnips happened now?" my mother asked when she saw me on crutches.

"You mean you haven't heard? My latest adventure hasn't made the gossip rounds yet?"

Thank those blazing turnips for small favors, I thought.

Mom put her hands on her hips. "What adventure?"

Just then, Colleen's little green VW bug parked behind Linc's truck. An unexpected bubble of joy spread in my chest. I'd missed my friend. And although Linc was a good sounding board for my current troubles, Colleen was free from embarrassment and residual crush-like feelings.

"Thanks for the lift, Linc. I'll see you tomorrow to clock more service hours."

He helped me onto the porch step by gripping my uninjured elbow to steady me. I ignored the little jolt of heat emanating from that skin-to-skin contact and focused on not falling down.

"See you tomorrow. Mrs. Lightwood," he addressed Mom with his mother-killer smile. She practically melted. "You look lovely as always. Be sure Alex elevates her ankle and keeps ice on it."

"Of course, Lincoln. Thanks for taking good care of her."

"Anytime. I'll come pick you up tomorrow, Alex. Quarter to nine, okay?" I nodded. "Unless your ankle gets worse, and you want to rest it. Just text me. I put my number in your phone."

"When did you do that? And how did you get around my password?" I asked.

The dingbat winked at me and, with a small wave to Colleen who was walking up the porch, sprinted back to his truck. Alan Jackson blared from the speakers, and Fang's head hung out the back window as Linc drove off down the street.

"Now there is a boy who aged to perfection," Colleen commented as all three of us watched the truck turn out of sight.

"Whatever. I'll always think of him as the kid who shoved me in Mr. Albright's pond when we were eleven," I lied. I had one hundred percent noticed the man he had become. Like a puppy, he'd grown into himself.

Unlike me, who still couldn't manage to walk through a doorway without banging an elbow. Maybe that's why I liked the desert so much—nothing to run into.

"Okay, Peanut. Let's get you in the house," Mom said. "You can tell us both what the heck happened."

An hour later, hot tea mugs empty, cookies eaten, ankle fussed over, and story told, Mom left me and Colleen seated in the living room while she ran some errands. "Errands" were merely an excuse to gauge the scuttlebutt about town, but I took advantage of her absence to tell Colleen about the events of the weekend and my suspicions about Kelly.

"Okay, the timing is weird. But Kelly has definitely grown up since her mean-girl high school stage," Colleen said when I finished.

"But what if she's just acting all sweet and innocent, but underneath is a cold-blooded killer?"

Colleen pursed her lips. "You haven't known her these past years. She's changed. And why would she act now? Why not years ago?"

"I don't know. Maybe they got in some argument and Kelly finally lost it. She's been living in Missy's shadow since high school."

"So have a lot of people. If you ask me, I'd put the money on the husband." Colleen took another cookie from the plate. I scowled. If *I* ate any more cookies, the calories would go right to my hips. But Colleen could eat an entire cake and still be a rail. She was tall and thin and Irish to the core. I'd always been jealous of her thick curls and bright-green eyes. Colleen was vibrant like a kaleidoscope where I resembled the bland sands of the Sahara.

That's it. I was moving back there. I could stay with Abbas and help him rent camels.

"Earth to Alex," Colleen said, waving a hand in my face. "I said, I think Mike did it."

"Sorry. Zoning. Maybe I hit my head in the tumble this morning. Why Mike?" I shifted in my chair. The rest of my body was now feeling the aches of falling too.

"The husband always does it, right?"

"I'm going to need more solid evidence than that to get off Chief Duncan's list," I pointed out.

"Okay, how about this? I have it on good authority that Mr. Acting Mayor is having multiple affairs. Multiple! Maybe Missy found out, and he killed her so he could be with one of his side pieces." Colleen practically giggled. I caught the excitement.

"Oh, that is juicy. Do you know who any of the women are?" I asked. Maybe we could have a little chat with them, you know, being friendly neighbors and all.

"Only through rumors and speculation. But my dad plays poker with Mike and a bunch of other guys on Wednesday nights. I heard him mention that Mike hasn't been coming the last few weeks. But he has been telling Missy that's where he's going," Colleen said.

"We have to follow him," I blurted out. "Do you think he'll go tomorrow night?"

"Normally, I'd say no. His wife just died; you'd think he'd have a little more respect." Colleen tapped a purple nail on her lips. "But this is Mike Vandenburg we're talking about. Couldn't hurt to try."

"You're willing to go with me? Just like that?" I asked, genuinely grateful to have such a great friend.

"Are you kidding? Every episode of *Forensic Files* I've binged has led me to this very moment. Plus," she added with a smirk, "who's gonna keep you from falling through a window or smashing into yet another sign?"

"Ha ha, funny guy," I said, but I smiled too. Colleen wasn't wrong. I'd be even more impeded if my ankle didn't miraculously heal by tomorrow night.

"Soooo, I've been trying to think of a way to ask without sounding like a complete creep, but—" Colleen started.

I cut her off, "You want to see the picture."

"Please?" Colleen asked, wrinkling up her nose. I understood completely—the same morbid curiosity drove me to look more closely at Missy's body in the woods.

"Grab my computer and hard drive from my bedroom."

Colleen practically ran up the stairs.

"And some ibuprofen!" I added. If I was going on an adventure tomorrow night, I needed my body to cooperate. From a vast number of prior experiences, I knew I always hurt worse the day after a fall. Like the time I was taking pictures of a memorial procession in India, backed up to get a better angle, and stepped right off the edge of a small cliff. I saved my camera. My back and head? Not so much. I was stiff for a week.

Colleen made it back downstairs in record time. She fetched me a glass of water while I booted up the computer and navigated to the saved photos. Hard to believe this was only a few days ago. I took the pill and opened the photo file.

Colleen sucked in a breath, then let it out, and leaned closer to the screen. "What am I looking at? I mean it's a great picture of the birds, but is this the right photo?"

I zoomed in to the area behind the bush with the cardinals. I pointed to the lighter part among the grass and detritus covering the ground. "Here."

"Oh my goodness! That's it? How did you even notice that?" she asked, clearly disappointed.

"It was drawing my eye away from the birds. I wanted to see how easy it would be to crop it out," I explained. Again.

84

"Hmph. You can't even see the cause of death." Colleen flung herself back on the couch, arms crossed. "At least the birds are pretty. You can totally crop her out."

"Colleen! I'm not actually going to use this photo," I exclaimed. Just what I needed—some mommy blogger using this photo and then finding out later it was a crime scene.

"It's a great picture!" Colleen started scrolling through the rest of the shoot. "These are all great. Okay, fine. You have others that are equally as amazing."

"Thanks," I said.

"So, tell me all about your day with Linc," Colleen said.

"Nothing to tell. I cleaned up the firehouse desktop; he iced my ankle." I shrugged.

"Boring." Then Colleen's eyes sparkled. "Unless 'iced my ankle' is a euphemism for—Hey!" she shouted, catching the pillow I threw at her head.

"Honestly, I spent a good portion of the day searching for apartment rentals. I love my parents, but I need to get out of here. I'm used to being on my own." I thought of the apartment I'd shared with Wreck-it Rick for the last year. "Or mostly on my own."

"Come on, then. Let's go look! I'll be your chauffeur."

"I'm supposed to be icing and elevating," I said evasively, gesturing to my ankle. As much as I wanted to move out, I wanted to move out to New York, not find a place here in Piney Ridge.

"No excuse. You can bring the ice. And elevate when you get home."

I bit my lip. Was I ready to take this step toward permanence? Was I willing to not take that step and stay at my parents' house?

"Come on," Colleen whined. "I'm bored. We can drive by and at least look if you don't want to tour any."

Before I could respond, the front door slammed open, making us both jump. Nana K stood there in thick stockings, thicker glasses, and a scarf covering her shock of white hair. Or at least it used to be white.

"Nana K!" Colleen exclaimed. "What do you have going on under that babushka?"

She whipped off the scarf to reveal a pink- and purple-ombre pixie cut. "Whaddya think?" she asked.

I smiled so broad I thought my face might break. "Nana, I missed you so much. It looks perfect."

Nana K shuffled over to where I had my foot propped on the coffee table. She leaned over to give me a light kiss on the forehead. Then did the same to Colleen.

"The other ladies in the community think I'm nuts for this hair. I told them I may be nuts, but I'm not dead."

"Of course you did," I said fondly.

"Your mother called to tell me what happened," Nana K explained. "I came to see if you needed anything. Cheesecake? Pierogis? I'll make whatever you want."

Before I could open my mouth to say, "Yes, please," Colleen cut me off. "I'm trying to convince Alex to go look at some apartments."

I gave her a look. If Nana K agreed, there would be no begging off. Mom absolutely got her stubbornness from her mother.

I watched with dismay and amusement as all of Nana K's wrinkles rearranged themselves into a bright smile. The thick lenses of her tortoiseshell cat-eye glasses magnified her hazel eyes.

"Fabulous idea," Nana K said. "We can take my car so we can all go."

I sighed. No cheesecake for me.

Chapter 12

Our unlikely trio piled into Nana K's pale-pink Mercedes. She already had the convertible top down and the babushka tied back around her head by the time I managed to get myself and my crutches in the front seat.

"There are extra scarves in the glove box. Buckle up, ladies, this baby likes to go fast." Nana K ground the gears into first and took off like a shot down the road.

"I didn't even give you an address!" I shouted over the wind.

"I know the perfect place," Nana K shouted back in her raspy voice. We sped through town—stop signs seemed to be optional—and ended up on the other side of the reservoir near the Bachman's Orchard and Farmer's Market. I pried my white-knuckled fingers from their death grip on the door handle as we screeched to a halt in the driveway. Glancing in the rearview mirror, I saw Colleen looked as shell-shocked as I felt.

"Why are we here?" I asked. "Hungry for a road snack?"

I wouldn't put it past my grandmother to detour miles out of the way because she craved a piece of Anita

Bachman's famous apple pie. My stomach grumbled. Apple pie wasn't my grandmother's homemade cheesecake, but it would be a fine consolation prize.

"Two birds, one stone," Nana K said. "I happen to know on good authority that Bobby Bachman has a room to let in the loft of the barn. He's been saving it for his wayward son, Tony. But everyone knows Tony does not want to take over the family business. Not that he'd be any good at it anyway. So the beautiful space is sitting there empty, collecting hay dust and cobwebs."

"Sounds charming," I mumbled, hobbling on my crutches after my grandmother. For an octogenarian, she sure was spry.

Colleen stayed by my side as Nana K bustled along ahead of us. "Was this place on your list?" she asked me under her breath. I wasn't sure if Colleen was trying to keep her voice down or if it was leftover anxiety from the car ride here. My heart still pounded from the near-death experience by the Scoop's intersection. Did Nana K even see that stop sign?

"Nope," I answered her. "Wasn't even listed on any of the websites I looked at. I'll just wait for an opportune moment, make an apology, and steer Nana K toward the pies. I mean, how does she even think I'm going to be able to look at a loft with a bum ankle?"

"No kidding," Colleen chuckled. "You can barely climb a ladder on a good day."

By the time we caught up to Nana K, she'd already cornered Bobby Bachman and his mother, known to everyone under the age of 60 as Mrs. Anita, at the back of the market space where they were restocking fresh-picked strawberries from their fields.

"No, no. Don't give me that nonsense about Tony. We all know he isn't coming back anytime soon," Nana K was saying.

I gave Mrs. Anita an "I'm sorry" look. Anita Bachman, only a few years younger than Nana K, smiled back.

"You're letting that place sit empty when you could be renting it. For money. And Alex is as quiet as a mouse. You'll never even know she's here. You might even convince her into taking some professional photos of this place. Your advertising could use some sprucing up," Nana K continued, unabashed.

"Nana!" I admonished. "I'm sure their advertising is fine."

Nana K shook her head and hitched a thumb at Bobby. "Bobby here takes the photos with his phone and uploads them right to the website. Without any filters. I know; I follow them on Instagram."

"She's not wrong," Mrs. Anita said. She turned to her son. "That loft has been sitting unused for quite a while. No reason we can't rent it out while we wait for Tony to make up his mind."

Maybe this could work. If there was the threat of eviction at any moment, then there wouldn't be a long-term lease. Which meant I wasn't pressured into staying in Piney Ridge.

I said, "I'm looking for some short-term lease options anyway, so that isn't a deterrent."

"Why are we standing around gabbing? Let's go look at the space, then," Nana K said. She grabbed Mrs. Anita by the elbow and marched her out the door.

"Your gramma looking for a job?" Bobby asked as we followed the two matriarchs. "She could sell a glass of water to a drowning man."

Instead of a ladder, like I imagined, a sturdy set of wooden stairs with an elegantly crafted handrail led from the outside of the well-kept barn to a door on the second level. With Colleen's help, I managed to hop up the steps without spraining another ankle. Bobby pushed the door open to reveal what in New York would be considered a studio apartment. Except this was nothing like I would have found in New York.

The space dwarfed the one-bedroom apartment I'd shared with Rick. The exposed rafters of the barn ceiling added to the spacious, open feeling. It was longer than it was wide—running about half the width of the barn below, but beautifully renovated. More log cabin than stinky, old barn, which was the image floating through my mind when Nana K described it. And, to my delight, not a cobweb to be seen.

"Wow," Colleen said on a breath. "I'll trade you."

"Not much to see, but I'll take you on a tour," Bobby said. I could hear a sense of pride in his voice despite his humble comment.

"Did you do all the work yourself?" I asked. The wooden floors and walls shone with fresh lacquer. The dents and scuffs in the age-worn wood only added to the rustic, authentic vibe.

"Mostly, but I had some help. The same guy that's gonna fix the Welcome sign. He helped some," Bobby said.

Mrs. Anita leaned in toward me and Colleen and whispered, "Bobby mainly stood around and replenished water bottles. Occasionally fetched a tool. Bless his heart."

I hid a laugh behind a cough. The Welcome sign would be in good hands if the same man that crafted this space worked on it. I felt a little better about where my money was going.

"Bedroom is behind this partition," Bobby said, pointing to the right. I peeked in. Not a huge space, but definitely more than I was used to. A huge bay window let in ample natural light—something my photographer heart craved. A little cut-out closet with a curtain graced one wall. Nice touch.

"Next, we have the only fully separate room—the bathroom. I figured Tony wouldn't care one way or another, but Ma here had the ladies in mind. Hoping Tony gets himself one of those at some point," Bobby explained.

"Good thinking," Nana K said. "No tub, but this shower surround looks like the one at the spa in Mapleton. Alex, check out that tile."

"It's really lovely," I said, meaning it. River rocks and rough, natural tile intertwined to create the ambiance of the outdoors. A window in the ceiling bathed the space in light and warmth. The design was perfect and exactly what I would have picked for myself. A small pedestal sink, decorative round mirror, and normal boring toilet finished the space.

"Down this way is the living room area and kitchen."

We moved the rest of the way down the space to the far wall toward the kitchen. A fair amount of cabinet space, more than I would ever need for my two pots and three dishes, lined the wall above a deep farmhouse sink and counters in the same color palette as the tile in the bathroom. I turned in a circle to view the open space and gasped when I saw the fireplace inset into the wall.

"Is that real?" I asked at the same time Colleen asked, "Is that safe?"

Bobby chuckled. "Both real and safe. We had all the inspections done. There's a wood pile out back beside the barn."

"I don't think I can afford this," I said. Considering how much I paid for a run-down, water-stained, cockroach infested, third of this space in New York, I couldn't imagine what this brand-new, handcrafted space would cost a month. My lack of steady income suddenly seemed more of an issue. My savings, and the royalties from stock photography, was ample, but certainly not bottomless. Especially since it was currently unreplenished.

Nana K piped up. "I'm sure we can come to something agreeable. This space was sitting empty, so any amount is better than nothing. Throw in Alex's photography services, say once a season or for special events, and that could offset some of the cost. Of course, she'll pay for her own utilities."

"Sounds like you have this all figured out," I said, smiling.

Nana K shrugged. "It's a no-brainer."

"Sounds like a win-win to me," Mrs. Anita said, cutting off whatever Bobby was about to say. She named a price that had me gaping once again. This time in a good way.

"Are you sure?" I squeaked. Then cleared my throat and tried again. I couldn't even rent a parking space in New York for that little. "I don't want to take advantage."

"Keep in mind we're running a business here. No loud parties. No drugs or illegal activities," Mrs. Anita warned.

"Wouldn't think of it," I said, crossing my heart with a finger.

"And don't break anything," Bobby added. I nodded. Can't a girl run into one sign without everyone pegging her as Alex the Destroyer?

Okay, two signs. But who's counting.

"Tony gets priority. So if he suddenly decides to come back, you're out. Want to be clear up front."

"No problem. I have very little belongings. And I'm hoping this is temporary until I get another gig in New York," I explained.

"Sounds like it's all set. How long until she can move in?" Nana K asked.

"Coupla days?" Bobby suggested. "Just need to run the water and turn on the electricity again."

"Fabulous. Now let's go get some pie. All this negotiating makes me hungry," Nana K said.

Holy crap. Did I just lease an apartment? What did I do? I took a deep breath. I'd have a few days to think about whether I really wanted this commitment or not. But given the price and the condition, I'd seriously be an idiot not to take it. The only downside was how to get to town without a car or a driver's license for the next few months. I wasn't used to relying on people.

I gave my grandmother a sidelong glance. It was Nana K's fault I was here in the first place. I'd feel less guilty about asking her to escort me around for the time being. If my stomach could handle Nana K's driving, that is.

Colleen bumped my shoulder. "Stop overthinking it. This is an amazing deal. Much better than what I'm paying for my crappy rancher."

"Yeah, but you own your rancher," I pointed out. Like an actual adult.

"True. That money pit is all mine. If you can wait until the weekend, I'll help you move. I can borrow my brother's truck." She flashed me a grin. "I'm sure Linc would love to help."

"I'm sure Linc will be sick of me by the end of the week. I'm spending a ridiculous amount of time with him because of the community service. We'll both need a break from each other by then," I pointed out.

Nana K's small, bespectacled head popped out from the market door. She shouted, "You two slow pokes are gonna miss out on pie if you don't put a little boogie in your step. Get your skinny butts moving!"

Colleen laughed. "All right, hobbles, the sooner we eat this pie, the sooner we can get you back home to ice that ankle again. I need you a bit more mobile tomorrow night."

"What's tomorrow night?" I asked. "I'm not moving until the weekend, right?"

Colleen gave me a dumbfounded look. "Are you sure you didn't hit your head in the fall? We're following Mike Vandenburg, remember? Wednesday night is poker night, but his adventures take on a different meaning to poke-her, if you get my drift."

"Ew, Colleen," I said, but chuckled. "Are we really doing that?"

"You betcha. Mainly to help you clear your name. But also for the gossip," Colleen said, rubbing her hands together. "Working at a preschool doesn't usually give me a leg up in the juicy-gossip game. The book club is going to eat this up!"

I shook my head at her. I took one last look back at the outside of the barn that I would likely call home in a few short days. Maybe my luck was starting to turn around after all.

Chapter 13

I iced and elevated and iced and elevated my ankle all day Wednesday until it returned to almost normal size. The color was still as brilliant a blue-purple as my fish, however. I'd even begged off going to the firehouse so I could rest up for our spying tonight.

Bruising and swelling was the excuse I gave Linc, anyway. Really, I knew that as soon as he saw my face, he'd know I was up to something. Know I was hiding something. I didn't want to hear the lecture about snooping.

Colleen beeped the horn outside at exactly six thirty like we'd planned. The poker night started around seven, so we wanted to be sure to catch Mike before he left his McMansion. Halfway there, I got the jitters.

"This is silly. Why would he still sneak around with Missy dead? Couldn't he be more out in the open about seeing other women?" I asked. He wouldn't need the cover of the poker game without Missy.

"We'll never know unless we go. Stop being a Polly Pissypants. I'll get you ice cream on the way home," Colleen placated in her teacher voice.

"I'm not a child. I'm just wondering if this is a waste of time."

"Look. From what I understand of men, they are creatures of habit. If he has a standing date with some chick on Wednesday nights, he'll probably keep it. Plus, coming right out with a new relationship less than a week after your wife turns up dead isn't a smart move. If I were him, I'd totally still keep any affairs clandestine. Not only for my reputation, but also to keep the cops off my back."

"Fair point," I admitted. I tapped my fingernails on the doorframe as the town passed beside us. The Vandenburgs lived on the Hill, as the townies called it. A grouping of overpriced, cookie-cutter mini-mansions on small lots situated on a hill overlooking the reservoir. These were the types of impersonal dwellings that all looked the same and had rooms that no one ever used. The developers named all the streets after the trees they cut down to create the planned community.

I much preferred the comfort and personalization of my parents' smaller home in town. Although we didn't have a view of the reservoir since the surrounding pine forest blocked it, we did have immediate access to it through the backyard path. The Hill dwellers had to drive to get to the water. Not that most of these spoiled housewives would be caught dead in the woods.

I shivered. Except that Missy *was* found dead in the woods. What would she have been doing there in the first place? Did someone lure her there? How? Threaten her kids? Threaten to chip her manicure? I couldn't guess what motivated Missy to wander into the woods that day. I just wished she hadn't.

"Almost there," Colleen said, slowing so we could see the house numbers. She stopped a few houses away from the

Vandenburgs' and parked along the curb. "Now we wait to see if the target leaves the nest."

"You watch too much television," I said.

"Maybe you don't watch enough. I can't believe you didn't wear all black. You're such an amateur."

"I didn't have any black pants. And you know my mother doesn't have any that I could borrow. These cargos are close enough." I paired the darkest pair of green camo-printed cargo pants I owned with a black tank top. Seemed good enough to me at the time. But given the lack of actual foliage beyond the crisp landscaping, the camo wouldn't really help as much as I thought.

"If we get caught, I'm blaming your green—" She stopped talking as a light in the Vandenburg garage came on. "Look!" Colleen pointed at the house.

"I see it. I see it." I didn't know whether to duck down in my seat or tell Colleen to start the car. "What do we do? What do we do?"

Why was I suddenly a parrot?

"Follow him, of course. That's literally why we're here." Colleen sounded like she was speaking to one of the toddlers at the preschool where she worked. Again.

"Shoot. He's coming this way. Duck down!" I said. We both crouched down in our seats as the car drove past. As soon as the headlights moved away from the back seat, Colleen shot up and turned on the car. She rammed it into gear and made a tire-screeching U-turn while I tried to not throw up beside her. We raced down the hill after the car. How the heck did *I* lose my license when crazy drivers like Colleen and Nana K got to keep theirs? Mysteries of small towns.

"Cheese and crackers!" I exclaimed, holding tight to the handle above my seat as Colleen careened around a turnout of the neighborhood. "Would you slow down? We are supposed to *not* draw attention to ourselves."

Colleen eased up on the gas. "Sorry. This is all so exciting! And I don't want to lose him."

"You mean in all this traffic?" I gestured to the practically empty road around us. The Vandenburg car's taillights were clearly visible about a block ahead. "We don't even know it's Mike in that car."

"Who else would it be? The kids aren't old enough to drive. And it obviously isn't Missy," Colleen said.

I gaped at her.

Colleen shrugged. "What? It's true."

I mean, she wasn't wrong.

The Vandenburg car—something sporty and splashy—turned onto the Weather Streets. This neighborhood, unlike the one where the Vandenburgs lived, was an older neighborhood with mature trees, old Piney Ridge family names, and a mix of ranchers, Colonials, and split-levels. No cookie-cutter houses here, much like my parents' neighborhood. The lots were spacious, most having been fenced in over the years to accommodate pets and small children, and the porch lights were lit. I knew if the blood rushing in my ears would slow, I'd be able to hear the laughter of families enjoying the early evening air on their back porches.

Mike rounded the corner from Snowfall Way onto Sunshine Court. Colleen followed at a safe distance; no need to go too fast since Sunshine Court dead ended. We saw the car in front of a modest rancher at the end of the cul-de-sac. I whipped my eyes to the front porch in time to see a male—must be Mike—entering the house. The curtains were drawn in the front window, so we couldn't see in. Darnit.

"Who lives here?" I whispered.

"No idea," Colleen whispered back. She followed the circle of the court and parked her car opposite Mike's, facing the open end of the street. Smart move in case we needed a quick getaway.

"Now what?" I asked, still whispering.

"We wait a minute. Maybe we'll see some naughty shadows in the window. Or maybe they'll come out and go somewhere else," she said.

"Why are we whispering?" I asked.

Colleen laughed. Then said in her normal voice, "You started it."

I laughed too and felt a little lighter. "Well, there's one thing for sure. He was, and still is, lying about poker night."

We sat for a few more minutes staring at the house. No movement, no noise, no nothing.

"This is boring," I said. I was used to the hustle and bustle of big cities, the shouts and crowds of village markets, the shrieks and cries of the never-quiet jungles. This was equivalent to watching paint dry or waiting in line at the motor vehicle administration. Or organizing the desktop icons at the firehouse. Everything here in Piney Ridge was so quiet and so slow. No, not just slow, but still. Practically moving backward.

"So tell me about your plans," Colleen said, turning her attention to me instead of the quiet house. "I feel like we haven't caught up since you've been back."

I shrugged. "The more plans I make, the more this whole thing feels permanent."

"What's wrong with that?"

I could hear the hint of umbrage in her voice. Like me, Colleen had been born and raised in Piney Ridge. Unlike me, Colleen never had any desire to leave. She'd always loved the small-town vibe. So much so, in fact, she won the

Miss Teen Crab Princess crown when we were in high school. She wore that sash around like she was mayor—taking her duties and appearances very seriously. Unfortunately, a terrible case of stomach flu blasted through the contestants, effectively canceling the state-level competition and Colleen's rise to Teen Crab power.

"Nothing is wrong with it," I answered her question. "It just isn't for me. Toe-may-to, toe-mah-to and all that. I need to get back to *my* life. This feels like a layover."

"At least you won't be laying over at your parents' house much longer. Can't say Connie and George in the next room is very conducive to an adult relationship, if you know what I mean." Colleen waggled her eyebrows.

"And who would I even be having an adult relationship with?"

"I know a certain firefighter who's single. And who you used to have a huge crush on."

I rolled my eyes and looked out the window so Colleen couldn't see the blush creeping up my neck. "That was a lifetime ago," I mumbled.

"Listen, the way he looked at you the other day says he's interested too."

I shook my head. "The only thing he's interested in is seeing how much more awkward I can be. I'm like a one-woman circus, and Piney Ridge has front-row seats."

"So? All I'm saying is a hot guy is interested in you—for whatever reason. Don't squander it."

I snorted and was about to respond when movement in the house caught my eye. "Look!"

Colleen turned her head to peer out the window.

"They're moving around back. I really wish I could hear what they were saying. Let's get closer," Colleen said.

Before I could react and tell her it was a terrible idea, Colleen had scrambled out of the driver's side and ran halfway across the street. She moved in a low crouch, which totally drew more attention than if she walked like a normal person. When Colleen reached the other side, she looked back and motioned impatiently for me to follow her. I sighed, grabbed my crutch, and got out of the car. I hobble-ran as fast as I dared across the street. Colleen was practically apoplectic by the time I reached her, dancing from one foot to another.

"Do you have to pee?" I asked brightly. "You should have thought of that before class."

"No! I'm excited. And you are taking your grand ol' time. I should've left you in the car."

"Why are we standing here yapping? Let's do what we came to do," I said, moving toward the tall privacy fence on the side of the yard. The slats were over six feet tall and almost touching. While that meant we couldn't see the backyard, it also meant Mike and his alleged mistress couldn't see us either. And really, we only needed to hear the conversation—or whatever else they were doing.

I pressed my ear to the wood. Colleen's face appeared in front of mine a moment later, giving me a little jump. I furrowed my brows at her; Colleen shrugged. We could hear faint music playing and the murmur of voices.

"Can you hear what they're saying?" Colleen said so quietly I had to read her lips to decipher what she asked. I shook my head. Collectively, we shuffled closer to the house. I got my crutch stuck in the mud and almost fell over but caught myself just in time. I stifled a giggle. Now it was Colleen's turn to snap her eyebrows together in warning. I clamped a hand over my mouth and pressed my ear to the fence again.

Snippets of conversation drifted through the fence now that we were closer to where Mike and his mistress were talking.

"... can be together," a woman's whiny voice said.

"... cool off for a bit until..." a man's voice answered.

Then the woman's voice, louder now and higher pitched as the conversation grew more heated. "Why, Mike?"

Colleen raised her eyebrows. We just got confirmation the male voice belonged to Mike Vandenburg.

The woman continued, "The crazy cow is gone. You said once she was out of the picture, we could be together."

I raised my eyebrows to match Colleen's. Did we just hear a confession? Too late I thought about recording on my phone. Dangit—but maybe they would continue the conversation and drop even more incriminating nuggets. Better late than never—I turned on the camera and held the phone next to my ear by the fence.

"... voice down," the man was saying.

"Who is going to hear? Who is going to care? No one even liked her."

Mike shushed her and lowered his voice. "... murdered... pin it on me... just for a while."

"Come on, say her name," Colleen wished out loud beside me.

I flicked her arm. When Colleen looked at me crossly, I pointed to my phone and mouthed, "I'm recording." I'd rather not have our voices on the recording just in case I needed to send it anonymously to the police. Was that a thing? I hoped it was a thing.

Colleen's confusion turned to excitement. "Good idea," she mouthed back and stopped rubbing her arm where I'd flicked it to give me a thumbs-up.

"I'm not going to wait forever. I deserve better than to be your side piece," the woman said, her voice as loud as before.

"Let's go inside if you're going to continue to act like a crazy person," Mike said, his voice clear as a bell.

I snickered. That wouldn't sit well with the side piece.

"Excuse me!" she shouted. "Now *I'm* the crazy one?" She paused for a moment, and I swore I heard her breathing heavily. But when she spoke again, her voice sounded much calmer and at a pitch everyone, not just dogs, could hear. Maybe she realized screeching did make her sound a bit crazy.

"Fine. I've waited this long; I can wait a bit longer. But not forever, Mike. Don't make me give you another ultimatum. I don't like being that woman," she said. I heard a chair squeak.

"*Another* ultimatum?" I mouthed to Colleen. "Another" implied a first. Could that first ultimatum have been getting rid of Missy? How did she put it earlier? Once Missy was out of the picture? Well, she was out of their vignette and into her own gruesome version of a still life.

The couple behind the fence were quiet for a while, then began murmuring again. I turned off my phone; we'd probably gotten all we were going to get for the evening. Colleen thought the same; she motioned for us to head back to the car. I nodded and, after putting my phone in my back pocket, hobbled after Colleen back across the street.

We managed to hold in our excitement until we got in the car, but as soon as the doors were closed, we looked at each other, happy-screamed, and danced around in our seats.

"I can't believe we just did that," Colleen gasped between laughs.

"I can't believe we got away with it," I said.

"Okay, okay. Deep breaths." Colleen took her own advice. "He totally did it, right?"

"Oh my goodness, totally. This definitely proves motive! And will hopefully get the police off my back. Adultery is a much better motive than high school rival."

"We should go into business as private investigators. You already have the camera gear," Colleen said. "We've already proven how great we are at it by getting away clean tonight. Despite your green pants."

Colleen had such a smug expression on her face, I almost didn't have the heart to tell her how ridiculous that was. We were only trying to prove my innocence so I could go back to living in anonymity.

"Don't be ridic—" I started, but a sudden rap on the passenger window had us both jumping and screaming again. Though this time from fright.

Chapter 14

Injured ankle or not, I practically climbed over the console to get away from my window. The shadowy figure standing there yanked open the door, and I instinctively kicked out. Unfortunately, I used my injured ankle and the screams of fright turned into yelps of pain as I connected with something solid.

"Hey, hey, hey," a male voice said. "It's Lincoln. Calm down."

Colleen's scream died out, but her breaths came in short rasps. I stopped whimpering and opened my eyes. Sure enough, Linc was leaning his broad body into the car. He held out his hand to help me right myself. Reluctantly, I took it.

"I'm afraid to ask, but what are you two doing here?" Linc asked when we were both sitting back in our actual seats and breathing normally. He squatted beside my open door, rubbing his stomach.

"Was that you I kicked?" I asked, astonished. From the solidity of the object, I thought I hit the door. Man oh man, the boy worked out.

"Answer the question, Alex," Linc said, ignoring my question.

There were a few things that really irked me into a slightly less than homicidal rage: being mean to defenseless animals, chewing with an open mouth, and social media filters, to name a few. But top of that list was being treated like a child. And that had happened a lot since I'd been home. The only person who got a pass was my mother—mainly because I was her actual child. I narrowed my eyes at him. Add to that I was getting rather annoyed that Linc always managed to show up at the most inconvenient times.

"I could ask you the same thing. Are you following us?" I asked, turning the accusation back on him.

"I live over there." He pointed to a house a few doors down from the one we were watching. Of course, Linc, forever bemused, lived on a street named Sunshine. I felt my righteous indignation slip a little.

But I wasn't going to let him know that. I doubled down.

"Still, sneaking up on two women in the dark is not a great idea. We thought you were an ax murderer."

"And sneaking onto someone else's property is any better?"

I shifted my attention out the front windshield. "I don't know what you're talking about. Colleen? Do you have any idea what he's talking about?"

"Nope," she confirmed without hesitation. "We were just sitting in the car talking, laughing, catching up on old times."

"Really?" Linc asked, dripping with sarcasm. "So there just happens to be another woman with fiery red hair sneaking around my neighborhood at night?"

"Must be," Colleen mumbled. "What a coincidence, huh?"

"And don't get me started on you, Gimpy McHopalong," he said to me. "You're about as subtle as a rhino in a china shop—and that's even without the added awkwardness of a crutch."

"Okay. Now you've insulted us enough, and you can be on your way. Colleen, start the car." I tried to reach around him to shut the door, but he was like a freaking bull—all muscle and broad shoulders and unmoving.

"Excuse me," I said, looking into his face. Bad idea. He wore that irresistible half-amused smirk. He looked like he couldn't decide whether to join us or to scold us. His expression was a perfect mix of devilish, rebellious boy meets responsible, handsome man. I couldn't look away.

Luckily, he stood and peered over the top of the car, leaning his arms on the roof. Unluckily, this put me at eye level with his midsection and parts south. I gulped and tried to pry my eyes away from that delicious expanse of skin that appeared between the bottom of his T-shirt and his low-slung jeans. Even in the dim light, I could make out the outline of that muscular V men have pointing toward their—

"I'll give you a dollar if you lick his abs," Colleen whispered beside me. Her voice broke into my thoughts and made me jump about a mile. I accidentally hit Linc in the upper thigh with my flailing arm. At least I thought it was his thigh. I scowled at Colleen whose eyes lit with amusement.

"Ow," he said, leaning back down. "What was that for?"

"Sorry," Colleen said. "My fault. I said something and it scared her."

"You guys wouldn't happen to be coming from the house with the sports car in front of it?" Linc asked.

"What? No, of course not," I said at the same time Colleen said, "So what if we were?"

107

Linc simply raised an eyebrow. We held our tongues.

"I find it oddly coincidental that you, Alex, happen to be sneaking around the same neighborhood that Mike Vandenburg's mistress lives in," he said.

My mouth dropped open. "You knew he was having an affair?"

"Everyone knows. I'm sure Missy knew. As I'm sure Mike knew about her affairs."

"Missy was having an affair too?" Colleen asked, equally as shocked.

Linc rolled his eyes. "Get out of the car, Alex."

"Why would I do that?" I asked.

"Maybe he wants to punish you," Colleen whispered under her breath. I smacked her chest.

"So I can get in the back seat," Linc said. "I'm tired of having this conversation out here on the street. I'm sure half the neighborhood is spying out their windows by now after all the screaming earlier." I didn't move. "Come on, Alex. Either that, or you get in the back."

Getting into the crammed back seat with my hurt ankle was less than appealing. Besides, seeing Linc try to squeeze his tall body into the back of the VW would be funny. He deserved it for treating us like common criminals. Or worse, children.

"Fine," I huffed. I swung my legs out first, grabbed the top of the doorframe to try to lift myself out of the low car without the aid of my crutch. Linc grabbed me under an armpit to help. He placed my hand firmly on the roof.

"Don't let go." He gave me another unreadable look and folded himself into the back seat of the VW bug.

When he was stuffed back there, I awkwardly plopped back into the front seat.

Colleen put the car in gear. "Where to?"

We ended up in a back booth at Plum Crazy Diner. Again, nostalgia hit me like bird poop hits a shoulder—unexpected and unwanted. How many times had the three of us sat here just like this over milkshakes and fries? Too many to count. We'd been almost inseparable in elementary and middle school. I was the glue that held our trio together. I'd been friends with both Linc and Colleen individually first, then introduced them to each other. Later, after Linc joined the Snob Blob in high school, it had been me and Colleen. He tried to join us a few times, but we quickly found we no longer had that much in common with him. I focused on photography and art classes; Colleen had her early childhood internship. And Linc had sports and parties with the "in" crowd. Parties that Colleen and I were not invited to. Nor did we care to be.

Or at least that's what we told ourselves.

Linc helped me slide into the booth beside Colleen. He propped my crutch against the wall beside us, then took the bench across. Colleen sat with head lowered and hands folded on the table as though about to get scolded. I drummed my fingers on the table as we sat in awkward silence.

Linc looked about to say something when Ms. Peggy Sue—yes, that was her actual name—wandered over to take our orders. Her hair may have had a bit more gray in it and her hips a bit wider, but her bright, welcoming smile and raspy, I-smoke-a-pack-a-day voice was just as I remembered.

"Well, look what the cat dragged in," she said. "I haven't seen you three in here since before the last president."

"Hi, Ms. Peggy Sue," I said. "Long time no see."

"No kidding. Still want the sweet and salty, or do you have more adult palates now?" she asked, remembering our usual order of milkshakes and fries.

"I mean, I don't think you're ever too old for a milkshake," I said, smiling. "Make mine a double-thick malt. And can I actually see a menu?"

Peggy Sue pointed to the laminated rectangles sticking up from the napkin holder. Of course. This wasn't New York where anything not nailed down would walk. Here, in Piney Ridge, you could leave the napkin holders with menus and even condiments right on the tables.

I looked over the choices while Colleen ordered a Coke and a piece of apple pie, and Linc ordered a coffee—black.

"You ready?" Peggy Sue asked, eyebrows raised toward me.

"I think so. You might want to write this down; I'm a bit hungry." My stomach rumbled in confirmation. I hadn't had much to eat today, since moving from the couch to the kitchen was a bit of a production with my ankle.

"Honey, I've been working this diner for longer than you've been alive, and I haven't written down an order yet. Hit me with your best shot."

"Okay. But don't say I didn't warn you." I ran my finger down the menu. "I'll have the honey-glazed chicken, but can I substitute the pepper jack cheese for provolone? And add a side of seasoned fries and an egg over medium."

"That all?"

"And some bacon. On the side. And a piece of wheat toast with butter," I added, replacing the menu where I found it.

"One bee's knees sub round for spicy, sassy fries, sloppy eggs and wheat, and pig parts. Got it," Peggy Sue repeated and sauntered away.

I looked from Colleen's astonished face to Linc's amused one. "What? Spy work makes me hungry."

"Ah-ha!" Linc said, pointing a finger at me across the table. "You admit you were spying tonight."

"So what if we were? Whose house was Mike visiting?"

"Nope. I'm not helping you two on your path to self-destruction. And I'm not ratting out a neighbor." Linc sat back with his arms crossed. Like the mature, world-savvy adult I was, I stuck my tongue out at him.

Peggy Sue brought over our drinks and some complimentary bread. As I watched her dole them out, I got an idea. Didn't Linc mention that everyone knew about Mike's affairs? And didn't everyone in Piney Ridge end up in Plum Crazy Diner at one point or another?

"Isn't it awful about Missy?" I asked Peggy Sue as she placed the milkshake in front of me.

"A life ended too soon. And in such a violent way. Things like that don't happen in Piney Ridge," Peggy Sue said and made the sign of the cross.

"And poor Mike. He must be devastated to lose his wife."

Linc sat up a little straighter, not trusting me.

Peggy Sue snorted. "Yeah, right. He might not even notice."

"Really? Why is that?" I tried my best to look innocent and wide eyed.

"Please. That man didn't even wait for the ink to dry on his marriage certificate before he cheated on Missy. And about as discreet about it as a catfight."

"Wow. I missed so much gossi—er, news, being away."

I waited a beat, then gasped as though I just thought of something. Linc rolled his eyes at my theatrics. I ignored him.

"Do you think maybe the mistress killed Missy, so she could have Mike all to herself?" I asked.

"Who, Crystal?" I tried not to look too smug. Linc frowned. "She wouldn't hurt a fly. Besides, even with Missy out of the way, she wouldn't have Mike all to herself."

"Oh, because of the kids," I said, shaking my head in mock pity.

"Them too. But mainly on account of Mike having more than one bed to warm in town. Even though Crystal is his main fling, he never met a pretty woman he didn't try to seduce. And he was successful more times than not, from what I hear."

"Order up!" a voice called from the kitchen. Peggy Sue excused herself to grab the order.

"Crystal, huh?" I said. "Is that the woman from tonight?"

Linc pressed his lips together and shook his head.

"Come on, Linc," Colleen said. "We're just gonna look it up online. You're merely delaying the inevitable."

"Fine. Her name is Crystal Coyne. And yes, she's my neighbor. She also volunteers at the fire department. And, her affair with a married man notwithstanding, she's a very nice woman."

"I didn't say she wasn't," I said defensively. "But sometimes love makes people do things they normally wouldn't do."

"Yeah, like trying Thai food or jumping out of an airplane. Not murder," Linc shot back.

"But someone did murder her, Linc," I said, gentling my voice. "I realize I don't know these people as well as you two do, so I'm sorry for suspecting them. But someone did murder her."

Linc sighed and took a sip of his coffee. "I know. I just can't imagine anyone in Piney Ridge doing it."

"Listen, Linc," Colleen said. "I don't want it to be anyone I know either. But we overheard Crystal say something about an ultimatum."

"Yeah," I added. "She also implied that she and Mike could be together when the—and I quote—'crazy cow' was out of the way."

Peggy Sue interrupted us to bring our food.

"I'll give you a dollar if you eat all of that," Colleen said, pointing at the stacked plates in front of me.

"Just watch me."

"Where do you put it all?" Linc asked, astonished. "You're like the size of my little finger."

"Mostly in my hips," I said around a mouthful of chicken. "Help yourself to some fries."

Linc picked up the conversation while I ate. "If what you said is true, then Mike is definitely on the suspect list."

"Duh," Colleen said, dipping a fry in some ketchup. "He'd be on the list regardless of the conversation. The people closest to her always are."

Linc was quiet for a moment. He watched me eat with his half smirk. I tried to ignore him; his constant scrutiny made it hard to swallow.

"What?" I finally asked, wiping my mouth with a napkin. "You never see anyone eat before?"

"You never cease to amaze me," he said, shaking his head. He reached across to grab a piece of bacon, but I slapped his hand away.

"I said you could have some fries. But touch the bacon and you may lose a finger."

His smirk turned to a full-on smile as he wrapped his hands back around his coffee mug. "Are you going to be well enough to come back to the firehouse tomorrow?" he asked me. "If you can roll out of bed after all this food, that is."

"Sure. What grunt work do you have for me to do?"

"I thought we could get started on the calendar. It's Crystal's day to volunteer. I can tell her to come prepared."

"And we can question her!" I said, almost knocking over my milkshake in my excitement.

Linc glowered at me. "We can have a conversation. A light, non-accusatory conversation."

"Sure, sure, sure," I said. "This'll be great."

"I'll draft a list of questions tonight," Colleen said. "And then call me immediately when you finish. Man, I wish I could be there."

Linc groaned. "I have a bad feeling about this."

I shot him a wide smile. This could be the break I needed to completely wipe my name off Chief Duncan's suspect list. I went to grab another fry, then realized they were gone. I sucked down the last bit of my milkshake and held out my hand to Colleen.

"Do you want a high five?" she asked.

"No, you owe me a dollar."

Chapter 15

Armed with a list of questions from Colleen and a welcoming smile, I tottered my way into the firehouse the next morning. Nana K had graciously agreed to be my chauffeur in the mornings. I'd have to rely on my parents or Linc for the way home. At least for this week. When I moved to the loft, I'd be out of everyone's way. I made a mental note to call about the safe-driving class later. Even though I'd lasted months without driving in New York, I'd had umpteen number of taxis at my immediate disposal. I would bet Lash that Piney Ridge didn't even have rideshares, much less a taxi service. And I was really attached to my fish.

But those were worries for another day. Today I needed to focus on what to say to Crystal.

I contemplated my approach. The conversational "I'm new to town" schtick worked fairly well with Peggy Sue. I could definitely do that again, although Crystal was younger and might see through the innocent act, so I could try a more direct approach to catch her off guard.

Wrapped up in my thoughts, I ran right into someone in the lobby of the firehouse. Too soft to be Linc, too broad to be Crystal.

"Still running into things, I see."

"Chief Duncan," I said, taking a step back away from him. My good mood faltered a little.

"I thought I told you to stay out of trouble," he said. I tried to move around him, but he blocked my path to the engine bay where the photoshoot would happen.

"I am. I'm here to do my court-ordered community service."

"Mike Vandenburg mentioned a green VW bug followed him last night. Know anything about that?" The chief put his ruddy hands on his hips and puffed out his chest. Well, tried to puff out his chest. Instead, his large belly mushroomed even larger. I took another step back to avoid being knocked over by his moving girth.

"Nope. Colleen and I were out and about. We ended up at Plum Crazy." Not exactly a lie.

"Stay away from Mike, Alex. Stay away from this case. I'm only going to warn you this one time."

I almost said "Or what?" but caught myself just in time. He may be a dingbat, but he was still chief of police. Best not to poke the bear.

Instead, I said, "Sure thing, Chief. Hey, did Mike happen to tell you where he was going when he saw the VW?"

"Wednesday night is poker at the lodge. He didn't have to tell me."

"Interesting. Now, I know I've been away for a while, but unless the lodge moved, he was heading the opposite way when we saw him," I said, adjusting the camera bag on my shoulder.

The chief's face got a little red. He poked a pudgy finger at my chest. "No worry of yours. Keep your nose out of it. Leave the police work to the professionals."

"Of course. Good to see you, Chief. Have a great day," I said, my voice dripping sweetness and innocence. When I stepped around him, I saw Linc leaning against the door to the engine bay with his signature smirk.

He waited until the door shut between us and the chief, who still stood in the lobby, giving me the stink eye, before he said, "I didn't think anyone's eyes could roll so far back in their head. You know, if you keep that up, they'll stay that way."

"Thanks, Dad," I said. I caught myself rolling my eyes again and stopped midway. "Is Crystal the only one I'll be photographing today?"

"Officer Martinez volunteered to have hers done today. And we could do one of my shots, if you want," he offered. "The humane society will be here soon with a few furry friends. And Fang is around here somewhere."

As if on cue, Fang, a tornado of black and white fur, barreled toward us at full speed. Linc put himself between the excited dog and my crutch-supported body. Man and dog wrestled for a moment, then Fang turned his attention to me.

"Sit," Linc commanded. Fang complied and lifted his paw to me.

I shook it and patted his head with my non-crutch hand. "What a good boy. Such a gentleman. Can we get some shots with him too?"

"Maybe. We usually keep it to adoptable animals. Another advertisement for the humane society. Fang doesn't usually sit still either. Just ask Andrea. She actually had the joy of trying to pose with him when he was a guest at the animal shelter. Before I adopted him."

"Did someone say my name?" Officer Martinez called. She made her way across the bay to where we were setup. Fang barked and ran circles around her legs. She gave him a pat on the head, and, satisfied, he disappeared into the recesses of the engine bay.

"Hey, Andrea," Linc said, flashing her his full smile. He pronounced it "Ahn-drey-a," of course, because she wasn't exotic enough as it was.

They embraced in a friendly hug, and I felt an inexplicable wave of jealousy. Linc could hug anyone he wanted to. Even if that anyone was a mahogany-skinned, fit, twentysomething with the sleekest, healthiest hair I had ever seen. It didn't matter that he hadn't hugged me since I'd been back. I hadn't even noticed.

Andrea held her hand out to me, her grip firm and strong. "We didn't get to really meet the other night," Andrea said. "We really appreciate you doing this for us. The calendar is one of our biggest joint fundraisers. And to have someone of your caliber shooting it brings an added level. I saw your photos of the Puerto Rican hurricane damage. They were amazing."

"Oh, no." I waved away the compliment, embarrassed. "I always seemed to be in the wrong place. The spread in *National Geographic* was much better."

"I didn't see that one. All I know is you showed the humanity and the destruction with such grace and reverence. Without them feeling exploitative."

"Wow. Thank you," I said, warming to her immediately. "That is probably one of the nicest things anyone has said about my photography."

"My grandparents live there, so I have an added interest," Andrea explained.

"Oh, I'm so sorry. How are they doing?" I asked. Having seen the destruction firsthand, I immediately felt a connection.

"Much better, thank you for asking." She laughed to lighten the mood. "I guess doing a silly photo shoot with local first responders and some fluffy adoptees is a bit boring compared to other things you've seen."

"Everyone has a story to tell. Some are more dramatic than others, sure, but each one is unique. That's what I like to capture. So, we'll take this more like a documentary approach instead of a posed shoot. I'm gonna set up my gear and get some settings."

I moved toward the area where Linc indicated they usually took the photos. I took a moment to scan the space. The concrete corner was impersonal and rather dark. I'd rather shoot with the bay door open, letting in all that natural light, and with the fire trucks in the background barely in focus. It would add color and personality and context.

I turned to tell Linc and was surprised to find him watching me.

"You know you mumble to yourself as you work," he said.

Great. Another notch in my Alex is Awkward belt. Out loud I said, "How important is that spot to you?" I pointed to the corner.

He shrugged. "Not at all. That's just where we've always done it."

"Not this year. Can we open the bay door? The middle one here. And is it possible to pull that ambulance a little farther into the garage? To leave a little more space between the door and the truck?"

I was in the zone now. Asking for little adjustments, but not really asking. Linc moved around the space accommodating my every request with barely a question as to why. I half believed he would have found me a juggling act had I requested it. This was quite different from working with Rick who, instead of helping me, would tell me what he thought was the best angle. Basically, mansplaining my job to me.

This was also quite different than photojournalism where I could manipulate nothing and was at the whim of the weather, the lighting, and the environment. Being able to control the setting was a refreshing change of pace.

Linc's laughter caught my attention. I glanced toward the sound, pushed aside the fog of jealousy, and held the camera to my eye. He was completely relaxed while chatting with Andrea, one foot resting on the bumper of the fire truck, his hands folded languidly across his chest. The light put a little sparkle in his already jovial eyes. I snapped away, glad I'd opted for my telephoto lens so I could zoom in a little without getting too close.

I backed up to get Andrea in the shot too. Their contrasting uniforms and Fang jumping around their feet might be the perfect calendar cover. Linc saw my movement and turned his sculpted face toward me. I snapped a few more shots before his expression changed from amusement to trepidation.

"What are you doing?" he asked.

"Testing the light and the settings." Not a complete lie. Untrusting, he narrowed his eyes.

A cacophony of barking drew his attention away from me and toward the open bay door. A frazzled woman holding three excited dogs and a cat carrier tumbled through the door. Linc rushed to help her with Fang at his heels.

"Oh, thank you, Linc. I was only going to bring Louie"—she gestured to the golden retriever—"but these two were giving me the serious puppy dog eyes when I snapped Louie into his harness. I couldn't leave them."

"These two" referred to a small fluff ball and a medium-sized teddy bear. I bent to get some candid shots of the dogs playing and loving on Linc. He laughed and roughhoused with them a little.

"Which one do you like, Andrea?" Linc asked. "You can do your shoot first. I'm sure you have duties to get back to at the police station."

She pointed at the retriever, the calmest of the three. "Where do you want us?" she asked me.

"In this general area. Try to stay on the edge of the shadow line." Andrea moved into position and stood there stiffly holding Louie's leash. I put the camera to my eye and waited for a moment. Andrea stood stock still and unmoving with Louie sitting dutifully at her feet. I lowered my camera.

"Andrea. Act natural. Interact with Louie. You can bend down to pet him if you want," I suggested. I wasn't used to directing people. And Andrea was clearly not used to being photographed. Which was a shame because she had amazing bone structure.

After a few more awkward moments, I dropped my camera again. "Shoot. I think I need a different lens. Why don't you and Louie get acquainted while I change it out."

I made a show of hobbling slowly over to my camera bag. I didn't need to change my lens, but I wanted to give Andrea some time to loosen up. And possibly sneak some shots while she didn't think the camera was on her. Effective—yes. Sneaky—double yes. But it got results. I'd made my career by being discreet and invisible. And a bit of a creeper. Minimal interaction was why I'd chosen photojournalism.

I fiddled with my camera bag as I watched Andrea out of the corner of my eye. Linc engaged her in conversation again. I admired that about him—how he could make anyone feel comfortable. Small talk, a personal nemesis of mine, seemed to come so naturally to him. Andrea looked looser already. She bent down to give Louie a rub behind the ears. I quickly snapped a bunch of pictures, then moved over a little to get a better angle.

When Andrea noticed me, she immediately stiffened. I said quickly, "Perfect. Scratch his head again. Tell him a deep, dark secret you wouldn't want your mom to find out."

Andrea laughed, a blush rising on her cheeks. "The dog?"

"He's the perfect secret keeper," I said. I crouched down to shoot them straight on as Andrea laughed into the dog's silky fur. The moment was so sweet, I barely noticed the pressure on my ankle. Everything else faded away as I focused on the scene through the viewfinder. On autopilot, I adjusted the settings to accommodate the changing light. I shot some with the fire trucks in focus behind the duo and some without. I had way more options than I needed for a simple calendar, but like that day in the woods, I felt back in the zone. Back in my comfort zone. Dare I say it, back in myself.

"I think we got it," I said, checking the back of the camera to be sure I got some with Andrea's eyes open.

"Wait? That's it?" Andrea asked. "No sitting still and trying to get the dog to look at the camera?"

"That's not really my style," I said slowly. Imposter syndrome set in once again. Was I getting this all wrong? Did they want boring, posed shoots?

"Okay. That was actually fun," Andrea said. She looked sternly at Louie. "Don't go telling my secret now." Louie licked her hand.

"Your turn, Linc," I said.

"Didn't you get enough earlier?" he teased.

"Practice shots," I reminded him. "None with the animals. They're probably throwaways anyway," I lied. No picture of Linc would be a throwaway unless it was completely out of focus. But I'd only admit that sentiment to Louie.

Linc grabbed the two other dogs. "Where do you want me?"

"Uh..." I stuttered. That was a loaded question if I ever heard one.

Chapter 16

I fiddled with my camera to give myself a moment of recomposure and then cleared my throat. "These two seem to have a ton of energy. Why don't you start against the far wall and walk them toward me?"

He nodded and led the dogs to the other end of the engine bay. I got a few action shots and gave him a thumbs-up. He bent down to pick up the small fluff ball. The juxtaposition of the tiny dog in his large arms had me quickly taking some more shots. The little dog, as if on cue, stuck out its tiny, pink tongue and lapped at Linc's nose. He squinched up his nose and laughed. And I knew I had my shot.

"Perfect," I said, smiling at the back of my camera.

A clack-clack-clacking of heels accompanied by a huff announced the presence of someone new. Whatever I expected Crystal to look like, it wasn't this. She was tall—like, really tall—like taller than Lincoln tall. Made even taller with her three-inch heels. She made me feel like a munchkin from *Wizard of Oz*.

She was also—I struggled to put it into words—not pudgy or even fat, just thick. She was the picture beside "big-boned" in the dictionary. And she wore it well. She exuded confidence with a touch of aloofness. Maybe because she literally had to look down her nose at everyone.

She didn't wear firefighter gear, instead sported a tight-fitting, cheetah-print tube dress. It clung to all her very womanly curves. Her heels were a matching print. I had seen outfits like this in the clubs of New York—heck, I'd worn outfits like this when my hips and I were in our early twenties—but this was Piney Ridge. A firehouse in Piney Ridge in the middle of the morning, to be exact. Seemed a bit out of place.

"Hi," I said, holding out my hand. "I'm Alex Lightwood, the photographer."

Crystal squeezed my fingers limply in her own, gave me a dismissive look, then focused her full attention toward Linc.

"I don't have a ton of time," Crystal said. "I have an appointment. Where do you want me to sit?"

"I actually have a more organic approach," I tried to explain.

One derisive look from Crystal had me faltering. She looked at Linc for help as if to say "Where did you dig her up?"

As if reading her mind, Linc handily brought over a chair. Crystal plopped herself in it. She held her hands out. I wasn't sure what that meant. Did she want a hug?

"The cat?" Crystal said impatiently. The frazzled humane society worker gently placed a feline in Crystal's lap. With this warm welcome, I'd be lucky to get any information pertaining to Missy out of her.

I took a page from Crystal's book and ignored her. I talked to Linc instead.

"So, you really think Mike has been acting suspiciously, Linc?" I asked as though we had been in the middle of a conversation. I gave him a pleading look from behind my camera, hoping he'd just go with it.

"Oh, uh, totally. Like I was saying"—Linc cleared his throat but played along—"Mike hasn't even called to ask about the autopsy yet. What kind of grieving husband wouldn't be banging down the police station door demanding information." I could've hugged him.

"Weird."

Through the viewfinder, I saw Crystal shift in her seat. Her fake smile—the one she put on when the camera started clicking—faltered a little.

I pressed on. "The first suspect is always the husband."

Crystal huffed. "That's ridiculous," she mumbled.

I pretended not to hear. "Good thing he's protected by being acting mayor. Otherwise, Chief Duncan would probably already have him in custody."

"Don't be stupid," Crystal huffed.

"Did you say something?" I asked, lowering the camera.

Crystal scowled at me. "Mike didn't do it. He's too soft."

"You think? I don't know. People have snapped before. I heard he cheated on Missy. Sounds like a motive to me."

"Just because he wanted a break from his demanding, annoying wife doesn't make him a murderer." Crystal scowled.

"Oh." Linc snapped his fingers like he just thought of something. "Maybe his mistress did it? Maybe she got tired of sharing."

I shot him a warning look when Crystal narrowed her eyes at him. She'd gone completely still except for her chest rising and falling with each labored breath. We were definitely getting to her. I just didn't want to press her too far.

"I happen to be close friends with Mike's mistress," Crystal said, lifting her chin in defiance. "And not only is she one of the sweetest people I've ever met, but during the afternoon of the murder, she and Mike were together at her house. Nowhere near the reservoir."

I tried not to snort at her description of her "friend" as the "sweetest person" she knew.

Crystal handed the cat back and stood up. Guess we were done with the shoot. Linc had derailed it with the mistress comment. For the record, Mr. We'll Just Have a Conversation pushed it too far. Not me.

"If you ask me," Crystal said, as she brushed cat hair off her dress, "the police should be looking closer at who Missy was cheating with."

"Wait. Missy cheated too?" I feigned surprise. I was getting good at that, in my opinion.

"Oh yeah. Big time. With someone right here in the firehouse, right, Linc?"

I felt the color drain from my face. Was Missy cheating on Mike with Linc? Was that why Linc got so upset about us snooping in his neighborhood? Because all his neighbors knew about his affair with Missy?

"What are you talking about, Crystal?" Linc asked carefully. I held my breath for the reply.

"I mean, that's why Alex has to do the photo shoot this year, right? Because Becky caught Missy and her husband together?" Crystal said.

I breathed a loud sigh of relief. Not Linc. He gave me a weird look, then said, "Becky's husband was cheating with Missy? I had no idea."

"Yup." Crystal's face broke into a smug smile. What was it with people being the first to hand out gossip around here? It was like verbal currency or something.

"But that was months ago. Why would it trigger a reaction now?" Linc asked.

Crystal shrugged. "There are plenty of people who aren't losing sleep over Missy Vandenburg being dead." And with that statement, she shimmied her skirt down her thighs and stalked out.

Lincoln stood beside me to watch Crystal leave. "If your eyebrows go any higher, they're going to blend right into your hairline," he whispered.

I lowered them. "That was interesting. From start to finish." I turned to him. "She volunteers here? What does she do?" I certainly couldn't picture her wearing the firefighter gear. Nor could I picture anyone effectively fighting fires in a tube dress and stilettos.

"She helps in the office sometimes," Linc said absently. "And rides the truck in the parades."

I raised an eyebrow. "Sounds like an amazing contribution."

"We take what we can get," Linc said.

We farewelled the humane society lady and the pups before resuming our conversation.

"Do you believe her?" he asked as he closed the bay door.

"About being with Mike the afternoon of the murder?" Linc nodded. I shrugged. "I don't know. If she is telling the truth, then both Mike and Crystal are off our suspect list."

"It's such a bold thing to lie about. Does she honestly believe people don't notice a flashy sports car like Mike's parked in front of her house? Not many people drive that kind of car in Piney Ridge. I mean, I noticed," Linc said.

"Cheaters stay in a constant state of denial. They think they're so discreet. Some cheaters even deny it when you catch them red-handed. Then they gaslight you into believing you didn't actually see what you saw. They build on the fact that you don't want it to be true," I said, my voice rising with each sentence.

"Why do I get the feeling we aren't necessarily talking about Mike and Crystal any longer?" Linc asked.

I shook my head and attempted a smile. "Sorry. I had a bad experience right before coming back home. It's still a little raw."

"You caught your boyfriend cheating?" Linc asked quietly as we walked toward the door to the office. He propped it open so Fang could run between the two areas.

"Ex-boyfriend. Very ex. And yes. He cheated with a younger colleague at his magazine. A younger colleague with much bigger breasts and much less travel-weary wrinkles than I have." I waved a hand to clear the entire room of the memory. "But I'm over it. Or at least mostly so."

"I'm sorry," Linc said.

I shrugged. "It happens. I'm more angry at myself for denying it for so long. There were definite signs before I actually caught them. But I believed his excuses."

"So, you think Missy and Mike knew about each other's affairs?" Linc asked, bringing the conversation back to the present. I appreciated him for changing the subject before the tears of humiliation, anger, and hurt welling unbidden in my eyes spilled over. I'd shed enough tears for Wreck-It Rick, I didn't want to spend any more emotional energy on him. I brought myself back to the present too.

"In a town as small as this, I don't see how they didn't." Remembering Crystal's comment about Missy's affair, I asked, "Do you know Becky? Could we talk to her?"

"She'll be in later this week for her calendar shoot. We could approach her similarly to Crystal today," Linc suggested.

I nodded. "That could work. Even if Crystal is lying about their alibi, Becky and her husband could both be suspects. Think we could get the husband—what's his name?"

"Danny," Linc supplied.

"Think we could get Danny to come consult on a few shots? Be a second shooter? Not for Becky's turn, of course," I suggested.

"Oh no. We told him, in no uncertain terms, that he was no longer welcome on the premises."

"No exceptions? Even to clear me of murder?" I asked, trying to nail the puppy dog eyes.

"No exceptions. I think Chief Duncan and I scared him so bad, he has PTSD even driving past the place."

"Fine."

I dropped into a chair in the office. Linc automatically brought me a stool to prop my ankle on, then went to fetch me a bag of ice. I mulled over how I could weasel my way into talking to Danny. Honestly, Becky was the stronger suspect—a woman scorned and all that. But Danny could have blamed Missy for the end of his marriage. I needed to learn more about Becky and Danny's relationship prior to their breakup. The best place to do that would be to follow my mother to one of her many clubs. The mere thought gave me hives, but I'd suck it up. Especially if prison was the other option.

Linc came back with the ice.

I smiled up at him. "Thanks."

I reached for the bag, but he knelt down beside my leg. He rolled my sock down to look at the bruise, still blue, but fading to green around the edges. Linc ran his fingertips lightly around my ankle before braceleting it neatly between his thumb and middle finger. He chuckled lightly and gave it a little squeeze, replacing his fingers with the ice. He'd always been fascinated by my petite frame. I could never understand why—it's just genetics.

When he looked at me, his expression was guarded, but dark. Serious.

"Whoever cheated on you, Alex, is the stupidest man alive."

Chapter 17

On Saturday morning, I looked out at the clear blue sky dotted with cotton-ball clouds drifting in the slight spring breeze and frowned. I'd secretly hoped for rain. Or a tornado. Or the apocalypse. Anything to get me out of moving. Moving meant commitment and permanence.

It meant defeat.

Even my stupid ankle felt a lot better so I couldn't use that as an excuse.

"Even though I'd prefer you stay, we couldn't have asked for a better moving day!" my mother exclaimed happily when I finally dragged myself out of bed and toward the inevitable.

"Don't remind me," I mumbled around a mouthful of cereal.

"Now, Peanut, if you don't think the loft is right for you, you can always stay here. Your father and I have loved having you home again, especially after so long away."

And there it was—the rock to match my hard place. If I didn't move, I'd still be stuck here. I loved my parents and had missed them equally as much. Staying at their house also meant the added benefit of my mother's cooking—not good for my waistline but perfect for my appetite. But being a thirtysomething living out of my childhood bedroom screamed failure even more than moving into a Piney Ridge apartment. I ought to take out a neon sign that read "Pathetic."

"Thanks, Mom," I said. "I really appreciate it. But Lash needs more space. She's fiercely private, and us sharing a room isn't working."

As I threw the last few things into a box, I reminded myself it had been less than two weeks since I'd been back in Piney Ridge. I couldn't actually expect to put my entire life and reputation back together in that short a time. Not to mention that I'd been dealing with other problems—a wrecked sign, a hurt ankle, a murder. You know, the usual.

When I heard the beep outside, I grabbed the box from the dresser and met Colleen as she was coming up the walk. True to her offer, she'd managed to borrow a truck. Colleen took the box from my hand after we exchanged greetings, and that started a sort of assembly line for the rest of the boxes. Luckily, I hadn't unpacked much since I'd been home, so it was only a matter of moving the already full boxes from the garage into the back of the truck.

"Where's the rest of it?" Colleen asked after my corner of the garage was emptied.

"That's it," I said. If I thought looking at my belongings stuffed into the back of the Fiat was bad, looking at it taking up just over half of the truck bed was even worse. The "Pathetic" sign blinked on and off a few times in my mind, just to remind me it was still there. I thanked my past self for not calling Linc to help; this was one embarrassing moment he wouldn't be privy to.

"Gah, I wish I had the willpower to have so little stuff. My house is so cluttered, I'm about to classify myself as a hoarder."

"This is going to look absolutely ridiculous in that large, gorgeous space," I said forlornly. I hugged Lash's bowl a little tighter to my chest.

"Are you kidding? This way you can always see the amazing woodwork. It won't be covered in junk!" Colleen said. I looked in awe at my friend, wishing I could bottle some of her optimism.

"We do still have the bed frame and mattress. That'll take up a little more room," I said. But only a little. I was using my childhood twin bed until I could afford an adult-sized one.

"We'll follow you over there, Peanut," Mom said, shooing my father into their car. "We can't wait to see it! The way Nana K talks, it's an oasis."

"Come on," Colleen said, bumping my shoulder. "I'll bet once you have these boxes unpacked, you'll fill more space than you expected."

The unpacked boxes did not fill a lot of the space at all. Nearly all the kitchen cupboards were empty. My clothes closet remained only half-full. The entire place echoed from lack of furniture as we talked. The only upside? We finished in less than two hours.

My parents went out to get some lunch and groceries as Colleen helped me unpack the last few boxes.

"These are really great," Colleen said as she unpacked some framed photos. "I really need to remember to print more photos. All my recent shots are in phone jail at the moment. Or on social media, scrolled through and forgotten."

"As are most of mine. Although not on my phone, but on my computer." I walked over to pluck a frame out of the box. It was an eight by ten of the sunset over the Saharan sand dunes. I'd always meant to print it larger and hang it over my bed, but once I moved in with Rick, I'd never gotten around to it. He preferred signed football memorabilia and generic art prints to my work. That should have been red-flag number one that our relationship was doomed from the start.

"I forgot to ask if I could hang pictures," I commented now. "It almost feels like sacrilege to hammer a nail into this wood."

"I'm sure it's fine. It adds character, right? And you could always fill the holes in later. Make this place your home, Alex. Even if it is temporary."

I smiled at her. "I missed you, Colleen."

"Missed you too."

We were interrupted by a knock on the door. "Hello?" a voice called. "It's Mrs. Anita."

"Hi, Mrs. Anita!" I called. "Come on in."

I smelled the fresh baked apple pie before Mrs. Anita even rounded the corner. My mouth salivated.

"I've brought a welcome-to-the-neighborhood pie. I hope you like apple," she said, presenting the most perfectly browned apple pie. The top crust boasted a lattice-work pattern with a little capital A in the center. I carefully took the offered pie with the potholders Mrs. Anita brought. Good thing because I didn't have any. I added them to my mental shopping list.

"Thank you so much. You didn't have to do this," I cooed. I placed the pie on the kitchen counter since I didn't have a table.

Mrs. Anita looked around the space with a bewildered expression. "Feel free to find Bobby or one of the farmhands when you need help hauling up the furniture."

"I just have a bed frame and mattress. My father and I can handle that," I explained.

"Oh, okay," Mrs. Anita said slowly. Then laughed. "When you said you travel light, I didn't think you meant this light."

"My apartment in New York was about the size of a postage stamp. And I wasn't there very often anyway."

"Feel free to make this place feel like home. If you want to hang pictures or add throw rugs, that might help make it homier. We just ask that you don't paint the walls."

"Oh, thank you! I was going to ask about hanging pictures," I said. "And I have no intentions of painting this wood."

Mrs. Anita smiled and started making her way to the door. I followed. "If you need anything, just holler. We're usually in the market or the fields until dusk, then at the house. You'll find the contact numbers in the lease."

"Thank you so much. This whole thing is really very kind."

Mrs. Anita patted my shoulder. "We're happy to have you."

Colleen already had the pie cut by the time I walked back to the kitchen area.

"Help yourself," I said, laughing.

"I did. Want a piece?"

"Of course. We'll have to eat standing up. Or sitting on the floor."

Colleen shrugged. "Grab your computer. Since Mrs. Anita said you could hang pictures, we should pick some more recent shots too. Make good on the promise to print more. And I need some too."

I booted up my computer while sitting crisscross applesauce on the floor by the fireplace. Colleen joined me with two slices of pie. "Too bad we don't have ice cream," she quipped. I added that to my growing shopping list.

"Let's start with your reservoir shoot and work backward from there. I'm sure you got some amazing local shots. Maybe you could even convince Mrs. Anita to let you set up a little display in the market. She's done it for other local artists," Colleen said.

"That's a great idea. And would help supplement my income. I got the quote from the mechanic." I rolled my eyes. "Apparently Fiat parts are hard to come by. I asked if I could pay with the promise of my firstborn son, but that was a no-go."

"Do you need a loan?" Colleen asked.

I looked up from my keyboard. "Thank you so much for offering. Really. But I'm okay. I have some savings from my last pro shoot. And the mechanic has a payment-plan option. I can't drive the stupid thing until I take that stupid safe-driving class anyway, so what's the difference."

"Tell me how you really feel about it," Colleen laughed. Then she pointed to the screen where I was scrolling through my flagged shots from the reservoir. "Oh, that one is lovely."

She pointed to one with the water lapping against the rocks on the reservoir edge. I had lain on my belly to capture the exact moment the small waves broke against the shoreline. The angle made them seem larger than they really were. Colleen pulled the laptop into her lap to get a better look.

"You took this at the reservoir? It looks like ocean waves," Colleen remarked.

"It's all about the angle and the lens." A bright bit of bokeh caught my eye in an otherwise darker part of the frame.

"What's that?" I asked, pointing to the bright spot. Colleen zoomed in.

"Hard to tell," Colleen said. She put her face inches from the screen. "Probably some kind of metal. Jewelry, maybe?"

"Let me see." I pulled the laptop back in front of me. I used the exposure and dehaze sliders in the editing software to bring down the glare a little bit. The shape of a locket came into focus. Goose bumps broke out over my arms.

"Looks like a locket," Colleen confirmed.

"I think so too. Guess who shoved a locket into my face the day I took these pictures?"

Colleen's eyes went wide. "Missy? Shut up. We have to go look for it!"

"I'm sure the police already collected it," I said, but my heartbeat threatened to pump right out of my chest.

"But what if they didn't? What if it's evidence?" Colleen asked in a hushed tone.

"Then we should call the police and tell them about it," I said without any conviction. I didn't trust Chief Duncan as far as I could throw him.

"You don't even believe that," Colleen said, reading my tone perfectly. "Besides, we need to verify that it's there and that it belongs to Missy before we call the police. Otherwise, they'll think we're idiots."

"Too late for that," I said, thinking of how Chief Duncan looked at me that first night. I saved the files, closed the program, and shut the laptop cover. "Okay. Grab my camera. Let's go look for a locket."

Chapter 18

We opted to park in the reservoir parking lot since that path was more worn. My ankle felt loads better, but with moving today, I didn't want to press it. I texted my parents to tell them we were going out "for supplies." Yes, I was thirtysomething, but I didn't want them to worry if they came back to an empty apartment. And, given their history of missing children, they would definitely worry. We made our way to the spot where I'd taken the picture. I sat on a tree stump to rest my ankle and pointed in the general direction.

"Somewhere over there," I said, massaging the aching muscle. Probably I'd overdone it today what with moving and now hiking. I made a mental note to ice it when I got home. If I could find ice in my new place.

Colleen poked around in the grass and rocks. Then her head popped up suddenly. "I think I found it!"

"Don't touch it! Let me take a picture of it first. That way, in case it is Missy's, we will only be in a little bit of trouble from the police," I said. I limped over to Colleen and shot from several angles.

"We should have brought gloves," Colleen said in a hushed whisper as if we were superspies.

I replied in my normal voice. "For what?"

"There could be fingerprints on it! We don't want to contaminate the evidence when we touch it. 'Cause we're totally gonna touch it, right?"

I looked down at the locket. The smart thing to do would be to call the police. Of course, if this did turn out to belong to Missy, Chief Duncan would find it super suspicious that I was once again the one to find it. Definitely not a plus in the Alex is Innocent column.

On the other hand, if I didn't tell them about it and it did turn out to be evidence, that looked just as suspicious. Rock and a hard place. Again. I'd found myself in that particular spot too often for comfort lately.

"Find a stick," I said. "A pointy one."

"Are we going to poke at it?" Colleen asked with a chuckle. "People usually do that with dead bodies not jewelry."

I scowled at her. "If I can see the front, I could tell you if it belonged to Missy or not. Then we can decide if we're going to open it."

"Fine," Colleen conceded. She disappeared into the brush returning a moment later with a pointy stick. "Will this do?"

I took it from her and bent down to turn it over. But between the weight of the camera around my neck and trying to balance on one foot, I almost tipped face forward into the dirt.

"Let me do it," Colleen said. She took the stick and easily flicked the locket over. Not only was it Missy's locket—the engraved MVP on the front clearly visible—but the chain was also broken. I took several more pictures, making sure to get one of the clasp still locked tight.

"Of course, Missy would switch her initials so the moniker read MVP. Who else would be so vain?" Colleen asked.

"It's hers all right," I confirmed, still staring at the locket.

Missy was definitely wearing it when I saw her at the salon. Was it on her body when they found her in the woods? Only her leg was visible in the picture, so that didn't help. I closed my eyes to conjure the image of Missy's body on Sunday night as I swept the flashlight to her face. Thinking about it like a photograph helped me remember the details my mind tried desperately to forget. I pushed aside the blood and bruises to focus on Missy's neck. I was almost positive it was clear—no necklace. Which would make sense if it were in the grass when I took the shots by the reservoir.

I let out a breath. That was a futile exercise. Of course, Missy wasn't wearing it. Still, I'd found her body farther up the path and her necklace by the water—several feet away. Had it been broken in a struggle? Had someone tried to drag Missy up the path and given up? Had I interrupted their efforts?

That last thought sent a shiver down my spine. I could have been here at the same time as the murderer. Right after Missy was killed.

"Oh, for goodness' sake," Colleen cried when I had been silent for a while. She bent down and picked up the locket by its broken chain.

"Colleen! What are you doing? What about preserving evidence?" I cried, astonished at Colleen's impulsiveness.

"Whatever. I'm not even sure Piney Ridge has a fingerprint machine or however they do it. I swear I saw Chief Duncan photocopying someone's hand once."

I laughed. "Well, you might as well open it."

Colleen did. Inside was the picture I remembered from the salon. Two smiling kids that looked to be about elementary school age. They were pretty cute, now that I could focus since it wasn't held right under my nose. I could see the resemblance to Missy, especially with her daughter. The other side did not hold a picture of Mike Vandenburg like I originally assumed. Instead, Missy's little sister, Jodie, smiled back at me.

"I'd have thought the other side would be her husband," I mused.

"No kidding. I mean I love my siblings, but I don't feel the need to wear their picture around my neck," Colleen said. I could relate. I'd even lost a sibling, and although I have a faded picture of us together in my wallet, I don't carry one on my body.

"Wait a minute. This has to mean trouble in paradise," I said, excited again. "Missy must've known about the affairs or, at the very least, was unhappy in the marriage. Why else wouldn't she have her husband's picture in a heart-shaped locket?"

"Totally," Colleen agreed. "I mean, if they were both cheating, they couldn't have had a happy marriage, right?"

"Exactly. I think this puts Mike back on the top of the list. Put the locket in my camera bag for safekeeping. I don't want to touch it. The less my fingerprints show up on things, the better."

"So it's okay for my fingerprints to be on evidence?" Colleen asked.

"You're the one who picked it up! I didn't tell you to do that," I reminded her.

Colleen tucked the locket into the side pocket of the bag, then turned in a slow circle to survey the area. "Where did you find Missy?"

I pointed up the path. "In the brush there. A little way off the path."

"So how did her locket end up down here?" Colleen asked, voicing my thoughts from earlier.

"I wondered the same thing. Did you notice the broken chain?" Colleen nodded. I continued, "What if Missy and her murderer argued down here by the water. Their fight turned physical, and the murderer tore off the locket in the struggle."

"Yeah. He killed her here and then dragged her into the woods to hide her body," Colleen added. "Or maybe she tried to run, and the killer caught her up there on the path."

"Let's look for drag marks," I suggested. I had no idea if they would still be here even if they once were. It had been a week since the murder. How long did it take for grass to bounce back?

We looked around a little, then admitted defeat.

"I don't even know what I'm looking for," Colleen said.

"The killer could have used the path instead. Then there would be no drag marks." Some detectives we were.

I looked at the pictures I'd taken of the locket, on the back of my camera. I zoomed in on one of the locket's back, the way we'd first found it laying in the dirt.

"Look," I said, enlarging the area beside the locket. "What does that look like to you?"

"Drops of blood," Colleen said. "And there, too, on the corner of the locket."

"This could mean that she was killed by the reservoir and then moved up the path," I said. "What if the killer tried dragging Missy, but she was too heavy. It was taking too long, so they left her in the brush on the side of the path."

"That would pretty much rule out Mike," Colleen pointed out. "He's strong enough to throw her over his shoulder and carry her out."

I pursed my lips. "Dangit. You're right. What's another theory that makes him guilty?" I snapped my fingers. "Maybe someone came down the path, and he dropped her instead of having to answer questions."

"Alex. These are all theories. We probably should report the locket to the police," Colleen conceded finally.

I pouted for a moment, then huffed out a breath. "Fine. But I'm calling Detective Spaulding. Not Chief Duncan."

Chapter 19

I made the call as Colleen drove us back to the loft. I wanted to ask Colleen to take us back to the reservoir so I could put the locket back where we'd found it. We could just tell Detective Spaulding we came across it. Or call it in as an anonymous tip. Too late now. Better to be honest up front. How else would we be able to explain Colleen's fingerprints on it?

"He's going to meet us at the loft in half an hour. He promised not to bring Chief Duncan," I told Colleen.

"Good. I wonder what your mother got for lunch," Colleen responded.

"How can you be thinking about food? We just found a dead woman's locket," I admonished. Then my stomach growled, betraying me. Colleen laughed.

Nana K's Mercedes was parked next to my parents' car in the orchard parking lot, which didn't surprise me at all. I was more surprised it took Nana K this long to get here.

We stepped inside the loft to the noise and smells of family. My mother and grandmother laughed and talked as they opened containers and spread out food on the kitchen counter buffet style. I smelled fried chicken and coleslaw with an undercurrent of fresh coffee. My father sat on the couch holding a paper and a mug.

Wait. I had a couch?

"Where did that couch come from?" I asked by way of greeting.

"There you two are. We were ready to send out a search party. Either that or eat all this chicken ourselves," Mom said brightly, giving me and Colleen a hug.

"The couch?" I asked again.

"I've had that old thing sitting in storage for years," Nana K explained. "It's a bit beat up, but better than having company sit on the floor."

"That old thing" as Nana K described it was anything but. An ornate wooden curvature adorned the back of the midsized couch. The cushions were upholstered with a deep-purple, almost fuzzy fabric. Was that velvet? I didn't think so, but I wouldn't put it past my grandmother. Right now it sat facing the kitchen area. Ideal for this situation so we could all converse. But I could easily turn it around to face the fireplace. It would be a good visual buffer to separate the space, especially once I found a table and chairs for dining.

"Thanks, Nana," I said, embracing my grandmother and placing a kiss on the top of her pink and purple hair. I wasn't tall by any means, five foot three and a half—the half was important—but I felt like a giant compared to Nana K, who stood no more than five feet tall if she stretched her neck out. Part of our coming of age in my family was growing taller than Nana K. Out of all of my cousins, I took the longest. My cousin Greg passed Nana K at the budding age of eight. He held the record. I hadn't reached Nana's height until middle school. And even then, my parents weren't sure if I'd actually surpass the matriarch. Luckily, due to a three-inch growth spurt in the ninth grade, I

146

sprouted passed Nana K for good. Then added another inch and half for good measure.

"Come get lunch," Mom said. "We stopped by Solomon's for chicken and the market for dessert."

My mouth watered. Colleen said, "Don't have to ask me twice to eat Solomon's." She practically ran for the counter.

Solomon's was the local butcher and game processor. People came from all over Maryland for their fresh-cut bacon, fried chicken, and locally sourced venison. The attached restaurant overflowed with patrons for lunch and dinner.

"Great choice," I said. I couldn't believe I hadn't demanded Solomon's as soon as I came home. I was too caught up in my feels at the time.

Mom and Nana K joined my father on the couch to eat, balancing their plates precariously on their knees. Colleen and I leaned against the kitchen counter. Conversation lulled a bit while we all enjoyed the meal and concentrated on not dropping our food. A sharp *rap-rap-rap* on the door jolted me out of my food coma.

"Expecting someone?" Mom asked.

"Detective Spaulding," Colleen and I said at the same time.

"Why would Detective Spaulding be here?" Mom asked. She wiped her hands on her apron and went to open the door. She expertly replaced her confused expression with one of warmth and welcome as she swung it open.

"Welcome, Detective. We were having lunch from Solomon's. Come in, come in." Mom stepped aside to let the detective into the loft.

"Thank you, ma'am." His cop eyes immediately evaluated the space. It didn't take long until they landed on me with a mixture of concern and curiosity. I placed my plate on the counter behind me as he approached.

"Ms. Lightwood," he greeted me with a firm handshake. "Thank you for contacting me."

"Please. Call me Alex. Do you want some lunch first?" I asked. I purposefully avoided my mother's questioning glances.

"Actually, I just might, if you don't mind. I've heard amazing things about Solomon's chicken, but haven't had the chance to partake."

Dad stood to make a spot for him on the couch.

"We were just going," my father said before Mom could resume her seat. "Alex, we put some supplies in the fridge. Call us later, okay?" It wasn't really a question; his tone meant I had better call him later to explain the situation.

"Thanks, Dad. I will."

"But I haven't had any pie yet, and—" Mom started. But Dad cut her off with a look. She pursed her lips, but acquiesced. A rare move for Constance Lightwood. Then again, Dad didn't ask too much of the ladies in his life, so when he put his foot down on something, we usually complied.

After my parents left, Detective Spaulding turned to Nana K, who still sat comfortably on the couch with no outward intention of following her daughter and son-in-law out the door.

"I'm James Spaulding from the Maryland State Police," he said, holding out his hand. "I don't think we've met before."

"I'm glad we've met now," Nana K said. She rose from her seat, which didn't change her height much, and gave him her hand. "Regina Klafkeniewski. I'm Alex's very single, very young-at-heart grandmother. And you"—she made a show of looking him up and down—"are one tall drink of water."

Detective Spaulding blushed and ducked his head to hide his laugh.

Colleen quipped, "Nana K, everyone is a tall drink of water to you."

Nana K ignored her. "Come sit down, James. I'll get you a plate."

"No, please. I can do it. I don't need to be waited on." Nana K didn't have to be asked twice. She gestured to the spread on the kitchen counter and resumed her seat on the couch. Colleen joined her.

I took a moment to assess Detective James Spaulding with fresh eyes as he loaded a plate with chicken and sides. The last time I saw him I had just found a dead body and became suspect number one. Now, with a relatively clearer head, I could see what my grandmother was talking about. He was rather tall, just shy of six feet if I had to guess, and broad shouldered. His sandy-blond hair held a military cut— high and tight around his ears. He carried a little weight around his middle, but who didn't really. Well, besides Linc, whose body probably had a built-in machine that immediately turned carbs into muscles.

When Detective Spaulding turned around with his plate, he caught me staring and smirked. Instead of averting my eyes, I smirked back, surprising us both. His green eyes went wide, and the other side of his mouth hitched up as well. He had a great smile. It lit up his face and created little smile lines beside his eyes. His hands looked large on the small, disposable plates my parents had provided. I had the sudden urge to reach across the space and trace the scar on his chin.

Nana K, an expert in the art of subtlety, said, "Alex is single, you know. She moved into this big space today all by herself." I shot daggers out of my eyes and scowled.

"Just moved in. That explains the—" He struggled for a non-offensive word, but eventually gave up and waved his fork around in a circle.

"Sparseness?" I supplied. He smiled and nodded. "Unfortunately, what you see is what you get. I moved here from New York City. Not a lot of storage space there, hence the minimalist style."

"I see," he said, taking a bit of his chicken. His eyes went wide again. "Wow. This is really good!"

Even though his demeanor seemed light and his bearing relaxed, I sensed that he operated in cop mode all the time. He took in everything we said, every move we made, and made a mental note. All of this would go in a report at some point, or at least help him to form an opinion. His eyes were shrewd and sharp. I recognized that look. I felt the same way when hunting for the perfect shot on location. I had to be careful despite liking him immediately.

"We've ruined chicken for you forever. Definitely stop on the way back to the city for a to-go bucket. It is just as good cold on a sandwich tomorrow," Colleen said. She, like Nana K, had dreamy eyes for Detective Spaulding.

He turned his attention back to me. "What did you want to see me about?"

"You called him?" Nana K asked.

"Yes. And Nana, if you can keep a secret, you can stay. Otherwise, I'm kicking you out too," I said, pointing my finger at my grandmother.

"Cross my heart," she said, and did.

I left to fetch my camera bag from the floor by the door where I'd left it. I nearly jumped out of my skin when someone knocked.

"Alex?" The door opened a crack. "Can I come in?" Linc.

I sighed. I was bound to tell him about the locket at some point anyway. I hauled the door open all the way. He nearly tumbled inside. Fang ran by me, a blur of black and white.

"Whoa," I said, putting my hands on Linc's chest to stop his momentum. "I'm the one with the clumsy schtick, remember?"

"Sorry. I didn't expect you to be right here," he said, righting himself. He handed me a bouquet of wildflowers. "Housewarming gift."

"Oh, these are lovely, Linc. Thank you," I said, breathing them in, touched more than I could explain. I couldn't remember the last time I'd gotten flowers from someone other than my parents. Definitely never from Rick. He wasn't really a hearts and flowers kind of guy.

"Is it okay if Fang comes in?" he asked, even though by the sounds of oohing and aahing from the kitchen, he'd already made himself at home.

"Of course," I said, moving back to let Linc in fully.

"Is that Solomon's I smell?" Linc asked.

"So, that's what led you here. Following your nose," I teased.

He didn't deny it. "Any left?"

"In the kitchen." I pointed in the direction. I followed him down the hallway. I noticed he didn't even really look at the space, unlike everyone else who came through.

"Isn't the woodwork amazing? It's what sold me on this place."

"Sure," he said. "If you like that sort of thing." He noticed the group in the kitchen and stopped short. "Oh, sorry. I didn't know you had company."

"Lincoln Livestrong, the firefighter and EMT," Detective Spaulding said, pushing off the counter where he'd been leaning and holding out his hand.

Linc shook it, but his face remained unreadable. Fang had settled himself by Nana K's feet, eyes trained on her plate, hoping for a handout.

"Detective Spaulding," he said stiffly. "What are you doing here?"

"I called him," I explained.

Linc blinked at me, expressionless—what was his problem?—then turned his attention to Nana K. His face transformed back into the charming, amused Lincoln I knew.

"Nana K," he crooned. "It's been too long. You look gorgeous as always."

She gave him a tight hug from her seat. "Two handsome young men in the same room in one day. Have I died and gone to heaven? Alex, pinch me, quick."

We all laughed. I busied myself putting the wildflowers in a commemorative plastic Yankees cup I had in the cupboard. I heard Linc snort behind me.

"You're seriously going to put my flowers in a Yankees cup?" he asked.

I smiled as I fluffed them in the makeshift vase. Linc was a die-hard Baltimore Orioles fan.

"It's all I have at the moment." I set the bouquet on the fireplace mantle.

"Don't tell me you've joined the dark side. That would break my heart," he said, putting a hand over his chest in mock pain.

"Honestly, I'm not a huge sportsball fan at all. Unless I'm taking action shots at the game. Which is why I have this cup." I turned my attention back to Detective Spaulding. "I don't want to take up any more of your time," I said.

"Colleen and I discovered something by the reservoir today. We thought the police would be interested."

I motioned for Colleen to take the locket out of the camera bag. I still didn't want to touch it. Detective Spaulding immediately reached for it with a napkin. Colleen placed it in his outstretched hands. He brought it to his face to examine, using his fingers and the napkin to rotate it. I pulled up the pictures of where we found it on my camera.

"MVP," he said, reading the inscription.

A cloud passed over Linc's face, but I ignored him. When recognition dawned on Detective Spaulding, his expression changed.

"Why do you have Missy Vandenburg's locket?"

Chapter 20

All eyes were on mine, except for Colleen's. Hers were examining her chicken bones as if they held the location to Atlantis, leaving me on my own to explain this.

"Well," I said slowly. "We were looking through the pictures from the reservoir shoot to see if there were any I could print. Colleen suggested I put together a display of local shots for the market downstairs. And we both agreed that no one printed pictures enough anymore—"

"Alex," Linc cut me off. "Get to the point."

"The point. Right. Similarly to how I noticed Missy's, um, leg, originally, something bright in a patch of darkness caught my eye. When I adjusted the settings, it looked like a locket," I explained.

"So you just decided to go get it? A little Saturday afternoon treasure hunt?" Detective Spaulding's voice had an edge to it now.

"I, uh, I knew Missy wore a locket because she showed it to me at the salon that day," I explained. Before the detective could ask, I said, "We didn't want to call in the police right away because we weren't sure who it belonged to. It could have been left there forever ago. We wanted to be sure before bothering anyone."

"And once you realized it was Missy's, you thought bringing it back here was better than leaving it where you found it?" Linc's voice held a similar edge—equal parts sarcasm and disbelief. In hindsight, taking the locket did seem a bit hasty.

"We weren't really thinking," Colleen admitted. "But Alex took lots of pictures of where we found it."

"How kind of you," the detective said sarcastically. "Show me."

I did. I zoomed in on the picture where we thought we saw blood. As soon as he saw it, he called his crime scene guys and asked them to meet him by the reservoir.

"Wait at the top of the path in the parking lot. I'll meet you there," he said before disconnecting. Then turned his attention back to me. "I'm going to need copies of those photos. Do you happen to have them date and time stamped?"

"Of course."

"I'll also need everything you took that day at the reservoir."

"Every picture? There are over a hundred. Some of them aren't very good." I hated showing people my raw images. Even those I submitted as a photojournalist still had a bit of color correction and contrast adjustments.

"Every picture, Ms. Lightwood," he repeated. Uh-oh, we were back to Ms. Lightwood.

"If you wait a moment, I can put them all on a thumb drive for you now."

"That would be great. Bring your computer out here so I can be a witness to the chain of evidence."

I swallowed. "Chain of evidence" sounded terrible. I had been trying to help myself, but now I was in even more trouble. I took my time walking to my bedroom to gather my laptop and the extra thumb drive. I wanted a moment to collect and bottle my emotions.

"What were you thinking?" Linc's low growl behind me made me jump and squeal. He grabbed my elbow and spun me around to face him.

"Cheese and crackers, you scared me. I should get you a bell," I said, willing my heartbeat to slow.

"Answer me. Why would you go looking for evidence?" he asked. His eyes were darker than I'd ever seen them. Like the sky before a storm.

"We were just trying to help. Like I said, I didn't want to feel like an idiot if it turned out to be nothing," I repeated.

"Not a great idea, Alex. You seem to keep forgetting this is a small town. And there are very few secrets in small towns. Word is going to get out that you're poking into this," he explained.

"So?" What was the big deal?

"So, there is still a murderer out there." His voice had gotten louder, and we heard conversation stop in the other room. He took a deep breath and backed away from me a step before continuing. "If they feel like you're getting too close, they could come after you next."

The color drained from my face. I hadn't thought of that. Still, I hated being treated like a child.

"It was the middle of the day. I had Colleen with me. We weren't in danger."

"Great." He threw up his hands. "A pixie-sized photographer with a bum ankle and a preschool teacher with hair you can see from space. Quite the menacing duo."

I narrowed my eyes at him and poked a finger into his chest. "I have survived just fine on my own for the last decade in places much more dangerous than Piney Ridge. And I don't need your guilt trip. I already feel bad enough for not leaving that locket where we found it." I grabbed my laptop off the bed and elbowed past him.

"Dammit, Alex," I heard him say behind me. I didn't stop moving.

Detective Spaulding asked Colleen questions while Nana K sipped on a lemonade, looking amused. I set up the laptop on the kitchen counter and began transferring the images from my camera to the thumb drive. As they loaded, I scrolled through the folder with the reservoir pictures to take out any that were completely out of focus. I had a little bit of dignity left.

"Tampering with evidence aside," Detective Spaulding said, leaning over my shoulder as I worked, "these photos are really great. I love the ones by the water."

"It's really hard to mess up something as beautiful as the reservoir," I said, diminishing his compliment. "I just shoot what I see."

"You have a very good eye. I would have never thought to get down on eye level with the rocks."

"I guess laziness pays off sometimes," I joked. When the last picture transferred, I removed the thumb drive and handed it to him. "If you need explanations of where any were taken or whatever, just ask."

He looked from me to Colleen and back again. "Tampering with evidence is serious. How do we know you didn't plant this necklace?" He held up a hand before we could protest. "I might be crazy, but I believe your story. For now," he added ominously. He checked his watch. "I've got to go meet the crime scene crew."

He walked to the couch to address Nana K. "Ms. Klafke-Klafken-Klafski—" he tried.

She laughed and interrupted, "It's pronounced Klahf-ken-ev-ski. Everyone calls me Nana K. You, my darling, can call me whatever you want, just don't call me late for cocktails."

"Okay, Ms. K," he said, smiling. "It was really great to meet you. Try to keep your granddaughter out of trouble."

"Usually it's the other way around," I murmured.

Detective Spaulding made his farewells to Colleen and Linc—a warning to stay away from evidence for Colleen and a stiff handshake for Linc.

"Detective Spaulding?" I asked as we walked to the door. "We thought maybe Missy was killed by the water and then dragged into the brush. We looked around but couldn't really see any drag marks or anything."

He rubbed a hand over his face. "I probably shouldn't be telling you this, but I think you need to know. It'll be in the papers soon enough anyway. She was dragged. We noticed mud on her heels and disturbed brush the night we discovered her. By finding this necklace, you might have helped us pinpoint the actual murder spot." He opened the door to leave, then turned and added. "You shouldn't be looking into this on your own. Next time you even think you find evidence, call me first. Your boyfriend was right about that."

I nodded but felt compelled to add, "Linc isn't my boyfriend. We knew each other in high school."

We turned to look back toward the kitchen where Linc paced back and forth with a scowl on his face. He ran a hand through his hair when he caught us looking his way.

"Huh," Detective Spaulding said. "Well then, he has some major big-brother issues happening where you're concerned."

"It's because I'm so short. People feel like they have to treat me like a child."

He looked down at me with his green eyes glowing. "Ms. Lightwood, you are anything but a child."

Then he left. Dazed, I wandered back to the kitchen. What did that even mean? If I didn't know better, I'd have thought he was flirting. But that was ridiculous since he totally thought I was a murderer.

"I don't like the way he looked at you," Linc said. "Like a predator."

"He is hunting a killer. And I keep putting myself in the crosshairs," I said, falling onto the couch beside Nana K. Without asking, Linc got me a bag of ice for my ankle. Ever the EMT. Although this time he handed it to me instead of applying it himself. He must really be angry.

"What did he say to you?" Colleen asked.

"He told me our assumptions were right," I said. "She was dragged." I frowned, realization dawning. "Would that eliminate Mike? Couldn't he carry her?"

"Maybe," Linc said. "Unless he was trying to hide her and not take her out of the forest completely. But," he added, holding up a finger when my eyes lit up, "I managed to drop Crystal's alibi into conversation with my nosiest neighbor. She confirmed Mike's car was parked in front of Crystal's house all day."

"Well, poo. Two suspects essentially crossed off the short list. Now I really need to talk to Becky and her ex-husband," I said, already forgetting the detective's warning to stay out of it.

Linc opened his mouth to undoubtedly remind me of that warning when Nana K piped up for the first time since the revelation of the locket. "In my experience, I find that people are often willing to let their guard down more around unassuming citizens and old ladies than the police. And there is no harm in being friendly and talking to folks. That's what we do in small towns."

"You aren't helping, Nana K," Linc said. "It isn't safe for Alex to be snooping around. For any of you to be."

"Talking, not snooping. You need to change your mindset," Nana K clarified.

"Unbelievable," Linc said, running his hands through his hair again.

"Okay. How about a compromise?" I said, trying to keep him from blowing a blood vessel. "You can be the one to ask Becky a few questions on Monday. I won't even open my mouth except in terms of the shoot."

He gave me a long look. "You aren't going to let this go, are you?" he finally asked.

I shook my head. "I can't."

"Fine. Not one word from you even if you think I'm not doing it right."

I mimed locking my lips with a key and throwing it over my shoulder.

"Sit down and have some chicken, Linc," Nana K said. "You're making us all nervous with your pacing."

He followed orders and sat on the other side of Nana K on the couch.

I tried to lighten the mood. "You'll never believe what Detective Spaulding said by the door."

"That he wants to show you how else he can use handcuffs?" Linc mumbled.

"What? Don't be ridiculous."

Nana K guessed, "That he wants to marry me and make my final years heaven on earth?"

"Not quite," I said, laughing. "He thought Linc was my boyfriend. Isn't that silly?"

Linc stood up from the couch abruptly. "Silly. Right." He stomped toward the door. "See you on Monday at the firehouse, Alex. Stay out of trouble until then. Fang, come."

The frame rattled as he slammed out the door. So much for lightening the mood.

"What was that all about?" I asked.

Colleen shrugged and heaped another scoop of coleslaw on her plate. Nana K sat back on the couch with a bemused smile on her face.

Chapter 21

An obnoxious noise woke me out of a difficult dream. I reached over to silence my phone alarm, but no amount of button smashing would stop the intermittent noise. Groaning, I rubbed at my eyes. I had a moment of panic when I opened them in a strange room before remembering I was in the loft at the orchard. I glanced at the time on my phone and nearly fell out of bed. Six thirty in the morning. On a Sunday. I hadn't been awake this early on the weekend since my mother made me attend early morning Mass at St. Joseph's.

So, if the noise wasn't coming from my phone, where was it coming from? I went to the window to look outside. Below me a flock of chickens pecked around by my steps. As I watched, one particularly fluffy one stretched his neck and crowed. I'd found the source of my impromptu alarm clock— a rooster.

"Well, Lash," I said to my fish on the dresser beside me. "I guess farm animals are the trade-off for the amazing price of this place."

As I dropped some fish flakes into Lash's bowl, I added earplugs to my mental shopping list. A list growing exponentially each moment. A list I should probably consider transferring to a note in my phone so I didn't forget anything.

I shuffled into the kitchen to find some breakfast.

"Thank you, Mom, for knowing me so well," I said, as I pulled a box of sugary cereal from the cabinet. Maybe the sugar would wake me up a little and help me shake off my dream.

In it I was stuck in a room with Linc, Detective Spaulding, and Rick. Linc and the detective each pulled on one of my arms. Linc, with his stormy-gray eyes and adorable grin, kept reminding me of the kiss we shared in his truck in high school. Detective Spaulding, with his sharp, green eyes and intriguing scar, told me over and over that I was anything but a child. Wreck-it Rick stood in the background laughing his head off. I didn't need Freud to help me figure out what that meant. What bothered me was why I dreamt about these men at all. I wanted nothing to do with the opposite sex. At least not in a romantic way. Rick had ruined that for me for a while.

Not that it mattered. Neither of those handsome alpha males would give an awkward pipsqueak like me a second glance in real life.

To take my mind off it, I contemplated a way to talk to Becky's ex-husband, Danny, without being so obvious. And to figure out where Danny lived.

Begrudgingly, I called my mother.

An hour later, I had showered in the beautifully tiled bathroom, all the while pretending I was at a spa, and slapped on some light makeup, mainly to hide the bags under my eyes from lack of sleep. I put on my least-threadbare cargo pants and an unwrinkled T-shirt. For once

I left my hair down around my shoulders instead of pulling it up into a messy bun on top of my head. I was headed to the Ladies' Auxiliary Sunday luncheon. My mother would be here to pick me up in ten minutes. Just enough time to pack my go bag of camera essentials—I never went anywhere without it—and head down the steps to meet her.

When I opened the loft door, a tan-colored chicken stood at the top of the steps as though waiting for me. It cocked its little head to one side and looked up at me.

"Well, hello, there. How'd you get up here?"

The chicken made a little coo sound in its throat and looked at me with the other eye.

"Okay, then. Don't poop on the steps, please," I scooted around it to descend. I guessed I'd have to get used to having farm animals visit.

My mother pulled up a moment later, scoffed a little at my outfit without saying anything, and zipped us off to the luncheon.

Mom reintroduced me to her friends—it had been several years since I'd seen any of them. Noticeably missing was Laura Poledark, Missy's mother. A fact that didn't go unnoticed by the other women either.

"Poor Laura. She can't bring herself to get out of the house yet," Judy Gosling clucked.

"And poor Jodie too. The sisters were really close. I mean, Missy practically raised her since Laura was always busy with her charities and... things," Anne Fletcher added. Everyone knew "and things" meant getting drunk on cheap wine and passing out on whatever barstool she found herself on.

"Not to mention Michael Junior and Patsy," my mother said, mentioning Missy's kids. All the women made affirming noises and shook their heads as they passed the pitcher of mimosas around the table.

"I'm going to take Laura a casserole," Anne said definitively. Everyone agreed that would be a wonderful idea. They made a schedule to feed both Laura and Mike and the kids.

Slowly, their conversation moved to the actual murder. It was the most exciting thing to happen in Piney Ridge, and everyone felt like they had some sort of personal connection to the crime. I sat back and listened intently. Most of the women regurgitated what had been printed in the paper. Others spouted theories and gossip. Most thought Mike did it.

When it seemed like they weren't going to talk about Missy's infidelity, I tried to steer the conversation that way. "I heard Missy was having an affair as well."

"Oh, yes. With Daniel Tidwell. But that ended a while ago," Anne Fletcher said.

"Didn't it break up the Tidwell's marriage?" I made sure to repeat the surname so I would remember it later.

"Yes. But honestly those poor kids were heading for divorce anyway, in my opinion," Victoria Munhouse chimed in.

"I heard that too," Anne confirmed. "They had a pregnancy scare a few years ago that had them get hitched in the first place. When that turned out to be a false alarm, the marriage seemed doomed. Becky tried to make it work for a while. But when you trick a man into marrying you like that, the trust is never going to be there."

"I saw her coming out of Wyatt Fielding's office about a month before she found out about Missy," Victoria said.

"Who's Wyatt Fielding?" I asked.

"He's a lawyer. Specializes in divorces," my mother explained.

"But I heard she and Danny had a huge blowout when she found out about Missy. That's why Danny isn't doing the first-responder calendar this year."

"No calendar?" Anne asked. "What a shame. I love that calendar. Mainly for the animals, of course."

Mom huffed. She leaned in and whispered in my ear. "Animals, my dupa. She has her calendar set perpetually to August. I'll give you two guesses whose month that is."

I only needed one. "Linc?" Mom nodded. I grinned.

"I'm doing the photo shoot this year. You'll still get a calendar. Although it might look a little different. I think Danny and I have different styles," I explained. The ladies let out a collective sigh of relief.

"How wonderful," Victoria commented. "It'll be nice to have a change of style. They were getting a bit redundant over the last few years."

"I'm guessing Becky and Danny aren't still married? Linc indicated he wasn't welcome anywhere near the firehouse," I said.

"Nope. Becky got the house. Danny tucked his tail back to his parents' house. When Becky kicked him out, he lost her and Missy," Anne said.

"That's right." Mom laughed. "Nothing puts out a flame like moving back in with Mommy and Daddy. No offense, Peanut," she added for my benefit.

I rolled my eyes. "I managed to move out in less than a month," I reminded her. "What's taking Danny so long?"

"Lack of motivation. He likes having women take care of him," Victoria said. The ladies chuckled. Then the conversation moved to all the ways they cared for their husbands.

I tuned out to process the information I learned. If these ladies were correct, Becky didn't really have a motive to kill Missy. They were headed toward divorce well before she knew about the affair. And the affair ended months ago. I felt a little better about my compromise with Linc. It didn't matter what he asked her; my gut told me it wasn't her. That would be a dish of revenge served very cold.

Danny, on the other hand, had lots of motive. He'd risked and ultimately lost his marriage for Missy only to have her dump him the moment he found freedom. Now he was stuck at his parents' house and the butt of a lot of town gossip. It wasn't hard to imagine a man stewing in his childhood bedroom plotting revenge on the woman he loved and lost. The woman who'd cost him everything.

The more I thought about it, the more I liked the theory. I had to find a way to talk to Danny.

"Good luck with the calendar, Alex," Victoria's voice cut into my thoughts. I looked up to see the woman standing in front of me. "I can't wait to see what you come up with."

I stood to say farewell. Victoria took my shoulders and put an air kiss on both of my cheeks.

"So good to meet you, Ms. Munhouse," I said. "Thank you all for inviting me to the luncheon."

"The more the merrier. Tell Lincoln we said hi when you see him next," Anne said. She followed Victoria out the door, and the rest of the ladies followed soon after.

"You didn't tell me you were doing the calendar shoot," my mother admonished me as we drove back to the loft. "Your first Piney Ridge job. How nice!"

"Not exactly a job since it's part of my court-ordered community service."

"Pish-posh," Mom said. "Any publicity is good publicity. Once people see your work, they'll be banging on your door for photo shoots of their own."

"Great. Just the way I wanted my career to go." I pouted. "Taking pictures of babies and housewives."

Mom was quiet for a moment, then said, "I've had about enough of your little pity party, young lady."

"What?" I asked, surprised. Usually my mother pointed her ire outside her own family.

"You once told me that you loved capturing real moments with real people. Piney Ridge may not be as tragic as some of the villages you've been to, or as exciting as the big cities, but the people here are as real as anyone else. And they deserve to have their images captured for the next generation same as everyone else. Family portraits may not win you any awards, but they will undeniably be treasured by generations of the family you gift them to."

I stared at her. I never really thought my mother "got" my profession. Apparently, she did. And better than me lately.

Mom looked over at my astonished expression. "What? I'm right. And not only that, but family portraiture also pays the bills. That sign isn't going to fix itself. And you can't continue to barter photos for rent forever."

"I know. I'm still bitter about how the whole thing ended. I didn't do anything wrong, and yet I'm the one paying the price."

"Yup. It sucks. But are you going to continue to let Rick knock you down? Or are you going to put your Lightwood on and not give up?"

I sighed. That was the million-dollar question. Was it selling out if I went commercial? Was it just another form of defeat? I could look at it like a means to an end, I supposed. An "in the meantime" professional detour to help me put food on the table—after I got a table—and not a permanent career move.

"I guess you're right. I have to do something while I wait for the magazines to grovel on my doorstep begging for my return," I said. That was what I wanted. I wanted the photojournalist world to realize what they were missing without me and seek me out. I wanted them to see Rick for the lying, cheating idiot he was and blacklist him instead. I wanted my integrity and reputation to be restored immediately.

In the meantime, I might have to take pictures of babies.

Chapter 22

Nana K's Mercedes, parked in the orchard lot, twinkled at us under the bright afternoon sun.

"What is she doing here?" Mom asked. I shrugged.

"Maybe she brought me some more furniture?" I suggested. A table would be nice. Or a desk to put my laptop on. Or a comfy chair to curl up in with a good book. Those things would require a lot of squirming toddler pictures to purchase myself.

"Your father and I have bowling league in a bit. I hope you don't mind me dropping you off. If I go up there, it'll be an hour before she lets me leave," Mom said.

"No problem. I have no plans because my life is currently in the toilet," I said brightly. I reached across to give my mother a kiss on the cheek. "Thanks for letting me tag along today. It was fun. You have really nice friends."

"Thank you, darling. Use dinner at our house as an excuse if Nana overstays her welcome."

I waved to the retreating car as I mounted the steps to my apartment. I kept an eye out for chicken droppings but didn't see any. Thank goodness.

Nana K, still clad in her babushka and light jacket, got up from the couch as soon as I walked through the door. "Don't drop your bag, we're going out."

"I just got home," I protested.

"You need supplies. I could see you making your mental list yesterday. Besides, I need some things too."

I couldn't argue with that. As we drove to town, I told my grandmother about what I learned at the Ladies' Auxiliary lunch.

"Obviously, you have to talk to Danny Tidwell," Nana K confirmed.

"Right!?" Finally, someone agreed with me. "I just need to think of a reason. And figure out where he lives."

Nana K swerved the Mercedes into an illegal U-turn in the middle of the street without so much as a blinker or a brake pedal. I screamed and held on to the dashboard.

"What are you doing? You're gonna get us killed!" I shrieked over the blaring horns from other drivers.

"I know where the Tidwells live. If Danny is still living there, he'll for sure be home on a Sunday afternoon."

"Could you at least give me a warning next time?"

"This way is more fun. Puts some color in your cheeks."

I shook my head in disbelief. "What am I going to say to get him to talk to me? I don't have a plan."

"I find that sticking as close to the truth as possible is always a good idea," Nana K suggested.

I snorted. "Somehow I don't think 'Hi, did you murder Missy Vandenburg?' is a great way to engender conversation."

"Of course not. But what is your connection to him?" Nana K asked.

I thought about it a moment. "I guess we're both photographers."

"And..." Nana K prompted.

"And we've both worked on the firehouse shoot." I snapped my fingers. "That's it! I'll ask him for advice on the shoot. Men love when you play up to their ego, right?"

"Not only men. Everyone. Compliments catch more flies than vinegar," Nana K said, butchering the idiom.

"I think it's honey, Nana," I corrected.

"Call him whatever you want. Just figure out if he was bitter enough to murder Missy."

Armed with my camera and a bright smile, I rang the doorbell to the Tidwell residence. Nana K stood beside me for moral support. And to distract Mrs. Tidwell so she didn't hover while I talked to her son. She had a reputation of being a little overbearing even though Danny was in his twenties.

But Danny answered the door. "Sorry, no solicitors," he said and started to shut the door.

"Wait. We're not solicitors," I called. The door paused mid-swing. "I'm Alex Lightwood. This is my grandmother, Regina Klafkeniewski. I'm doing the first-responder calendar this year." I held up my camera as though that were evidence enough. It seemed to be because Danny opened the door again.

"Why are you here?" he asked.

"I was hoping you could help me. I've heard such amazing things about past calendars, and I don't want to mess it up. I'd love any pointers or, like, tips or tricks that have worked for you in the past. How do you get the pets and the people to look at the camera? I'm not used to directing," I babbled. I saw his face soften a bit and held my breath.

"Sure," he said finally. "Come on in."

Nana K and I gave each other a high five behind his back.

"Is your mother home, dear?" Nana K asked. "I wanted to show her a new technique in Bridge."

"She's out right now but should be back soon."

After settling in the living room, I listened to Danny blather on about flashes and strobes and posing—all things I had no interest in using. I made the requisite agreeable sounds occasionally.

Finally, when I couldn't stand it any longer, I interrupted to ask, "Do you have a copy of last year's calendar? I'd love to see these techniques in action."

When he left the room to fetch the calendar, I rubbed my temples. Nana K leaned in. "Did you understand all that?"

I nodded. "It's basic stuff. All of which I know and none of which I'll use. But I'm building rapport, right?"

"Could you hurry up? I want to get to the pharmacy before they close."

Danny came back with the calendar. I flipped through the pages. They all looked pretty much the same— gray background, subject leaning on a stool, animal either sitting on the ground or in the subject's lap. Everyone had fake smiles that didn't reach their eyes. None had anything personal. Danny had even managed to make Linc look a bit dull.

They were well lit and evenly composed. But they lacked life and vibrancy. This is what I feared my photography might turn into if I started family portraits. The same poses in the same places with the same fake smiles. Cookie-cutter portraits to match the cookie-cutter houses on the Hill. I felt myself shrink a little.

Out loud, I oohed and aahed at the photos. When I flipped to October and saw Mike Vandenburg, I almost laughed out loud at my good fortune. This would be the perfect segue into talking about Missy.

"Oh, Mike. Poor thing. So sad about Missy. I graduated high school with her," I explained.

"I wouldn't waste too many tears on feeling bad for Mike," Danny said, practically spitting his name. "He treated Missy like crap."

"I heard he cheated on her. But still, losing a wife so violently," I said and shuddered. I only had to half fake that.

"They were going to get divorced anyway. She cheated on him too. With a much nicer guy who treated her right." He flipped the page away from Mike. I studied Danny's face. There was anger there but directed more at Mike than Missy. He sniffed once, and I saw the tears welling in his eyes.

"Do you think Mike did it?" I asked, pretending not to see his distress.

"Probably. He has a temper."

"I still can't get over where it happened. And right in the middle of the day," I said, remaining vague on purpose. Maybe he would let something slip—like that she'd been killed by the water, not in the woods. That happened all the time in *Law and Order*.

"I wish I'd been here," he said quietly, looking out the front window with unfocused eyes.

"Where were you?" I asked, equally as quietly.

"Mom and I went antiquing in Annapolis. I didn't hear about it until the next day," he said.

"That must have been hard," I said. Danny sniffed again and then turned his attention back to me. He blinked me back into focus and seemed to realize what he said.

"Hard for anyone. Everyone loved Missy."

"Of course. I remember her fondly from high school." I practically choked on the words. "Well, thank you for your time. And your wonderful advice. I feel much better about the calendar shoot now."

I stood and pulled my almost sleeping grandmother up with me.

Danny walked us to the door. "Glad I could help. It's nice to talk shop with someone else who knows photography. I'd be happy to help you choose the final images after you're done."

"Thanks so much for the offer," I said, plastering on a fake smile of my own. "I'll definitely keep that in mind."

When we got back in the car, Nana K said, "You'd think he commissioned the *Mona Lisa* with the way he talked about his photographs. His calendars are not that inspiring. The only reason people buy them is to look at Linc. I told him last year if Linc took his shirt off, he'd sell a lot more calendars."

She wasn't wrong.

Chapter 23

I awoke Monday morning to the dulcet tones of the rooster crowing his head off outside the barn. I'd forgotten earplugs on my shopping trip yesterday. Nana K had distracted me with other frivolous things like real plates and towels. Could I shove the towels in my ears? Maybe roll up some of the washcloths Nana insisted I buy. Why one person needed a twelve pack of washcloths, I'd never understand. But they were in my closet, taking up space where earplugs could have been.

Now I had an extra hour to sulk about not being able to find a ride into town today for my community service. All of my usual contacts had fallen through. Even Nana K had plans this morning. My mother had given me her bike when we moved on Saturday as a just in case. I didn't think I'd need to use it so soon.

I was still sulking an hour later since I couldn't find any rideshare opportunities in the area. No surprise there. I laced up my boots for the bike ride into town. I wanted full ankle support before getting on that thing again. Then a *tap-tap-tapping* came from my front door. Did someone take pity on me and come to get me after all? Could I be that lucky?

"Coming!" I called as the tapping continued. It was too light to be Linc, not that I really thought it would be him. He had barely answered my texts all weekend. I still didn't understand why he was so angry with me. Was it really because of the locket?

When I opened the door, no one was there. A movement by my foot caught my eye and I glanced down. The same chicken stood there looking up at me expectantly.

"You aren't coming in."

I knew as much about chickens as I did about cars, but I didn't think letting it into the house was especially sanitary. The chicken made the little noise again and pecked at the ground. I could have sworn it was telling me it wanted food. I eased the door closed and went back to the kitchen to get some bread. Did chickens eat bread? They were birds, and the pigeons—also birds—at my old apartment loved bits of bread. I half expected the hen to be gone when I opened the door again. But there it stood, pecking and scratching at the stairway landing. I leaned down and offered it some bread. The greedy little thing took it right out of my hand with no hesitation.

"Aren't you friendly." I offered another piece, then reached out a hand to see if I could pet it. The hen didn't even flinch, just let me run a hand over its feathers. Softer than I would have thought. I broke up the rest of the bread and scattered it on the landing.

"Don't tell your friends," I warned as I stood. "I don't want a bawk party up here." I giggled at my joke. "Get it? Bawk party... like block party?" The chicken ignored me.

I went back inside to wash my hands and grab my camera bag before heading down the steps to the bike.

Thirty incident-free minutes later, I arrived at the firehouse—a little sweaty, but otherwise unscathed. Linc barely glanced at me as I came in. He shoved an envelope in my hands.

"The invoice for the sign," he said.

"Thanks." My bank account whimpered, so I tucked it in my bag to deal with later. "I found out some more interesting things this weekend," I tried, hoping to get him into a conversation.

"I don't want to hear it. I'll help you with Becky and then I'm done. I'm not going to continue to help you put yourself in harm's way."

"I wasn't in harm's way. I was at the Ladies' Auxiliary lunch. The best place to pick up on some gossip and backstory," I explained.

"Whatever." He clipped Fang to a lead by his desk and led me through a hallway toward the police station. I hated that he was mad at me. Besides Colleen, he was my only friend here in Piney Ridge. I couldn't even count my parents or Nana K because, as my family, they were obligated to like me.

I decided to let it go for now since the anxiety of being near Chief Duncan was already making my tummy hurt.

To add insult to injury, being here was my own stupid idea. Since I wanted authentic, personal shots, photographing the police officers in their environment made sense. In addition to Becky, I would also have the other police deputy and Chief Duncan as models today. I hoped Detective Spaulding hadn't told the chief about the locket yet. Wishful thinking.

The humane society provided another dog and a few more cats for the day's shoot. I could hear the scrambling of claws before we even crossed the threshold into the station.

Becky, one of the 9-1-1 operators, was first. I set up the shot at her desk. Becky chose a cat for her companion. Like most cats, this one made a beeline for the keyboard. I got a great shot of Becky laughing as she lifted the furry adventurer off the desk.

Linc stayed true to his word and coaxed Becky into conversation about Missy. Her face turned to stone at the mention of Missy's name, but Becky mentioned she'd been in Virginia with her sister all weekend. Nowhere near the reservoir. Cross another suspect off the list.

I tried not to be offended when Linc was his normal, jovial, fun-loving self with everyone else. He reserved his steel stare for me. And it wasn't only anger—disappointment laced every sigh before he answered my direct questions. Was he really that mad at me for wanting to know about the case? Wouldn't he want to try to figure out the mystery if he were one of the prime suspects?

I mulled it over as we walked to Chief Duncan's office. I didn't realize my steps had slowed until Linc called, "Stop dragging your feet," from a few feet ahead of me. To say I dreaded this was the understatement of the month. I was half tempted to pass my beloved camera off to Linc and wish him luck as I ran for the hills. If the thought of passing my expensive camera to anyone else didn't give me automatic hives, I absolutely would have.

I didn't want to show the chief I was rattled, so at the door, I gave myself a little shake and squared my shoulders. Linc looked down at me, his eyes softer than they had been all day.

"You okay?" he asked in a moment of cease-fire. "We can postpone until after the investigation if you want."

"No," I squeaked. Then cleared my throat and said more definitively, "No. I'm okay. I can't keep hiding from my problems."

"Okay," he said. "I'll do the talking. You just point and shoot."

I scowled at him behind his back as he rapped his knuckles on the office door. So many people diminished my profession to "just point and shoot." I didn't think Linc was one of those people, but he was full of surprises lately.

I pushed my frustration aside as the door opened. Chief Duncan's girth took up the doorway and spilled over behind the edges. He wiped crumbs from his shirt as he said, "Come on in. Let's get it over with."

We followed him into the room.

"Thanks for taking the time today," Linc said.

"I still don't understand why we have to do it here and not in our usual spot," he said, looking at me.

"This tells your story better. The chief of police busy at work in his office. The humane society even brought a German shepherd to be your companion."

The chief harrumphed, but I could tell he was pleased.

"Where do you want me?" he asked.

"Standing behind your desk. We'll sit the dog beside you. Your certificate frames will be the backdrop," I explained. The dog handler came in then. I repeated my request, and the dog sat by the chief's feet.

I snapped a couple of safety shots, then suggested Chief Duncan interact with the dog a little. His chair gave a little groan of protest when he plopped back down in it. I got a rare smile from him as the dog put two paws on his lap and panted into his face. Chief Duncan rubbed the dog's ears and neck while I snapped away from several angles. Fortuitously, the dog even covered some of the chief's weight.

When we finished, Linc walked out with the dog handler, leaving me alone with Chief Duncan. I could have cut the awkwardness with a knife.

"Thanks again for agreeing to pose for me. I hope you're pleased with the final shots," I said, one hand on the doorframe.

"Listen here, Ms. Lightwood," Chief Duncan started, the smile now vanished from his rotund face. "Spaulding might think you're innocent, but your lost-little-girl act doesn't work on me. Finding that locket is a little too convenient. I've got my eye on you, Alex. You'll make a mistake sometime, and I'll catch you."

I almost said, "Where is your other eye pointed?" but caught myself just in time. Instead, I said, "I hope you find the killer, Chief Duncan. And I will also expect an apology when you finally realize it wasn't me."

Chapter 24

Driver Improvement Program. More like Naughty Driver School.

According to the pamphlet I received when I registered, this program was usually assigned to people who accumulated over five points on their license or were driving egregiously. I'd barely driven my car at all during the last decade. And hitting the sign wasn't even really my fault—I'd been startled by the blaring horn. It's not like I aimed for the stupid thing. Or that I was going too fast. Or driving "egregiously."

I took a seat toward the back, thankful that the class would only last four to six hours. I hoped my instructor leaned closer to the four hours length. A few more people filled in around me—no one I recognized, thank goodness. It amazed me that this many people in Piney Ridge needed Driver Improvement Program. I honestly thought I might be the only one. Then again, if Judge Cockran assigned it to me with only one offense, he probably handed out this class as liberally as my mother traded gossip.

As the nine o'clock start time came and went, the group around me started shifting in their seats and looking from the clock to the door. Used to sitting still and waiting, I observed the room from my seat in the back. If I had my camera, I'd frame the gentleman at the front of the room with neck wrinkles so thick his index finger got caught in one as he scratched his neck impatiently. I'd also love to capture the look of pure annoyance on the face of the middle-aged woman seated a row ahead of me. Unlike me, this woman clearly had other things she'd rather be doing. Her bouncing leg reminded me of the popcorn Grampa Klafkeniewski used to make in the skillet on the stove.

"Is this like college?" a younger student asked. "Like, if the instructor doesn't show up in fifteen minutes we all get to leave?"

The annoyed woman scoffed and crossed her arms over her chest. "I don't want to leave. I want to get this over with. I had to make arrangements with my kids' daycare and work. It's highly inconvenient."

"Should we call someone?" the wrinkled gentleman asked.

Before anyone could answer, a blue blur that could have been a Piney Ridge PD uniform streaked into the room with a flurry of "I'm sorry. So sorry."

I smiled when the streak came to rest behind the desk at the front of the room. Andrea Martinez.

Andrea surveyed the group as she tried to catch her breath. Her eyes locked with mine. I smiled encouragingly. Officer Martinez's shoulders removed themselves from her ears as she visibly relaxed.

"Sorry I'm late, everyone. Thank you for waiting. We are in the middle of a big case, and things are starting to move," she explained, avoiding my eyes now. "I may need to excuse myself during class if I get a call."

The mention of the big case had us all sitting up in our seats. Obviously, she meant Missy's murder. That was not only the biggest case in Piney Ridge, but the only case as far as I could tell. But Officer Martinez was done talking about it apparently. She moved right into the first part of the program.

About an hour in, my eyes started drooping. I still hadn't managed to get any earplugs and those missed hours of sleep in the mornings were catching up to me.

That reminded me I also needed to add bread to list. Or maybe birdseed? Did chickens eat birdseed? My little friend, whom I'd nicknamed Nugget, came to visit me every morning for breakfast. This morning, I sat on the landing next to Nugget and placed some of the bread pieces on my legs. Without hesitation, Nugget jumped right up onto my lap. Inconceivably, I wished I could be more like the chicken—trusting and confident. Two things I used to be before the big wide world—with a little help from a missing brother and a final nudge from Wreck-it Rick—turned me cynical and wary.

I glanced at the clock on the wall for the millionth time. Only ten more minutes had passed since I last checked. I stifled a yawn. Mr. Wrinkles had his head resting heavily in his hand. Ms. I'm Too Busy not so discreetly played a game on her phone. We all needed some coffee or to at least splash some cold water on our faces to wake up.

As if I willed it with my wishes, Officer Martinez's phone rang. That woke everyone up.

She glanced at the screen and muttered an apology. "I have to take this. Take a ten-minute bio break, and we'll meet back here at ten thirty."

She stepped into the hall. I didn't have to be told twice. I shot up out of my chair to stretch and try to wake myself up. I didn't want to be rude to Officer Martinez by falling asleep on her. It wasn't her fault the material was as dry as an elephant bone in the Sahara. I wandered through the halls looking for the bathroom.

"The results are in already?" Officer Martinez's voice stopped me in my tracks.

I ducked around the corner so I could unabashedly eavesdrop.

"What's the murder weapon?" Officer Martinez asked in a hushed voice. She listened, her eyes going wide. "Scissors? The M.E. is sure?" Another pause. "Right now? I'm in the middle of Driver Improvement Class." I heard her footsteps as she paced up and down the hallway. "Okay. Okay. I understand. I'll be there in ten."

Forgetting all about the bathroom, I rushed back down the hallway in case Officer Martinez came my way. I sat on the edge of my seat, leg bouncing as hard as the annoyed woman's was earlier. Scissors were the murder weapon? Like hair-cutting scissors? Could this mean that Kelly was the killer after all? But she'd been at the salon all day. At least that's what she told the detectives. I really wanted to talk this through with Colleen or Linc.

My heart sank a little. It would have to be Colleen since Linc basically told me he was done with me, on Monday. We'd barely spoken a word to each other yesterday when I reported to the firehouse. He pointed to a stack of files and the filing cabinet and then disappeared with Fang to places unknown.

"It seems I need to apologize again. We're gonna have to cut class short today," Officer Martinez said when she reentered the room. Her voice was steady and clear, holding none of her earlier excitement. Very professional.

"What!?" annoyed lady cried. "I rearranged my entire schedule for today."

"I'm sorry. There's nothing I can do. You will be credited with the time you put in. I'll see if I can get the rest of your requirement waived." She grabbed her stack of folders from the desk and sauntered out of the room before anyone else could protest.

I, too, felt the flicker of annoyance—I couldn't get my license back until I took this class—but I was more excited about the information I just learned. I texted Colleen on the way out of the building.

Me: Can you meet for lunch? Exciting news to share
Colleen: Henry Cavill's in town & wants to marry me!
Me: Even juicier. Scoops?
Colleen: Be there at eleven

I checked my phone clock. I had about half an hour to bike to Scoops. I would be a sweaty, red-faced mess when I arrived, but I could do it. Man, I really needed my car back. I'd managed to pay off the repairs using last month's royalty check from my stock photography, but it still had to sit in car jail until I finished this class.

Colleen's VW was already parked in the lot when I arrived a little past eleven. In addition to ice cream, Scoops offered a small selection of deli sandwiches, mayonnaise-based salads, and homemade soup. No matter the season, I loved their homemade soups. I used to stop here on my way home from school almost every day to get a cone and a cup of soup—not to be eaten together.

I met Colleen at the counter where she undoubtedly ordered an egg salad sandwich on rye toast with extra black pepper and a pickle on the side. I looked at the daily soup offerings and gave a little shout of joy: jambalaya topped the list. My favorite. I ordered the soup—a large today so I could save some for later—and a huge fountain coke, then waited at a picnic table outside for Colleen to join me.

"So what's juicier than Henry Cavill?" Colleen said, taking the bench across from me. She unwrapped her egg salad sandwich and took a huge bite. I smiled. Some things never changed.

"I found out the murder weapon," I said. Colleen, eyes wide and mouth full of sandwich, waved her hand frantically for me to continue.

"Scissors! Missy was stabbed with scissors," I exclaimed. Colleen choked a little. She took a big swig of her own fountain soda to right herself.

"I mean, that certainly puts Kelly back on top of the list," Colleen said when she got her coughing under control.

"Right? Officer Martinez had to cancel driving class to rush somewhere. Do you think they're raiding the salon?"

"This is one time I wish I had a police scanner."

"I also wish I had a car. Then I could inconspicuously drive past. I'm a little noticeable on the bright yellow bike."

"So?" Colleen asked. "People bike down that road all the time. Hence the bike lane."

I pursed my lips. "Right. The other main suspect in the murder just happens to be riding by at the exact moment police are searching the place? Chief Duncan warned me he'd be watching my every move."

"But the murder weapon gets you off the hook," Colleen said. "It points the finger squarely at Kelly. I mean, I like Kelly, but her motive is ten times stronger than yours. She's completely erased any inkling of Missy from that salon in less than two weeks."

"True. Still, I have enough people mad at me right now. I don't want to borrow more trouble. I'll text Nana K and see if she heard anything on the scanner."

Me: Anything interesting on the scanner?
Nana K: Police activity at the salon

187

Me: Thought so. Murder weapon=scissors

Nana K texted back the wide-eyed emojis. I showed Colleen the exchange.

"Now I really wish I had a car," I said.

"I'd let you borrow my car, but we are hauling kids to the park later this afternoon."

I sighed and spooned my soup. "I thought maybe after today I'd start getting my life back. I'd have my car. I could maybe go into the city and see about freelance jobs at the *Baltimore Sun*. I could even try Washington, DC, although it's a longer commute. Now I'm stuck here until I can finish that class."

"You still have to finish your community service anyway."

"That's true. Although with Linc mad at me for some reason, I'm beginning to dread that as well. It's like there's this big cloud of yuck hanging over us. I can't figure out what I did to make him so angry."

"Did you ask him?" Colleen said, an edge to her voice.

"He barely talks to me anymore." I sighed, settling into my little pity party. "This is all Rick's fault. If he hadn't spread those lies about me, I wouldn't even be in this situation. I would be back in New York talking about my next assignment. Not here riding around on a yellow bike and contemplating taking Christmas card pictures for Mary Homemaker."

Colleen interrupted my pout by slamming her hand down on the table, making me jump.

"Really, Alex. I missed you and I love you, but you're being ridiculous. If you don't want to be here, move somewhere else. But stop putting down the people and the town I call home." She rose from the table. "Honestly, when did you become such a snob?"

I gaped at her back as she stormed away.

Chapter 25

I rode slowly back to my loft, wondering how I had gotten to this point. Yes, Rick was the reason I felt I needed to leave New York. His lies about my work and my integrity gutted the connections I'd made there. But I didn't *have* to leave. I chose to. And I chose Piney Ridge.

As much as I hated to admit it, I couldn't blame Rick for everything that had happened since I arrived. He was the catalyst to my current situation, sure, but I was the fuel. I was to blame for losing my car. I somehow alienated Linc. I just insulted Colleen's entire way of life. I'd even somehow managed to warrant a lecture from my mother. And Rick absolutely had nothing to do with me being a murder suspect.

Okay, so maybe the last one was simply bad luck—wrong place at the wrong time—but the others were undeniably, absolutely, irrevocably my fault. When I first came to Piney Ridge, I promised myself I wouldn't give another thought to Rick, wouldn't let him manipulate me any longer. And yet I was letting my one bad experience with him shape my relationships with others.

Stupid. In less than a month, I'd managed to push away almost everyone who tried to support me. Linc and Colleen had been nothing but kind and supportive and indulgent. I'd been a regular Sour Patch Kid.

I had to fix this. I could fix this. My attitude and the way I treated my friends and family were in my control. I just hoped it wasn't too late.

Chief Duncan rolled out of an unmarked police car as soon as my bike's front tires hit the orchard parking lot. His face waffled between scorn and satisfaction. He was trying to look businesslike and serious but had trouble hiding the small grin playing on his lips. All of that meant nothing good for me. I looked up at the clear, blue sky—the ominous shadow must be from whatever was about to happen to me.

"Ms. Lightwood," Chief Duncan said. "I need you to come with me."

"Why?" I asked. I walked my bike over to the loft steps and leaned it against the barn wall. My soup from Scoops teased me in the basket. Something told me I wasn't going to get to enjoy it tonight.

"We have a few questions you need to clear up. About Missy's murder. It's better if you come to the station for formal questioning," he explained, standing much too close behind me.

"Me? Why me?" I asked. When I turned to face him, handcuffs dangled from his fingers. My eyes bugged. "Am I"—I gulped— "am I under arrest?"

"Not yet," he said. "But we can do this the easy way or the hard way. Come with me voluntarily, and we won't have a problem. Like I said, just a few questions."

I didn't entirely believe him. If I weren't under arrest, I could refuse. There was nothing he could arrest me for. Still, not complying would surely make me seem even guiltier. Breathing made me seem even guiltier in Chief

Duncan's eyes. I sighed and followed him to his car. What else could I do?

"I knew you'd see it my way," he said smugly.

"Where is Detective Spaulding?" I asked. I needed someone on my side.

"Busy. He may swing by later," he answered. I felt my trepidation grow.

I texted my father and Nana K on the way to the station, told them everything was fine for now, but to have the lawyer on standby just in case. Since I wasn't under arrest, if I began to get uncomfortable with the questions, I could end the interview and leave.

When we arrived at the station, Linc was rolling out hoses in the adjoining parking lot. I wished I were there under different circumstances so I could appreciate the way his biceps rippled and flexed as he worked. He stopped what he was doing to watch as Chief Duncan held my upper arm and escorted me into the police station.

Joy, the receptionist, greeted us grimly. She obviously knew we were coming. Chief Duncan pulled me to the counter and stood behind me, essentially trapping me in place. An archaic-looking ink fingerprinting set took up space on the countertop. I arched an eyebrow at the chief.

"Just procedure. Like I said, you aren't under arrest, but having your fingerprints would help us in the investigation," he explained. I could see him practically salivating at the prospect of finding my fingerprints on the evidence. I instinctively balled my hands into tight fists.

Joy jumped in with a smile. "It's for elimination purposes, Alex. This is like a quicker version of DNA."

Yeah, right. I didn't *think* Chief Duncan would plant my fingerprints on anything, but he'd surprised me with his audacity before. Still, I knew for a fact my fingerprints weren't on the locket. And I hadn't touched a pair of scissors—whether from the salon or otherwise—since I'd been back in Piney Ridge. Against my better judgment, I held out my hand for Joy to take my prints.

Linc walked in as she finished rolling my last thumb.

"What's going on here?" he asked, his eyes darting from Chief Duncan to me and finally settling on the ink on my fingertips. His eyebrows knit together; his eyes turned to steel.

"Routine questioning. Nothing that concerns you," the chief said.

"Alex?" Linc asked, concern and anger edging his voice.

"I'm okay, Linc. Just trying to be helpful." I put on a bright smile to hide the swelling panic.

Chief Duncan left Linc standing there clenching and unclenching his fists as he corralled me down the back hallway. I thought we were going to his office where we took the calendar pictures earlier in the week, but instead he took me to a smaller, almost empty room on the other side of the hall. I knew an interrogation room when I saw one. The panic bubbling under the surface threatened in earnest to spill over. I swallowed it down, reminding myself that I was, in fact, innocent. And this was just questioning. If I told the truth, everything would be fine.

Although that didn't work too well with my career.

"Have a seat, Ms. Lightwood," Chief Duncan said, gesturing to a chair on the far end of the table. He took the seat by the door. A thin manila folder and a voice recorder lay on the metal table between them. Given the non-digital fingerprints, I was a little surprised it wasn't a cassette tape. Did they still sell those things?

Chief Duncan messed around with the recorder for a second until a little red light flashed on. "I'm going to record this interview." Not a question. "This is Chief Clive Duncan interviewing Alex Lightwood in regard to Melissa Poledark Vandenburg's murder." He stated the date and time, then placed the recorder back on the table between us.

"What can I help you with?" I asked, hoping my voice sounded calmer than I felt.

"I'd like to go over your timeline from the day of the murder." He opened the folder and made a show of reading the top sheet of paper. I waited for a question. None came. Instead, he took a pen and pad of paper out of his jacket pocket, then looked at me expectantly.

"Did you have a question, Chief?" I asked as politely as I could muster.

"Your timeline. Take me through your day. Be as specific as possible," he said. I opened my mouth to speak, but he added, "And remember, we already have statements from several other people."

I nodded. "I have nothing to hide. I woke up at my parents' house, and we had breakfast."

"What did you eat?" he asked.

"How is that relevant?"

"Answer the question, Ms. Lightwood." He tapped his pen impatiently on his pad.

I bit my cheek to keep from rolling my eyes but complied. "I had cereal—Cheerios, I think. My father drank cold coffee. And my mother had an apple cinnamon muffin."

"Continue," he said. I told him about my mother's frustration with all the calls, which prompted her making the hair appointment.

"So, you're claiming your mother, Constance Lightwood, suggested and then made the appointment?" the chief asked, eyebrow raised.

"That's what happened," I confirmed.

"But you picked the salon." Not a question.

"No. The whole thing was my mother's idea."

After a long scrutinizing gaze, he asked, "What time did you leave the house?"

"About eleven o'clock. We went straight to the salon."

"Which salon?"

I gave him an incredulous look. He knew which salon. I'd already told him I'd gotten my hair done at Missy K's the morning of the murder. Not only that, but Missy K's was the only real salon in town unless you counted Patti's Pizzazz and Pizza. But no one did. Patti ran a little side hustle out of her basement where you could get an 80s style perm or a slice of pepperoni. Those were your only options.

"Oblige me for the record," Chief Duncan said.

"It was Missy K's at the time. I think Kelly recently renamed it Shear-lock Combs," I said.

"That was the victim, Missy Vandenburg's, salon at the time?"

"Yes. But I didn't know that before we got there. Kelly told me about their business partnership while she cut my hair."

"How long were you there?"

"I guess about an hour and a half? I think we got back to the house a little after one."

"Anything else happen while you were there?" he asked.

"Missy did come in while we were there. We hadn't seen each other since high school. She told me about her husband and kids, then basically ignored me," I explained. Since Kelly didn't think the unpleasantries exchanged between me and Missy were a big deal, I felt no need to mention them now. If Chief Duncan asked me directly, I'd respond, but no more volunteering information that put me in a negative light. Not with Chief Duncan.

"Nothing else you want to mention?" he prompted. "Just got your hair cut and were on your way?"

"That's about it," I said. "Exactly like I told you before."

He slammed his hand on the table and then pointed a pudgy finger in my face. I recoiled immediately, almost tipping backward off my chair.

"Ah-ha! Your first lie," he bellowed triumphantly.

Chapter 26

"I didn't lie," I lied. Technically, it was an omission.

"Witnesses testified that you and Missy had a torrid fight at the salon that day. One of the other patrons said she was surprised you two didn't start clawing each other's eyes out."

"First of all, I wouldn't call it a fight, and second, it definitely wasn't torrid. She insulted me, like she used to do in high school, and I told her to grow up. The end."

"Witnesses said you threatened her. Then she turned up dead hours later."

"I didn't threaten her. She threatened me with interfering in my court case," I clarified, my anger amplifying to match his.

"So you did have a reason to be angry." He looked like a cat that finally caught the canary.

I crossed my arms and clamped my mouth shut. I'd already said too much and didn't trust myself any further. From here on out, call me Fort Knox.

"Fine," Chief Duncan said after he realized I wasn't going to confirm or deny. "Finish telling me about your day. What did you do when you left the salon?"

Darn, an actual question. "I went back to my parents' house. We had a late lunch, and my mother complained about small-town gossips. Then around four I went for a walk by the reservoir to take some pictures."

"Four o'clock. Did anyone see you?" he said, making a note in his pad.

I shrugged. "I noticed a few people on the paths, but I'm not sure if they saw me."

"Shame for you. What time did you get back to your parents' house?"

"I left the reservoir when the sun got too low. I guess a little before dusk? Maybe around six thirty or seven?"

"The call to the police didn't come in until after dark. At least an hour later." His eyes narrowed again. I didn't hear a question, so I remained silent.

"Answer the question, Ms. Lightwood."

"What question?" I asked.

"Are you getting belligerent with the chief of police?" he asked, incredulous.

I was about to tell him that his title alone didn't guarantee him respect; he had to earn it, when the door opened behind him. Detective Spaulding stood there looking from the chief to me and back again.

"I thought we were going to wait to bring her in?" he said to Chief Duncan.

"An opportunity arose," the chief said. I snorted.

"Alex, you aren't under arrest," Detective Spaulding explained.

"I know," I confirmed. "I was just saying my farewells. I gave Chief Duncan my timeline the day of the murder. Again."

"She confirmed the fight at the salon," Chief Duncan spluttered.

"We didn't fight. She insulted me; I told her to keep my name out of her mouth. The whole thing lasted less than a minute. Apparently lots of people exchange catty words with Missy on a daily basis. I'm not special in that regard," I said. I kept my eyes on Detective Spaulding.

"She had ample access to the salon scissors. And she has no alibi for the time of death," Chief Duncan explained.

My mouth dropped open. So that was his reason for hauling me in here for questioning. Missy must have been murdered about the time I was in the woods. Alone. The color drained from my face; my bones turned to ice. I flicked my eyes to the open manila folder to see if I could read the paper Chief Duncan seemed so interested in earlier. Beside TOD, the medical examiner had written "2pm-6pm."

The chief saw me looking at the paper and slammed the folder shut before I could see anything else.

I looked at Detective Spaulding. "You could narrow down that time even more if you look at the metadata on the photo I took."

"Metadata?" he asked, coming farther into the room.

"Yeah. I connect my camera to GPS tracking so I always know exactly where and when the photos were taken. It's essential in photojournalism. I never changed the settings. Pull up the picture on any gallery app and look at the file info. That will narrow that timeline."

"Thank you, Alex. We'll do that. Did you happen to see anyone else in the woods when you were there?" he asked.

Chief Duncan had asked the same thing, but their tones were so vastly different. Chief Duncan made it seem like I needed witnesses to confirm my location. Detective Spaulding's tone suggested I could help them catch who really killed Missy.

"Yes," I answered. I described the man with the book, the boy and his dog, and the running girl. Detective Spaulding looked disappointed when I finished. I couldn't blame him: none of those people fit the descriptions of anyone on my suspect list either.

"Thank you for your time, Alex. We'll be in touch," Detective Spaulding said.

"I'm not done asking questions yet," Chief Duncan said, rising from his chair when I did. "She admitted to having a long-lasting feud with the victim. I want to know more about that."

"I absolutely did not say anything about a 'long-lasting feud.' You can listen to the tape to confirm," I said defiantly. I popped my hands on my hips, an old habit to make me appear larger, and started to stomp out of the room. Chief Duncan made a move to stop me, but Detective Spaulding stepped between us. I sidestepped my way out of the cramped room.

"Alex," Detective Spaulding called.

I turned to face him, glad the chief wasn't in my eyeline.

"I'm sorry for this." His eyes were soft and sincere. "It shouldn't have happened."

"Thanks. But I will be going through my lawyer from now on."

"Understandable. I'll listen to the tape too. I'm sorry, Alex," he repeated. So, he was back to calling me Alex. Guess I was off his suspect list again. A small consolation.

On my way by Chief Duncan's office, I saw Kelly sitting on the edge of the visitor's chair. She chewed a fingernail while her eyes darted around the space like a trapped animal looking for escape. I felt a twinge of sympathy for her.

Detective Spaulding and Chief Duncan's heated words followed me down the hallway and into the lobby. I drew up short when I saw Linc sitting there.

"What are you still doing here?" I asked.

He scowled at me. "Waiting for you. I figured you'd need a ride."

"Thank you. I was going to call my dad," I said, holding up my phone.

"Well, I'm already here." He rose from the chair and walked out the door. I had no choice but to follow. As we rode in awkward silence back to my loft, I texted my family to tell them they didn't need to bail me out of jail.

I replayed the interrogation over in my mind. Had I said anything incriminating? Would my words be used against me in court? I tried to remember, but emotion clouded my memory. Maybe I could request a copy of the tape. Maybe the tape would be played during the *Dateline* episode about my life and crimes. Maybe Chief Duncan would plant my fingerprints somewhere. Great. Then I'd be the crazy one screaming about being framed by the police. I dropped my head in my hands and took a deep breath.

"Hey," Linc said softly, turning down the radio. "You okay?"

I lifted my head to look at his profile. He glanced at me, his liquid-metal eyes full of concern, before returning his attention to the road.

"I don't know," I admitted, trying and failing to hold back the tears. "I really don't know."

I turned my face to the window so he wouldn't see the tears spilling down my face. I wasn't usually a crier. I could probably count on one hand the number of times I'd cried in my adult life. Losing a brother really put a lot of things in perspective. But stress and fatigue had these rare tears streaming now. I willed myself to get it together before we got to my loft, but we were already turning into the parking lot beside the barn.

I tried to scramble out of the truck and run inside before Linc could follow, but my little chicken legs were no match for his long, muscular ones. He met me at the base of the stairs and grabbed my upper arms gently in his large warm hands.

"Alex, look at me," he coaxed.

I shook my head and kept it lowered. I tried to swipe at my face with the back of my hand but couldn't reach it with the way he held me. Could this day get any more embarrassing? First, I had to attend driving class like a speed demon; second, I insulted my best friend, then I got hauled into the police station for questioning in a murder, and now, I was crying in front of Lincoln Livestrong. So much for the independent world-traveling woman I purported to be. I was acting like the child I hated to be treated like.

"Alex?" he tried again.

When I sniffled and stood there, he gathered me in his arms in a hug. Our first hug in over a decade. That only resulted in me sobbing even harder.

"Okay. It's gonna be okay," he soothed.

I wrapped my arms around his middle and clung to him, tangling my fingers in his shirt. He held my head to his chest with one hand, gently stroking my hair, while the other spread across my back. His six-foot frame engulfed my small one. Usually this made me feel weak and childlike. Tonight, I felt protected and secure. I gave up trying to hold back the tears and let them come. He made all the right soothing noises but didn't try to stop me or tell me I was ridiculous. Which was absolutely how I felt.

When my sobs subsided, he leaned me back slightly to cup my face in one hand. He used a thumb to wipe away a lingering tear. His face held none of the annoyance and anger I'd seen there the last few days. Instead, worry lines crinkled his forehead while the rest of his expression was gentle and soft.

"Let's get you inside," he suggested. He tucked me under one arm and shuffled me toward the stairs. Somehow, we managed to get up the steps and into the loft.

"Thanks, Linc," I said between sniffles. "You don't have to stay. I'm okay now." But just saying the words brought on another onslaught of tears.

"Yeah, I can tell you're just fine," Linc said with the hint of a smile. He put his hand on the small of my back to lead me to the only piece of furniture, besides my bed, that I owned. He set me down on the couch and rummaged around in the kitchen. He came back a moment later with a glass of water and some napkins, both of which he offered to me.

"I couldn't find any tissues," he said apologetically.

I hesitated a moment before blowing my nose, then realized having snot dripping down my face was more embarrassing than the sound of it going into a napkin. I took a deep gulp of the water when I finished.

"Thanks, Linc," I said quietly, still not fully trusting my voice. "For everything."

"What are friends for," he said.

I looked up at him and took a deep breath. I was already embarrassed enough; I might as well go for broke.

"I'm so sorry, Linc. For the way I've been acting since I've been home. I'm angry at my circumstances and am taking it out on the people I care about most. I've made a mess of everything here. I'm so sorry."

He reached a hand to smooth a wayward strand of hair out of my face. "I'm sorry too. You've been under a lot of stress since you've been back. Dealing with my mood swings hasn't helped."

I couldn't quite manage a laugh, but I did muster up a small smile. "*Your* mood swings. What about my mood swings?"

"I haven't seen your moods swing," Linc said, catching my smile. "You've consistently been a big grouch since you've been back."

I halfheartedly smacked his chest. But I knew he wasn't wrong.

"You scared me tonight, Alex. When you came rushing out from that hallway, your face was ashen, and your eyes were as wide as saucers. I thought you were going to faint right there," Linc said. He took the cup of water from my hands when the tears welled again. I put my head back on his shoulder. "Can you tell me about it? What did Chief Duncan ask you?"

I sniffled again. "The gist of it is that I have no alibi for the time of the murder; I had access to the murder weapon, and I have a motive for killing Missy." I shuddered, and he hugged me closer.

"You and half of Piney Ridge," he commented.

"That's pretty much what Detective Spaulding said when he came in." I felt Linc tense at the mention of the detective.

"They took your fingerprints?" he asked, changing the subject.

"I let them. I am innocent. I didn't touch the locket, and I surely didn't touch any scissors," I said. "Hopefully when that is confirmed, it will throw some cold ice on Chief Duncan's suspicions."

"I hope so. Sounds like you handled yourself pretty well in there, Sexy Lexi," he said.

I sniffled again. "I guess. How did I even end up in this mess?"

"I don't know, Alex. But I'm going to help you get out of it."

I leaned back a little to look up at him. "You said you were done helping me. That I should leave it to the police and stay out of it."

"I know what I said." His jaw clenched and unclenched a few times. "But that was before Chief Duncan made it clear he wasn't actually investigating the murder. He's trying to fit the evidence to pin it on you."

"Detective Spaulding seems competent," I said.

Linc's jaw clenched again. "I don't trust that guy either. He seems all nice and unassuming, but he's smart. Don't trust him too much, Alex. Good cop, bad cop is a tactic because it works."

"I saw Kelly in Chief Duncan's office when I walked past tonight," I told him. I put my head back in the crook of his arm. For being so muscley, he was pretty comfortable. I could feel the weight of the day dragging me down. I was exhausted.

"They searched her salon and her house," he said. "Joy and Andrea were talking about it while I waited for you. I got the impression they weren't trying to keep their voices down."

I stifled a yawn. "Did they find anything?"

"Not yet. If the scissors were from the salon, the killer didn't return them."

"Smart. I wouldn't return them either. I'd probably chuck them into the reservoir," I said, already half-asleep.

"You must be tired. Rest a little while. I'll wake you for some dinner later," he said.

I fell asleep with Linc stroking my hair.

Chapter 27

Another morning; another rooster crowing. I rubbed my eyes—still a bit swollen from my crying jag and lack of sleep—then rolled out of bed. Nugget, my adopted chicken, would be pecking at the door soon for her morning snack. I shuffled sleepily to the kitchen to grab the bag of bread.

A movement out of the corner of my eye had me climbing the countertop. I forced my tired eyes to focus, then let out a sigh. Linc was draped over my couch fast asleep. His long frame did not even remotely fit on the Nana K-sized couch. He had one arm across his forehead, the other dangled onto the floor. One of his long legs hooked around the back of the couch while the other was bent and resting mostly on the cushions. His knee protruded off the side. He'd grabbed one of the extra pillows from my bed to tuck under his head.

My eyes went wide. I looked down at my threadbare He-Man T-shirt that I used for pajamas. I had not been wearing this when I fell asleep last night. I ran my hands over my body, breathing a sigh of relief when I realized I still had on my bra and camisole that I'd been wearing yesterday. And a pair of shorts.

Had Linc changed me? I certainly had no memory of putting on my pajamas. I looked back over at him. In sleep he more closely resembled the boy I once knew. I tiptoed back to the bedroom to get my camera.

Was it intrusive to take pictures of someone sleeping?

Probably. Did I care right now?

Not really. He'd seen me cry last night, so I could take his picture this morning. Equal opportunity vulnerability.

I changed the settings to silent shutter, set my exposure for the dim morning light, and framed the shot. One wide-angle to set the scene—large man on a small couch. With the flowers he gave me on the mantel in the background.

I moved in closer for some details: the ropy muscle of his bicep, his enviably long eyelashes resting on his cheek, the curve of his foot dangling behind the couch. As the light began to warm the room, I got down low to capture the rim light wrapping around his body, casting him in an almost silhouette. I moved in again to get another close-up of his face, this time focused on his lips slightly open as he breathed softly. I snapped the shot, switched angles, and got ready to take another.

"What are you doing?" Linc's gravelly voice made me lose my balance and fall backward on my dupa.

I immediately put up my defenses, then saw the characteristic amused smirk playing on his lips. The eye that wasn't covered by his arm winked open to stare at me sprawled on the floor clearly holding my camera.

"I'm knitting a sweater," I answered.

"Weird place to knit." He unfolded himself from the tiny couch and groaned as he stretched out his muscles. "You need a new couch."

"I wasn't expecting overnight guests so soon."

He shrugged. "I didn't want to leave you so upset. Then it got really late, and I was tired."

"Thanks for putting me to bed," I said quietly, suddenly shy. Something about saying "bed" to Linc made me blush from my toes to my nose.

"I can think of one way you can thank me," he said, raising on eyebrow.

I gaped at him.

He chuckled and said, "With breakfast. What did you think I meant?"

I pursed my lips at him. "I don't have much in the way of food. It's hard to get out to shop when I don't have a car."

"I'm not picky."

"Then help yourself to whatever you can find. I'm gonna put my camera away."

I walked back toward my bedroom.

He called, "I'm going to want to see those pictures."

"Over my dead body," I mumbled. Sometimes photographs revealed secrets about the subject. Other times they revealed more about the photographer. I feared this series of Linc sleeping would be the latter.

When I disconnected my lens to put it in the side pocket, I felt a sharp prick on the side of my finger. I pulled my hand away to study the spot. A thin line of blood appeared—like a paper cut.

Weird. I didn't usually keep loose paper in that part of my bag. I stored my notebook in a different pocket.

Carefully I reached in again and extracted a wrinkled envelope. Then I remembered: the estimate for the sign. I sighed. Might as well rip off this Band-Aid before I put a new one on my cut finger. I stuck the injured digit in my mouth and held my breath while I opened the envelope.

My eyes darted immediately to the bottom line; I whooshed out the breath I'd been holding. It was much, much less than I anticipated. Thank the lucky stars! Then another line caught my eye, the signature at the bottom for the woodsmith.

Lincoln Livestrong.

What the actual towncar was happening?

As though summoned by my thoughts, Linc appeared in the doorway holding a bowl of cereal. He leaned against the frame and studied me, hair tousled from sleep.

"Are you expecting company?" he asked. "I think someone is knocking on your door."

"That's just Nugget," I said absently. "What's this?" I held the estimate out to him.

He took a quick look. "Looks like the estimate for the sign repair."

"Obviously. Why does it have your name on it?"

"Because I'm the one who will be repairing the sign." He said it like it was the most obvious thing in the entire world.

"But Bobby Bachman said that the sign-repair guy was the same person who helped him renovate this loft."

"Yup," he said, taking a bite of cereal.

"But you're a firefighter!" I exclaimed.

"Even firefighters have hobbies. Mine happens to be woodwork."

"Since when?" I'd never known him to be into woodwork when we were younger. In fact, he had even gotten special permission to take an extra gym class instead of shop in high school.

He shrugged. "I guess about a year after we graduated. I got stuck in a class in college and it turns out I had a knack for it."

"A knack? A knack!? Linc, this place"—I gestured to the room around me—"is freaking gorgeous! I'd say it's more than a knack."

"That knack grew into a hobby which grew into quite a lucrative side hustle. Being a firefighter in Piney Ridge doesn't really pay the bills."

"I had no idea." I looked at him again with new interest. Who was this strange man that used to be my best friend?

"I'm sure there are a lot of things you don't know about me, Alex. You left town and never looked back. Never even tried to keep in touch," he said, suddenly finding something very interesting about his cereal bowl.

I had a sarcastic comeback on the tip of my tongue—something about the phone working both ways—but he lifted his eyes to mine for just a moment, stopping the words before they could form. They were not full of anger or bitterness like I expected; instead, they held hurt. I'd hurt him. Somehow, awkward, introverted Alex Lightwood had hurt popular, strong Lincoln Livestrong. If I hadn't seen it for myself, I'd never believe it. By the time he looked back down, the pain I'd seen there vanished.

"I know. I'm sorry. I was... unsure of what to say to you," I admitted. "I didn't even think you'd notice."

"How about 'Hi, Linc. I'm in New York. How are you?'" he suggested.

"You make it sound so simple."

"Why couldn't it have been? Colleen visited you."

Was he obtuse? He really thought that after the disaster of a kiss in his truck I'd ever be able to face him again. Especially after he completely ignored me the next day and hung out with the Snob Blob instead. He probably told them all about my awkward slobbery attempt. I'd wished it could be that simple. I wished I'd been able to forget all about the kiss instead of persevering over it for—well, I was *still* thinking about it, wasn't I?

"Who's Nugget?" he asked when I didn't respond.

"What?"

"Nugget? You said Nugget was at the door. Should we let them in?" he asked.

"No." I shook my head and laughed, thankful for the change in subject. "Nugget does not come in. Grab the bag of bread from the kitchen and meet me by the door."

He gave me a wary look, but obliged. He came back carrying the bread but not his bowl. I took a piece of bread, opened the door, and knelt down. Nugget immediately jumped onto my knee for her morning treat.

"Huh. I wouldn't have guessed that scenario in a million years," Linc said.

Chapter 28

Linc's cell phone sounding from somewhere in the loft broke up our cuddle fest with the chicken. He was still shaking his head as he disappeared down the hallway to find the ringing phone. I smirked at the *Star Wars*-themed ringtone. Then frowned remembering our earlier conversation.

I looked down at the chicken pecking by my bare feet.

"What am I going to do about him?" I asked Nugget.

Nugget pecked my toe.

"Well, you're no help," I said, standing. I gave the bird one more pat on its feathered back and then wandered back inside. Linc's muffled voice drifted down the hallway from the kitchen. Not wanting to interrupt, I went to the bathroom instead. I wanted to wash my hands and face and brush my teeth. And I had zero idea what my hair looked like.

I groaned when I looked in the mirror. My mascara had puddled under my eyes and run down my cheeks creating an Alice Cooper Meets Rocket Raccoon look that wouldn't even be attractive on a Kardashian. My hair, usually flat and boring, decided this was the morning to stick up in any number of directions out of the hair-tie knotted on top of my head. Not quite the look I would've picked for waking up with a hot guy in the house. No chance of moving out of "like a little sister" zone with this look. I quickly scrubbed my face and ran a brush over my teeth and finger-combed my hair.

I was wrestling the last wayward strand back into a low ponytail at the nape of my neck when I heard Linc call my name from the hallway.

"Be right there," I called back. My face was a bit splotchy from where I washed it, but it was a thousand times better than looking like I was auditioning Halloween costumes. I wished I'd had time to change into something a little more mature than He-Man, but he'd already seen me in it, so I let it go.

I met him back in the kitchen where he was finishing his bowl of cereal. I poured myself my own bowl and sat beside him on the couch.

"I like your jammies," he said, tugging on the tattered sleeve.

"No one is supposed to see me in this," I said defensively.

"I've seen you in worse in our years together," he reminded me.

"Yeah, but seeing a kid in something crazy is different than seeing an adult in something embarrassing."

"Aww. It's almost like you care what I think."

"Don't get ahead of yourself," I lied. I totally cared what he thought. I just couldn't figure why I cared so much. The thought made me uncomfortable, so I changed the subject. "Who was on the phone?"

"Oh. Right. I got distracted by He-Man. That was Andrea," he said.

I couldn't fix my face to hide the scowl fast enough.

Linc must have thought I was confused because he clarified, "Officer Martinez?"

"I know who Andrea is," I snapped. Then took a breath and tried for sweetness. "Why is she calling you so early? Wondering where you laid your head last night?"

"Why would she care about that?" he asked. I raised an eyebrow. He said, "We're gonna circle back to that. First, though, she informed me that the Vandenburgs and Poledarks are having a memorial service for Missy tonight at Mike's house. I think we should go."

"Oh no. I'm not going there."

"Why not?"

"I was just brought in for questioning in suspicion of her murder. I'm sure that's all over town by now."

"Well, I'm going. If you want to hide here, that's your choice. But I told you last night I would help you get out of this mess, and I meant it. The memorial will be a great place to see all the key players in one setting."

I sighed. He was right. I'd have to suck it up and face the uncomfortable stares. Means to an end. The sooner I figured out who really killed Missy, the sooner I wouldn't have those accusatory stares directed at me.

"I knew you'd come," Linc said, reading me perfectly. He put a hand on my knee to push up off the couch. I felt the skin to skin contact in my gut. The blush from earlier rekindled and overtook my neck. Luckily, Linc wasn't paying attention. He was washing his bowl out in the sink.

What was wrong with me? I hadn't turned into a puddle over a guy since—not since Linc in high school. I must still be embarrassed about my crying jag last night. That was all.

"I've got to head to work. I'm late already, not that anyone else is there to notice. Why don't you take the day off from your community service? I'll pick you up around seven for the memorial."

"Thanks. I do need to apologize to Colleen and face my parents. I'm surprised they aren't here banging down the door already."

I walked him to the door. Even though I'd known Linc practically my whole life, I suddenly felt awkward and unsure around him. Almost like this was the end of a first date with a stranger.

Linc turned at the door, one hand on the frame. My traitorous eyes flicked down to the edge of skin exposed by his lifted shirt. How did he still look so fabulous? He was the one wearing yesterday's clothes after being crumpled on my small couch. Yet I looked like a disaster while he looked like a god. It wasn't fair.

"Thanks for breakfast," he said. "Best cereal I've ever eaten."

I rolled my eyes. "Only the best at Chéz Lightwood." My smile faltered a little. "Thanks, Lincoln. For last night. For forgiving me even though I've been a grumpy jerk. For not price gouging the sign repair."

He surprised me by reaching out to pull me into a hug. I hesitated a moment, then wrapped my arms around him.

"What are friends for," he said. He gave me another tighter squeeze, then chuckled. "I always forget how short you are without your shoes on." I lifted up on my toes a little and heard him chuckle again.

When he released me, I took a step back into the shadows of the interior to hide whatever expression might be playing on my face.

"I'll pick you up at seven. No chickening out," he said. "No offense," he added to Nugget, then disappeared down the steps.

After a shower and a fresh, non-cartoony T-shirt, I wandered down to the orchard market to sit at one of the picnic tables outside. It was a beautiful spring day. I hoped the fresh breeze and bird songs would carry over into my mood. And help me get through the conversations with my parents and Colleen.

I called my father's cell phone. That way he could put me on speaker, and I'd only have to have the conversation once. Mom and Dad were equally angry at Chief Duncan: "To think I allowed him to eat at my table," and worried about my mental health. "Do you want me to bring you some tea? Or a warm compress?" I assured them I was fine and not officially under arrest. After promising to keep them in the loop, I disconnected and braced myself to call Colleen.

A simple, heartfelt apology worked with Linc—along with crying like a blubbering baby on his shoulder—so that would be my approach with Colleen as well. Minus the crying.

Of course, I forgot Colleen was an actual adult with an actual real job, so I got her voice mail. I left a message for her to call me back.

I gave myself a little pep talk to get back on my bike for a ride to the store. I desperately needed those earplugs if I ever wanted to sleep again. I should probably also look for another chair or some sort of table.

Colleen called me back when I was headed back from the store. I'd found earplugs and some more bread but struck out on the furniture.

"Hey," I breathed into the phone, steering with one hand. "Thanks for calling me back."

"Sure. What's up?" Colleen's voice sounded clipped and irritated. Not a great start.

I pulled over and stopped the bike. "I wanted to apologize for being an idiot. I've been in a funk since I've been home, and I'm sorry for taking it out on you."

"Go on," Colleen said, her voice softening a little.

"Being bitter about being here has nothing to do with Piney Ridge and everything to do with my expectations for my life. I love Piney Ridge. That's why I chose here to sulk back to. I'm an insufferable snobby grouch. But that stops now."

"I'm still listening," Colleen said. I could hear a small smile in her voice.

"And to make up for it, I'll buy you Scoops milkshakes for a month," I offered.

"Deliver them to work when I ask?"

"As soon as I get my car back," I promised.

"And you get to listen to me complain about things next time we have lunch."

"Deal. I really am sorry, Colleen."

"I forgive you. And I'm sorry for calling you a snob."

"I was a snob! And I needed someone to call me out on being one."

"What are friends for?" Colleen asked, echoing Linc's statement from earlier. I hadn't had true friends in such a long time, I'd almost forgotten what it felt like.

"Hey, are you busy tonight?" I asked.

I told Colleen about Missy's memorial. She agreed to meet Linc and I there. As I disconnected, I felt a weight lifting from my shoulders. Sure, I was currently, technically, the primary suspect in a murder, but the people whom I cared about most believed in me. With my family and friends by my side, I felt like I could conquer anything.

Chapter 29

Little black dress? Check.

Styled, curled hair? Check.

Subtle, classy makeup? Check.

Killer high heels? Check.

Although maybe I should alter that last description given the circumstances for wearing said heels. I paced up and down the hallway of my loft, both to practice walking in the heels, which I didn't wear that often, and because I was antsy about tonight.

Linc texted a while ago to say seven o'clock was still a go. I had three minutes until I lost my mind.

Was I crazy for going? I was accused of Missy's murder. Even if the entire town believed in my innocence, which I highly doubted, showing my face at the memorial was a bold move.

On the other hand, if I didn't go, would that make me appear more guilty? Maybe I could hide behind Colleen and Linc—like sort of burrow into their backs. Maybe I should exchange my heels for flats so I was even smaller.

A honk from the parking lot startled me out of my contemplations. Too late now. Before I could change my mind, I grabbed my camera bag and started out the door. Linc waited at the bottom of the steps; I stopped midway down when I saw him. Since I'd been home, I'd only seen him in T-shirts and either jeans or his station-issued pants. He usually left his mass of dark hair unruly in a sort of purposeful bedhead look.

Now he wore a tailored, button-down shirt the color of his eyes with a sports coat overtop. Except for one rebellious strand that fell into his eyes, he'd tamed his thick, dark hair into waves. He looked up when he heard my heels *click-clack* on the wooden steps and placed a hand on his chest. His expressive gray eyes lit up as he gifted me one of his fully charged megawatt smiles.

"Sexy Lexi," he said on a breath. "All grown up."

I did a slow turn on the steps, swiveling my head to be able to see his reaction when he saw the back of the dress. Or rather lack of the back of my dress. Although the front was demure, the back dipped down from my shoulders into a V just below my waist, leaving the expanse of my back bare. It was one of the few dresses I owned and, truth be told, was more club than funeral. Still, I'd argue my backless black dress was still more appropriate than any crazy pattern I would have borrowed from my mother. Besides, I'd brought a cardigan to slip overtop when we got to the Vandenburgs' house.

When I finished my twirl, Linc held out his hand to me. I placed mine in it and he helped me down the rest of the steps.

"You look beautiful, Alex," he said, giving me another sweep of his eyes from head to siren-red painted toes.

I didn't want to admit how much I needed that compliment. Rick was more about corrections than compliments. Rick, I was really beginning to realize, was kind of a jerk. And a terrible boyfriend.

I pulled on the lapel of Linc's suit coat with one hand. "You clean up nice yourself."

He'd look good in a burlap sack, but the smoky-gray shirt really did do amazing things to his eyes. And with the added inches from my heels, I could appreciate them at a closer distance.

We stood like that for a minute before I became self-conscious about drool dripping down my chin. My hand, still clasped firmly in Linc's, suddenly felt clammy. I went to pull it away, but he held on tighter and took a breath as if to say something.

"Colleen is meeting us there," I blurted, cutting off whatever he was about to say. I couldn't explain why I didn't want to hear it, but something in the way he looked at me made my stomach flip-flop.

He smiled. "Okay. We'd better get a move on before fashionably late turns into a grand entrance." He tugged me to the truck.

Colleen waited for us by her parked VW in front of the Vandenburgs' house. The driveway and surrounding curbs were already full of cars and trucks. Safety in numbers? This actually helped assuage my growing anxiety about being here: the more crowded the house, the more I could blend in. Disappear. Go unnoticed.

I hoped.

"You look amazing! Much too nice to be at a Hill house. Linc, turn right around and take her on a proper date," Colleen said when we met her by her car.

"Would you?" I asked, suddenly hopeful for an excuse to not go in.

"Oh no, scaredy-cat. Our first date is not going to be an 'instead of,'" he said. I felt my stomach flip-flop again. He said it like he anticipated there would be a first date at some point in our future. But I was probably projecting again.

"What's our plan?" Colleen asked, back in spy mode.

"Divide and conquer?" Linc suggested. When he caught sight of my big, anxious eyes, he chuckled. "Or not."

"We'll play it by ear. I prefer to stand back and observe. Maybe lob a conversation starter and see where it takes us," I suggested. "Maybe I should run back to the truck and grab my camera. I could pretend to be photographing the event."

I made to turn, but Linc gripped my elbow firmly. "No running. Besides, photographing a memorial for a dead person is kinda macabre, don't you think?"

I shrugged. I really wanted to hide behind my camera instead of facing the gossip-hungry crowd.

"Do we go for the main players first? Or stick to the edges? See what the scuttlebutt is?" Colleen asked as we made our way slowly toward the entrance.

"I say main players," Linc said at the same time I muttered, "Periphery players."

Colleen agreed with Linc. I scowled at her. I'd only get her milkshakes half the time.

"Well, I still think Mike could have done it. He and Crystal could have slipped out with the neighbor noticing. Or Kelly. Or maybe one of them hired someone to do it," Colleen suggested.

"You think there are hitmen wandering around Piney Ridge?" I asked.

Colleen shrugged. "Stranger things have happened."

I caught a hint of sadness underneath her excitement and hope. It would be easier for the residents of Piney Ridge if the murderer was an outsider. Reason number one why I couldn't really fault them for easily believing it was me. I'd been gone—to the big city and beyond—for so long, I'd slipped out of their fold.

I tensed as we reached the door. I concentrated on Linc's warm hand on my arm, grounding me. I was innocent. I hoped I'd prove it soon. Then all the accusatory, judgmental people of Piney Ridge would move on to the next bit of juicy gossip and leave me alone.

"We'll start with Mike," Linc said. "It'll be easy because we need to give our condolences. He's low on the list because of Crystal's alibi anyway."

I let out a breath. My hand started trembling so much, I almost dropped my clutch. "Easy for you to say. You're not the one accused of killing his wife."

"I'm sure no one believes you did it," Linc assured me even as several pairs of eyes drifted our way.

"Darnit," I said, reaching for an excuse to leave. "I forgot my cardigan in the truck. I'm gonna run back really quick."

Linc gripped my arm tighter. "No, you don't. We're right here."

Colleen sized me up. "You do look really pale, Alex. Why don't you go to the bathroom, and we'll talk to Mike. I'll come get you when we finish."

I could have kissed her. Colleen won herself back the full promise of milkshakes.

"Thank you," I mouthed silently, detached myself from Linc, and hightailed it away from them before Linc could object again.

I wandered down a hallway but didn't see any rooms that resembled a bathroom. It was probably in the foyer that I just vacated. As I doubled back, I noticed a door partly open that wasn't so on my way past originally. Perhaps this was a bathroom that someone just vacated?

I pushed open the door to reveal a study instead. The furniture and décor screamed masculinity—dark wood, dark leather, sports memorabilia. This must be Mike's home office. I chanced a quick glance down the hallway. All clear. Before I could overthink it, I ducked inside and shut the door quietly behind me. Mike was hopefully engaged with his guests, so I could snoop a little.

I didn't really know what to look for—a receipt for a hitman? Did hitmen write receipts? Was that something you could write off on your taxes? I chuckled at myself. Clearly lack of sleep made me loopy.

I rifled through the papers on his desk, wishing I knew anything about invoices and accounts payable. Maybe Missy was killed as revenge for fishy business practices in Mike's seafood distribution. Except I'd never know because numbers made my head swim. I clicked a picture of a few of the sheets with my cell phone, then moved to the desk drawers.

Locked. Locked. Locked. Every last one of them. Darnit. I contemplated trying to pry the doors open for a nanosecond, then realized that was both out of my wheelhouse and totally obvious. I reached under the desk to see if he had taped an extra key underneath. A ripped-up document in the trash can under the desk caught my attention. Really the word DNA on one of the pieces caught my attention. I reached in to grab the ripped sheath of paper.

It looked like the results from a mail-away DNA ancestry kit. Those were a big hit at Christmas this past year, so not surprising that the Vandenburgs would have one. Out of curiosity, I held a few of the ripped pieces together.

"Where was your family from, Mike? Were you related to Nazis? Or were you on the right side of history?" I said to the empty room.

Except the name on the top wasn't "Michael Vandenburg"; it was "Jodie Poledark." Why would his sister-in-law's DNA results be ripped up in Mike's trash can? I tried to hold another piece together in place, but a sound from the hallway had me shoving the small pieces in my clutch and racing to the door.

The doorknob twisted under my fingers.

Chapter 30

I did the only thing I could think of—pulled open the door quickly. Mike Vandenburg stumbled right into me. Jodie stood right behind him, her bloodshot eyes open wide in surprise.

"Oh, goodness. I'm so sorry!" I cried. "Can you point me to a bathroom?"

"It's off the foyer," Mike said skeptically.

I didn't wait for any follow-up questions. Just gave a little finger wave as I moved past Jodie and walked away without looking back. I didn't stop, or breathe, until I caught up with Linc and Colleen in the great room. They stood huddled together drinking what looked like martinis.

"There you are," Colleen exclaimed when I approached. She handed me her glass. "Here, you look like you need this more than I do."

I took a big gulp and almost choked. "Is this an appletini?"

Linc rolled his eyes and nodded. "Signature cocktail. Apparently, it was Missy's favorite drink."

"Doesn't surprise me," I muttered. "Who has a signature cocktail at a memorial service? Isn't that usually reserved for weddings and bachelorette parties?"

"Why do you still look so pale?" Colleen asked, ignoring me. "You were supposed to, like, splash cold water on your face or something. Instead, your eyes are the size of saucers."

"We should probably go. Like now," I said, looking over my shoulder toward the hallway from which I came. "We need to go now."

"What's gotten into you?" Linc asked.

"I'll tell you in the car. Then you can tell me what you found out."

"We haven't talked to anyone but Mike so far," Colleen whined. I knew she wanted to play spy a little longer.

"Is Kelly even here? Or was she smarter than me and stayed home?" I asked, scanning the crowd while trying to look like I wasn't scanning the crowd. I took another small sip of the overly sweet drink in my hand.

"I don't think she's here," Linc said. "At least I haven't seen her. We could mingle, though. See what everyone is talking about."

By the looks the partygoers threw my way, I would bet my new 85mm prime lens that *I* was what everyone was talking about. Still, I was curious about the gossip. And even if—and that was a big if—Mike noticed the DNA results missing from his trash can, they may not even be connected to the murder.

"She's overthinking things again," Colleen whispered to Linc.

"I heard that," I said, but relented. "Fine. We'll take the long way out and hover by some conversations to hear what we can hear."

"That's the spirit!" Colleen said on a laugh. "Eavesdroppers unite!"

I gave her a rueful look and followed them around the room. Okay, more *hid* behind them, than followed, but I'd never admit it to them.

Snippets of conversation floated our way:

"So sad. Gone too young..."

"... never know what tomorrow will bring..."

"Patsy's already gone back to school. Can you imagine?"

"Jodie is staying here to help with the kids..."

I tucked that last one away. If Jodie moved in here with Mike to help watch the kids, then that might explain how her mail ended up in the trash can. I relaxed a little. Why would someone pay all that money for a DNA test to just throw it away? Then again, who knew why most people did most things? For all I knew, the company sent duplicate copies or a hard copy and a digital copy.

Someone stopped Linc to ask about repairing the sign. I turned my back to the conversation, hoping I wasn't recognized as the sign killer. When I turned, I met Jodie's eyes from across the room. I put on my best "My condolences" face—or at least I hoped I did. Jodie nodded once, and then her slightly unfocused eyes drifted away from me. She looked terrible, as I knew anyone who lost a sibling would look, especially one they were particularly close to. Her hair was a little out of place; her cheeks tear-stained and pale. She fidgeted with a bracelet around her wrist, turning it around and around by the little charm that hung from it. I made a mental note to reach out to her when she had a little more time to process. Since I, too, had lost a sibling, perhaps I could help her through the initial grief.

Just then I felt a warmth on my lower back. Linc had his fingertips on my skin. He slowly spread them until his entire palm was flat against my bare spine. I felt that warmth roll through me from my back all the way to my toes and the tip of my skull. Before I realized what I was doing, I leaned into his touch, inviting more. He stepped up close behind me, not moving his hand.

"Ready to go?" he whispered by my ear in his deep voice. I nodded and signaled for Colleen. We made our way out; Linc never removing his hand from my back.

Once we reached Colleen's car, she practically shouted, "What did you find out? What was so urgent?"

"Why don't we meet at Plum Crazy to discuss. I could use something to get the awful taste of those appletinis out of my mouth," Linc suggested.

"Ugh, fine," Colleen said. She pointed a finger at us. "No talking about it while you're driving. I don't want to miss anything."

Chapter 31

True to our promise, Linc and I waited until we were all seated at our usual booth at Plum Crazy before talking about the memorial. Peggy Sue shot us a raised eyebrow when we sat in silence as she took our order. I didn't blame her suspicions; we were usually boisterous and chatty. Something about the conversation we were about to have seemed important. Heavy, almost. And absolutely private.

As I sat there waiting for Peggy Sue to deliver the milkshakes and basket of fries we'd ordered, I thought about the time I had an assignment in San Francisco. The Californian city, known for its cascading hills, colorful townhouses, and the Golden Gate Bridge, also had the oldest running system of trolleys. Those trolleys ran on completely electric rails and the whole city crackled with it. A slight buzz constantly played in the background of my time there. At the time it made me feel a constant mixture of excitement and anxiety—a sense of anticipation that something big was on the horizon. That's exactly how I felt right now—buzzing with anticipation. My leg jiggled under the table and I tapped my fingernails on the countertop in a frantic rhythm.

As soon as Peggy Sue delivered our order and moved out of earshot, Colleen reached across the table to still my tapping hand. "What is wrong with you?"

"I feel like we're about to solve this," I said, eyes lit with excitement.

"Spill. What did you find out?"

I reached into my clutch and pulled out the ripped pieces of the DNA test. I explained where I'd found them— ignoring Colleen's astonishment and Linc's amusement— and what I'd been able to piece together on the scene.

On the scene—geesh, I was starting to sound like Colleen.

"Why would Mike have a ripped-up copy of Jodie's DNA results?" Colleen asked.

"I asked the same thing!" I exclaimed. "Now that we have the time and space, I thought we could puzzle piece the rest of it together."

Linc voiced my earlier skepticism. "Before you two blow a blood vessel in excitement, we should at least entertain the idea that this has nothing to do with Missy's murder."

Colleen waved him away. "Sure, sure, sure. But at the very least, we'll possibly have some juicy gossip. I never have gossip beyond whose kid is still wearing diapers."

We worked together to fit the pieces back into place as we munched salty, warm fries and sipped sweet, cool milkshakes. As the scraps formed coherent information, I felt that same buzz from earlier—my heart beat like a hundred birds trying to escape my chest. When I was photographing, my body reacted in almost the same way when I knew I got the shot. There was something important here.

I leaned across the table on my elbows to get a closer look. I practically bumped heads with Linc who was doing the same thing. He may seem all nonchalant and uncaring, but I could feel his excitement growing.

Colleen said, "This doesn't look like the results from a typical send-away DNA kit. One of the parents at the preschool had one done on her precious baby angel and it was much vaguer than this. Just listed countries of origin and possible genetic diseases to look out for. This is much more detailed."

"Interesting," I said. Why would any twenty-year-old need an intricate DNA report? An assignment for a college class? Or maybe she wanted to work at Quantico or the Pentagon. I knew plenty of people who had their entire lives picked apart for the privilege of working at those two places—both of which were within driving distance from Piney Ridge.

"Okay, not a lot of surprises in this first part," Linc said, scrutinizing the pieces. "She's related to the Poledarks. Very close relation to Missy—to be expected for siblings. But I don't understand this second part." He pointed to section two of the report where the results listed the paternal information.

According to the DNA report, Jodie was also related by blood to the Vandenburgs.

"Did the samples get mixed up? Are we sure this is for Jodie and not one of Missy's kids?" Colleen asked, leaning in now too. "It doesn't make sense."

"It's definitely her results," Linc confirmed. The information on the top was clear as day.

"So what could it mean? Let's assume there wasn't cross-contamination. Why else would Jodie be related to her sister's husband's family?" I asked. Colleen was right; even if this had nothing to do with Missy's murder, it was definitely juicy gossip.

"There's some sort of incestuous connection in the lineage of the Poledarks and Vandenburgs," Linc suggested. I made an "ew" face.

"Mike's father had an affair with Missy's mother, and Jodie is their love child," Colleen suggested, eyes wide.

"What if Mike had an affair with Missy's mother, and Jodie is their love child," I said, taking the idea one step further. "That's even more salacious."

Linc nodded. "Ms. Poledark was a looker back in the day, even with the drinking."

"Ew, Linc," Colleen and I said together. He shrugged, unapologetic.

"Having an affair with his wife's mother would be a motive for murder, for sure." I leaned back in my seat. "Although more so for Missy, not the other way around. If I found out my husband had an affair with my mother, I'd freak out and probably kill the scoundrel too." I looked at my friends' shocked faces and added, "Hypothetically, of course."

"Could they have gotten in a fight that went too far? Maybe the whole thing was an accident," Colleen said. "Scissors do seem like a crime of passion. If you're going to premeditate something, why not bring a knife or a gun?"

"True. Okay, picture this: Missy and Mike fought over the results. Mike lashed out in self-defense grabbing the only thing nearby—scissors." I could see it play out in my mind as clear as day.

"One small problem," Linc interjected into my mind movie. "Why was she in the woods? If they fought there, someone must have brought the scissors. You don't just find scissors laying around by the reservoir. Beer cans and chip bags, sure. But scissors? Not likely."

I felt myself deflate a little. We were still missing something. My buzz from earlier diminished to a dull ping in the back of my brain. Still there but much less intense.

Colleen must have felt the same since she said, "Maybe it is just juicy gossip and nothing to do with the murder."

"Could be," I confirmed. But I couldn't quite let it go. "But it is really coincidental. This report is recent." I pointed at the date at the top. "We're missing something."

Linc munched on the almost forgotten basket of fries, his eyes unfocused as he thought. We looked at him with anticipation. It wasn't like him not to offer an opinion.

Finally, he said, "Nope. I got nothing. I'm still on Team Kelly did it to take over the salon. Everything fits—the scissors, the timing, the renovations. Maybe this DNA report is just a—what do they call it? Pickled herring?"

"Red herring," Colleen and I said at the same time.

Linc nodded. "That's it!"

I sighed and finished my milkshake. "You're probably right. Keep your ear to the ground tomorrow at work about Kelly's interview last night. Charm your way into getting Joy to talk about it."

Linc gave me a sideways look, but a smile pulled at his lips. "Won't you be there too? You are falling way behind on your community service requirements."

I rolled my eyes, a habit that had gotten much worse since returning to Piney Ridge. "I don't really want to be anywhere near that place right now."

"Understandable. Maybe you can meet me by the sign, and we can get started on repairs."

Now it was my turn to smirk. "So not only would I be paying for the repairs, but I would also be helping to repair it? Something doesn't sit quite right there."

Linc shrugged, the hint of a smile turning into a real one. "I'll bet the carpenter would knock a few bucks off of the labor quote."

I threw a fry at him.

Chapter 32

Later that evening, I tossed and turned in my bed. My mind was racing, trying to connect the dots between Missy, Mike, and Jodie. It really was too much of a coincidence for the DNA results to come back almost the same day as Missy's murder. Someone—presumably Mike—was so upset about them, he or she ripped the report to shreds. No one ripped paper that much unless they wanted to erase what was on it.

The reservoir threw me off. If this had happened in the Vandenburg home or at Mike's office or at the salon, I could make my theory fit.

The salon! I sat bolt upright in bed. Of course. Missy had been at the salon that day. She could have easily picked up some scissors there. What if it wasn't Mike who came prepared with a weapon, but Missy? That fit with the "Missy was the angry one" scenario.

Or maybe she happened to have them in her pocket. I thought about all the times I found lens caps and cleaning wipes and SD cards in my pockets. People put work stuff in pockets all the time and forgot about them.

My scenario from earlier could make sense if Missy were the one to have brought the scissors. The couple fights over the affair, it gets out of hand. Maybe Missy remembers the scissors and pulls them to threaten Mike. He overpowers her, takes the scissors, and stabs her. Or they struggle for the scissors and Missy accidentally gets stabbed.

Mike obviously wouldn't want the scandal to get out. If he or his father were the culprit of the affair, the scandal would rock Piney Ridge and possibly affect their business. That would devastate the Vandenburgs, who thrived on their image and their current, lavish lifestyle.

A terrible thought occurred to me then. Would he also want to silence Jodie? Obviously she knew about the results; did she also figure out Mike's involvement in Missy's murder? If he were willing to kill to keep the secret of the DNA, he would absolutely kill again to cover up another murder. The stakes were so much higher.

I checked the time—not too late. I flew out of bed and threw on some clothes. Jodie would probably still be awake or even entertaining guests at the memorial. I had to try to warn her, to convince her to go to the police.

I cursed my stupid car for still being in the shop and contemplated calling Linc or Colleen to get a ride. Jodie's wide, bloodshot eyes and pale, tear-stained cheeks filled my head. There wasn't time. Tensions and emotions ran high tonight with the memorial. Mike, if he were anything like me, would be wound tight after putting on a false face all through the memorial. I couldn't risk the time it would take to have someone drive here to pick me up.

I grabbed the stupid bike and pedaled faster and harder than my poor body was used to. My legs were a gelatinous mess by the time I got to the Vandenburgs' house. Why couldn't they have lived somewhere called the Plateau instead of the Hill? Luckily, the house was still ablaze, and cars still lined the street. Free booze meant a long party whatever the occasion.

I leaned my bike against a tree across the street and made my way up the driveway to the back of the house. The eat-in kitchen had sliding glass doors that took up almost one whole wall. If I could catch Jodie in there alone, I could possibly motion for her to come outside. Not the best plan, but the only one I had at the moment.

Plan B would be to reenter the house, on the guise that I left something there, and try to pull Jodie aside. But I didn't want to draw attention to myself.

I hid behind some of the landscaping with an eye on the windows, poised to jump out and signal to Jodie should the chance arise. I'd been crouched there long enough for one foot to get those prickly, almost asleep tingles when my cell phone's shrill tone echoed in the silent dark, surprising me enough to make me fall backward into the mulch. I fumbled it out of my pocket all the while shushing it, as if that would help. I managed to silence it as I saw Jodie enter the kitchen—alone.

Quickly, I shoved the phone into my back pocket and lunged out of the bushes toward the house. I waved my arms like a crazy person, but with the light on inside and the pitch black outside, Jodie couldn't see me.

I took a deep breath, ventured onto the porch, and knocked on the window. Jodie jumped about a mile, her pale face getting even more translucent. I guess I wasn't the only anxious one.

I tried the sliding door. It was unlocked.

"Jodie," I whispered. "It's me, Alex Lightwood. I have to speak with you in private. It's urgent."

Jodie, of course, looked wary. "Aren't you the one accused of murdering Missy?"

I stood up to my full height, which wasn't much and was the point. I gestured to myself. "Do I look like I can murder anyone? It wasn't me. But I think I know who did it. Please, meet me outside so I can talk to you. Just for a moment."

Jodie looked behind her toward the great room. Then she looked back at me and nodded her head slightly. I let out a breath. I left the door open but moved back into the shadows away from the house to wait for her.

Jodie emerged from the house a moment later. When she got close to me, she said, "Follow me. It's more private by the pool house."

I followed her. She was right; no light from the house reached this part of the yard. The only light came from the moon that hung heavy in the night sky. We were completely secluded from the windows of the house. A tall fence surrounding the pool area cut us off from any prying neighbors too.

"What do you want, Alex? It's been an emotional day already." Jodie stood between me and the house with hands on hips.

There was no good way to say what I knew, so I just blurted it out. "I know about the DNA test results. That you are related to both Missy and Mike."

I saw surprise flash across Jodie's face followed closely by anger. Then it settled into the unemotional visage of a bored twentysomething again. She shrugged a shoulder.

"I think those results were what got Missy killed," I explained. "I'm worried that you might be next. If someone is trying to keep those results quiet, you are another person that knows about them."

"Thanks for your concern," Jodie said. "But it really isn't any of your business."

I felt my hackles go up. Here I was trying to help this girl, and I was getting the brush-off. "It kind of is my business since I'm accused of the murder. If you suspect Mike too, then you should say something. Not just for me, but for your own safety."

Jodie almost laughed. "You think Mike killed Missy?"

"Well, yes. It's the logical answer, right? He doesn't want any affair between his family and your mother to come out."

"My mother," Jodie scoffed. "My mother."

Her voice was full of so much sharp derision, it could have cut my hair as easily as the scissors used to kill Missy. Instinctively, I took a step back, although I couldn't really explain why.

"You want to talk about my mother," Jodie said, practically spitting the words.

I remained quiet. This conversation had derailed from what I expected. The tone was all wrong, and that feeling like I was missing something came back tenfold.

Jodie continued, "My mother is a lying, selfish piss goblin. She lied to me my entire life. She got what she deserved."

"Wait. What happened to your mother?" I asked.

"You didn't figure it out from the DNA results you somehow pilfered from us? Mike didn't have an affair with Laura. Neither did his decrepit old man. No, besides his indiscretions of late, he has always been under *my mother's* thumb," Jodie said.

Like the last piece of a puzzle, it all clicked into place. Missy wasn't studying abroad or at fat camp during sophomore year; the Poledarks sent her away to have a baby. Her loveless marriage, full of secrets and cheating, was no doubt forced upon them by their parents to keep up appearances if the truth ever came out. Her disregard for

Mike wasn't the reason his picture wasn't in the locket. Missy had pictures of her children—all of her children—in there.

"Your mother"—I took a breath as realization dawned—"is Missy."

Jodie started a slow clap, and I noticed something glinting in her hand. I squinted to bring it into focus.

A knife. A big kitchen knife. I felt my own face drain of color and willed myself not to faint. I had to keep Jodie talking until I found a way out of this mess.

"Some sleuth you are," Jodie said, taking a step forward. I took another one back. Pretty soon my back would be up against the fence. "You thought lazy, boring Mike would be capable of killing anyone? He barely gets off the sofa to go to the bathroom."

"Why?" I asked, keeping my eyes on the knife. "Why did you kill Missy?"

"Isn't it obvious? She lied to me my entire life. She let me believe we were sisters instead of proudly claiming me as her own. She brags all over town about Junior and Patsy, but she hides me behind secrets and lies. And all because she and Mike—excuse me, dear old Dad—were too stupid to keep it in their pants in high school. Like that was somehow my fault." Jodie began pacing back and forth as she spoke, her movements getting more and more animated. "She left me with that drunk woman instead. I never felt like she loved me—my *grandmother*. She either ignored me or yelled at me. I thought it was because I was an accident." Jodie laughed. "Which I guess I was. Just not her accident."

"What happened that day, Jodie?" I asked. Jodie must have been the girl I saw running on the forest path the evening of the murder. I wished I'd had the forethought to record this conversation on my phone. Too late now; I didn't want to risk a sudden movement by reaching for it.

"You heard her in that salon," Jodie said. "It was all Michael this and Patsy that and 'children are the most important thing.' God, I thought I was going to gag. I eventually got sick of it and stormed out. She followed me into the woods. When I yelled at her about the lie again, she had the audacity to get mad. *She* was mad at *me*! Can you even?"

I shook my head dutifully even though I didn't think Jodie was focused on me anymore.

"She told me I needed to find a way to get over it. The past was the past and all that bull. I suggested we could tell everyone the truth. That would help me get over it. She refused. Again. Then she tried to show me her locket." Tears fell from Jodie's eyes as she put on Missy's affect. "'I keep all my kids close to my heart,' she said. Puh-lease." Jodie swiped at the angry tears and gave a derisive laugh. "Like keeping my picture in a locket would make up for denying me all my life. She betrayed me—over and over and over. And was still betraying me, even after I found out the truth. I couldn't take it anymore. I-I didn't even realize I had the scissors in my hand until I swung them at her. They must have been in my apron pocket when I ran from the salon."

"I'm so sorry, Jodie," I said, meaning it. "The way she treated you was horrible."

Wasn't an excuse for murder—but I kept that thought to myself.

"That's right. It was horrible. And I'm not going to suffer one more day for her lies. So, I'm sorry, Alex, but you can't leave."

"I won't tell," I said quickly, taking another step away and feeling my back hit the wood of the fence. "Everyone knows there was no love lost between Missy and I. Frankly, I think you did Piney Ridge a favor. I promise." I crossed my heart with a finger. "I'm the best at keeping secrets."

"I don't know you, so I can't trust you. If only you'd kept your nose out of it, like Chief Duncan suggested. I'll work with their suspicion. I think you'll commit suicide over your guilt for killing Missy. How poetic that you do it right here at her house, on the very night of her memorial."

Jodie's dark eyes were now laser-focused on me, like a huntress on her prey. I shifted sideways down the fence as Jodie stalked me, knife raised in her hand.

I tried to focus, tried to see through my scared haze and concentrate over the thrum of the blood rushing in my ears and the roar of my racing heart. The moment I reached the corner of the fence, Jodie seized the moment and lunged. I held my breath and waited.

There was nowhere else to go.

Chapter 33

I ducked and rolled to the side as the knife passed my head. For once in my adult life, I thanked my Polish genes for my small stature. The knife got stuck in the fence, and as Jodie struggled to dislodge it—on a string of curses—I put my entire weight behind a kick to Jodie's knee. She fell to the ground, screaming in pain and holding her knee.

I ran blindly in the dark, trying to remember the location of the pool so I didn't accidentally fall in. I ran until I hit a solid object with an oomph. I ricocheted off and landed hard on the ground. A scream bubbled up in my throat. How did Jodie get in front of me? Hands reached down toward me. I clawed and kicked and scrambled and screamed.

Until a very familiar and very welcome voice broke through my panic.

"Alex. Lexi. Alex. It's me. Calm down. It's me, Alex. It's Linc."

I stilled immediately, blinking him into focus. Then, hearing a commotion behind me, bolted to my feet, grabbed his hand, and shouted, "Run!"

He gathered me in his arms to steady me and keep me still. My body was still in fight or flight mode, so I struggled to break free. He held on tighter.

"She's coming, Linc. She's right behind me," I screeched.

"Shhhh, Alex. I've got you. You're safe."

"Sh-sh-she has a knife!" I cried into his shirt. I clung to him, feeling my heart settle a little in his strong embrace.

"The police are here. Detective Spaulding," he added quickly when he felt me tense. "It's okay."

I leaned back to look up at him. "But... how? How are you here?"

"Your phone. I called earlier. You answered but didn't say anything. I heard everything," the last sentence came out on a choke. "I was afraid I wouldn't make it in time."

"I kicked out her knee," I said lamely.

I reached for my back pocket. The phone wasn't there. I must have dropped it during the scuffle with Jodie. I glanced back from where I ran. In the darkness, I could see figures emerging. I practically climbed Linc's body to get away.

"It's okay, Alex," he said again, smoothing a hand over my hair. "It's Detective Spaulding. He has Jodie in custody."

As they came into the circle of light from the house, I could see Linc was right. Jodie, spitting denials, limped along beside Detective Spaulding who had a firm grip on the cuffs encircling her wrists.

"It was her! It was all her! She attacked me!" Jodie screamed when she saw me. "I want to press charges. I think she tore something in my knee."

"We'll get it all sorted out at the station," Detective Spaulding said. He caught my eye and rolled his. I managed a small smile.

Linc and I followed them from the backyard. A large crowd had gathered on the back porch, watching the bizarre scene unfold.

Mike Vandenburg stepped forward when he saw Jodie in cuffs. "What's going on here?"

"Jodie Poledark is under arrest for the murder of Melissa Poledark Vandenburg," the detective said.

"I thought Alex was under arrest?" another partygoer called.

"Alex Lightwood is cleared of all suspicion. We have a recording of Jodie confessing. I'm not at liberty to say anything more."

"Jodie, I'll meet you at the police station," Mike said, turning to head back into the house.

"I don't want your help, *Dad*," Jodie spit at him. All eyes immediately turned to Mike.

"Let's get out of here," I said. "I've had about enough Vandenburg family drama to last me a lifetime."

I sat on the couch while Linc rummaged around my kitchen making tea. Once the adrenaline had worn off, I'd started trembling uncontrollably on the way home. Linc, ever the EMT, wrapped me in blankets to ward off shock and made me sit on the couch in front of the fireplace, which he'd expertly lit using the wood stacked outside. He'd wanted me to go to the hospital to get checked out, but I assured him I was fine.

Linc handed me the cup of hot tea and took the seat beside me, running his hands up and down my arms to try to stop the trembling.

"Thanks for coming to find me," I said quietly.

"Always." He turned me to face him. "Alex, when I heard her threaten you tonight, I-I've never been so scared."

"Me neither," I quipped with a wry smile.

"I'll bet," he said on a small laugh. Then his face turned serious again. He played with a strand of my hair, wrapping it around a finger and letting it slide through slowly. "I almost didn't make it to you."

"But you did. And I'm fine. A little shaky still, but okay. No silly twentysomething can take down this woman of the world." I tried again for levity, tried to bring back the signature amusement on his face. Serious Linc was much too intense for me.

"I don't doubt that. Adult Alex is pretty amazing," he said, a smile finally tugging the corners of his lips.

"Thanks. Adult Linc isn't so bad either." I stifled a yawn.

"Come on. Let's get you to bed," he said, standing and pulling me with him even though I was already pushing off the couch. The joint momentum propelled me right into his chest. His arms immediately wrapped around me. He held me there for a moment, one hand on the small of my back, the other cupping my head.

I sighed and allowed myself to lean into him. Had Rick ever just held me like this? I couldn't remember a single time. The only time he was cuddly was when he wanted it to progress to something more. And with that realization, I finally let Wreck-it Rick go completely. I'd never really loved him, I realized now. And he obviously had never loved me. We were shoved together through our jobs and acted on the convenience.

"Alex," Linc said softly. He moved his hand from my head to lift my chin. When I looked up at him, his eyes were the darkest shade of blue-gray I'd ever seen them. If I wasn't careful, I would drown there. His eyes flicked from my eyes to my lips, parted slightly as I tried to breathe, and back again.

"Alex," he repeated as he lowered his head to close the distance between us.

My eyes fluttered closed in anticipation. Did I want this? Did I want him to kiss me? Was he going to kiss me? I could feel his breath on my skin.

Then the door burst open with a bang, and we jumped apart. We stared at each other, each breathing heavily.

"Alex? Alex, where are you?" my mother's worried, loud voice sounded from the foyer. "Alex?"

I started laughing. I laughed so hard, tears dropped from my eyes. Linc shook his head at me but couldn't hide his smile. I'd moved out so my parents wouldn't interrupt "adult relationship time," and yet here they were. When I snorted and covered my mouth, he started laughing too.

"What in the turnip field is going on here?" Mom asked, following the sound of our guffaws to find us in the empty kitchen. She didn't wait for an answer, just gathered me into her arms and held on tightly. My father's arms came around me from the other side and I melted into their love.

"We thought we'd lost you too, Peanut," Mom said, "when we heard it on the scanner."

"I'm okay, Mom. I'm made of tough stuff," I assured them. Harrison was on all our minds.

Linc busied himself making tea for everyone. When my parents assured themselves that I was actually okay, they finally released me. Then bombarded me with questions. Although I'd already talked to my parents on the phone— Linc's phone since mine was confiscated by police—I again recounted the story, reassured them I was okay, and then reassured them some more. Linc handed out the tea as we stood around the kitchen area. Mom sat on the couch while the rest of us leaned against the counter.

"Who made the fire?" Mom asked when all their questions about the evening's adventure were exhausted.

"Linc did," I said. "Isn't it lovely? Almost feels like a home."

"You need a table. This conversation would be much easier if we had a proper place to sit."

"If I got a table, that would encourage people to come and sit," I said pointedly. My father smirked behind his coffee mug.

"Of course, dear," my mother said, completely missing my sarcasm. In Mom's world, everyone thrived on company. "Once I get you to join our book club, you could host a meeting. But not with this sparse seating," she added.

"I still have to pay for the sign and the car, so a table is low on the priority list," I explained. Before my mother could say anything else, I added, "I'm really tired. It was an exhausting evening. Both emotionally and physically. If you don't mind, I'm going to crash. Feel free to stay and finish your tea. Just lock the door on the way out, please."

I gave hugs all around, keeping the one with Linc short. I fell asleep as soon as my head settled on the pillow.

Chapter 34

A few weeks later, I sat on the hood of the fire truck, camera in hand, documenting the Welcome sign regaining its proper place as the sentinel to Piney Ridge. Colleen, leaning against the fender below where I clicked away, clapped, and whistled. The new acting mayor promised an official unveiling later in the week. Mike Vandenburg had quietly stepped out of the role to help focus on Jodie's upcoming legal problems. An ominous For Sale sign sat in front of the Vandenburg home. Rumor around the Ladies' Auxiliary was that he was packing up his children and moving to Baltimore, where Jodie was being held—probably for a long, long time. She finally got the attention from her birth parents that she craved.

I checked the histogram on the back of the camera. The sign really did look spectacular. Since it was flat on the ground for several weeks, a few townies took it upon themselves to touch up the paint that had been chipped and flaking for years. The new posts and new paint really did breathe new life into the historic sign. I smugly, and silently, congratulated myself on being the cause of the

249

transformation. At least my money had gone to something worthwhile.

And someone worthwhile. I snapped a few pictures of Linc, muscles flexing under his tight T-shirt as he worked with the other firefighters to secure the sign in place. We'd pretended the almost kiss in my loft never happened. That didn't mean that I didn't think about it. A lot. I mean even though our teenaged kiss was awkward and messy, it was still good. Linc knew what he was doing then. Kissing Adult Linc would have been even more inspiring, I was sure.

But that ship had sailed away as the wave of adrenaline and danger surrounding that night ebbed. I was officially back in the friend zone. Or even worse—in the "like a little sister" zone.

"Stop that," Linc said, catching me taking pictures of him out of the corner of his eye.

"Outtakes for the calendar," I said, even though I'd already finished the calendar and sent it to the printer. But I obliged. My file of Linc pictures was growing at an embarrassing rate. Having just been cleared as a murder suspect, I needed to be careful I didn't turn into a stalker suspect. I tucked my camera into the gear bag in my car.

Yes, *my* car. I'd gotten a reprieve on the safe-driving class and the rest of my community service from Judge Cockran. Much to my surprise, I also got a begrudging apology from Chief Duncan. I wanted to respond with a "You're welcome for doing your job for you." But my mother, knowing the snarky spark in my eye, gave me a death stare over Chief Duncan's shoulder. I wrinkled my nose at her and kept it at "Thanks for the apology."

Linc joined me and Colleen by the Fiat. "Congrats. You can officially wipe this black mark off your consciousness. Much like you wiped out the sign," he said.

I smacked his arm. So what if I let my hand linger there for a moment longer to feel his hard muscles. I may be in the friend zone, but I wasn't dead.

"Come on back to my place," I said. "We can sit outside and drink something cold to celebrate my liberation from all things criminal."

Stalking aside.

A large box sat at the base of the loft steps when we arrived. I checked the return address with a giddiness in my stomach. The first-responder calendars. And a day early.

"Are those what I think they are?" Linc asked, coming up beside me after parking his truck.

"The calendars! As soon as I figure out how to lug this up the steps, we can check them out." I looked around for a hand truck or something—they were always laying around the nearby orchard marketplace. I looked back to see Linc lift the box easily onto his shoulder and start up the steps.

"Show off," I teased.

"Hurry up with the key, will you?" he huffed. "This is heavier than it looks."

I scooted past him on the stairwell to unlock the door, then led him into the kitchen.

"Just put it on the table," I said. Then stopped short.

In the center of the once empty space sat a gorgeous table handcrafted from a piece of salvaged wood, the bark around the rough edges still showing under the light layer of lacquer. The small imperfections and knots in the surface mirrored the rustic look of the loft seamlessly. I ran my hand over the surface, reveling in the shape and texture and rawness of it all. It was exactly what I envisioned for the space.

Then, realization dawning, my eyes snapped to Linc's. His lips were curled into a hopeful smile. Anticipation shone in his eyes.

"Do you like it?" he asked.

"Did you do this for me?" I asked. He nodded slightly. "Linc. It's too much."

"Do you like it?" he repeated.

"I love it. It's the most beautiful thing I've ever seen," I said. "I can't accept it."

"Of course you can. Besides, I'm not hauling it back out of here." He moved forward to put the box on the surface. I almost squawked at him for scuffing the perfect, shiny surface.

I moved to him and touched his arm. "Thank you. It's the nicest gift I've ever received."

He put his hand over his heart in mock pain. "Six-year-old me is hurt. He thought the whistle he won you at the carnival was the nicest gift. He really, really wanted to keep that whistle for himself, you know."

I almost admitted I still had that stupid whistle in a box in my closet but decided that only added to the stalker vibe. Instead, I said, "Okay, the table is the second nicest gift. But only because it's going to give my mother an excuse to come over more often. And if I have to join her book club, so do you." I poked a finger in his chest. He grabbed my hand and held it to his chest. His eyes turned dark again, like they had the night of Jodie's confession.

And in a moment directly out of a rom-com, the door burst open again. Colleen bustled through.

"Sorry. I had to stop by my—" She stopped when she saw the table. "Holy cow! Linc, did you make this? It's amazing!" She spotted the box. "Are those the calendars already?"

Linc dropped my hand and moved to rummage in my kitchen junk drawer for scissors to open the box. I flinched a little as he brought them over to open the box of calendars. I wondered how long it would take before I could see scissors without thinking of Missy.

Colleen pulled the first calendar out before Linc even had the box all the way open. Her eyes widened at the cover shot—Linc and Andrea, both in uniform, playing happily with Fang and completely unaware of the camera.

"Alex. This is brilliant. You have both organizations represented on the cover. I'm in love with it already and I've only seen one picture," Colleen said. She eagerly flipped through to reveal all the candid shots I chose for the spread.

"You have to say that since you're my best friend," I said, downplaying the compliment.

"Why do you do that?" Linc asked.

"Do what?" I looked through a calendar too, noting a place where I dropped a shadow in one and realizing my composition was slightly off in another.

"Diminish your ability." I looked up at him, brows creased. He continued, "I've heard you do it at least three times. Every time someone compliments you on your photographs, you make some excuse for why it's not true."

"Do I?" I asked. I'd never thought about it.

"You do. I'm going to tell you this as many times as you need to hear it. You are an amazing photographer." He held up a finger, stopping the denial on my lips. "You are. You capture more than just pictures. Anyone can point a camera at someone in good light and get a shot with their eyes open. But you, Alex, you capture their spirit."

"Thank you," I said, truly touched. "I didn't realize how much I needed to hear that."

"He's totally right," Colleen confirmed. "You're gonna have every mother in Piney Ridge banging down your door down after this to take their Christmas pictures."

I waited for the slab of stone to weigh down my chest at the mention of becoming a family photographer, of opening a business in Piney Ridge. To my surprise it didn't fall. Sometime during the last few weeks, this place had seeped back into my being. Maybe taking a break from the go, go, go of my past and settling into the slow ebb and flow of this still life was exactly what I needed.

As I looked at my friends and the beautiful space around me, only one word came to mind. And that one word held so much promise, so much possibility, that it practically filled the entire room.

Home.

THE END

Keep Reading for Sneak Peek of
One Click in the Grave
Book 2 of the Alex Lightwood
Cozy Mystery Series

And don't forget—

Subscribe to Kari Ganske's Cozy Newsletter
for a FREE novella in the
Alex Lightwood Mystery Series
More information on her website:
kariganske.com

Excerpt from *One Click in the Grave*
Book 2 in the Alex Lightwood Cozy Mystery Series

Chapter 1

This was supposed to be an easy shoot. One to ease me into my new business adventure. The subjects were slow moving and therefor easy to capture in my sights. A couple hours tops, the client had promised and offered a generous fee for the few shots this would take. In and out. Easy, breezy. Payment upon completion.

What they forgot to take into account was my grandmother.

"Nana K? Do you need those glasses to see?" I asked her. She was wearing star-shaped, rainbow-colored glasses which were ridiculous in their own right, but the lenses were also causing a nasty glare in camera.

"No. But they do enhance the outfit. I'm not losing them," she answered, slamming her thin lips into a pout.

Her "outfit" consisted of a form-fitting rainbow unitard with interspersed sequins, a plethora of brightly colored plastic necklaces and bangles, and chunky bedazzled wedges that added a few inches to her five-foot-nothing frame. She colored the tips of her spiky white hair to match the rainbow pattern. For my mother's sake, I hoped it wasn't permanent.

"You can keep the glasses, but I'm popping the lenses out. They're causing a glare I'm not in the mood to edit out in post-processing," I said, snatching the glasses from her face before she could protest and popping the plastic lenses into my hand.

"You break 'em, you bought 'em," my loving grandmother said.

"They'll be fine." I handed her back the frames. "Now, what did you have in mind for the portrait?"

Normally, I would be the one directing the subject of a photo shoot. Or gently nudging, as I prefer to think of it. However, with my spirited 80-going-on-18-year-old grandmother, I knew she'd want to call the shots. Literally.

The other members of the Aged Pine Retirement Community had all chosen unassuming activities to engage in for the annual yearbook photo shoot. Beatrice Cornwallace showed me her knitting. Ethel Mayburn laid out a hand of bridge. Harold Martingale met me at the little fishing pond on the property. My grandmother, on the other hand, looked like she was about to strap on some roller skates and join a derby.

As I waited for her reply, I held my breath and thought about what lead me to this exact place. If you had asked me a few months ago if I'd still be in Piney Ridge, the teeny-tiny town in teeny-tiny Maryland that I left right after graduation, I'd have laughed in your face. If not for a douche canoe of an ex-boyfriend who ruined both my career and my personal life by blacklisting me from the photojournalist community, I'd still be living in New York. Or off on a shoot in an exotic locale. His lies and cheating prompted me to tuck tail and return to my childhood hometown to try to piece my life back together.

What I thought would only take a few weeks—surely the industry would realize they made a terrible mistake and bet me to return—had now turned into several months. And although I'd never admit it to my conniving ex or my ambitious eighteen-year-old self, I didn't actually mind it.

"Think we could find a cigar?" Nana K asked, pulling my attention away from thinking about a name for my new photography business. Since the first responder calendar shoot, residents had been tentatively asking when I was going into business so they could officially hire me for their events. Not a bad problem to have since my photojournalism income was now nil, and I had a needy betta fish to support.

"A cigar? You don't even smoke!" I said.

She shrugged a bony shoulder. "Yeah, but these old biddies don't know that. I like to give them a shock. Keeps them alive."

"Or you could give them a heart attack."

"When it's their time, it's their time." She noticed my gaping expression. "Oh, don't be such a prude, Alex. Death is a constant companion around here." She looked toward the residential buildings. "I bet Harold has a cigar hidden in his room."

"Nana K, I'm kind of on a timeline here. Do you have a plan B?" I crossed my fingers behind my back.

She pursed her lips like a disgruntled teenager. "Fine. I guess by the wishing well will do. I can pretend to climb in the bucket."

Faster than I would have thought possible for an octogenarian in three-inch wedges, she took off toward the front of the building. I grabbed my gear and scrambled after her, hoping I reached her before she fell down the well.

I caught her just as she leaned headfirst into the small well. I grabbed the elastic belt around her waist and yanked her back to standing.

"Aww. I wanted to see if I could reach any change," she whined.

"You know those are other people's wishes," I said.

Her smile broadened as she shrugged. "How would they know? Half those wishes no amount of pennies in a dinky old well will help come true. No twentysomething Clark Gable look alike is going to come strutting through the lobby looking for a sugar mama." She turned to the grouping of apartments behind her and yelled, "You hear that, Doris! You're wasting your pennies!"

If I had a penny, I'd wish for Doris to be out of earshot.

"Hey, maybe you could pretend to be making a wish," I said, trying to get Nana K back on track for the portrait. Her allotted time was almost over, and I'd yet to take a single picture.

"Perfect," she agreed.

I gave a sigh of relief and stepped back to get the full scene in the frame. She stood to the side of the well, leaned a hand on the stone edge, and raised a leg like she was kissing a lover. She looked down in the well and made a little "o" with her mouth. I may be bias because she is my Nana, but it was the cutest thing ever.

Until she turned, crossed her eyes, and stuck her tongue out.

"Nana K! You're worse than the preschoolers!" I scolded.

I'd photographed the end of year picnic for the preschool where my best friend, Colleen McMurphy, worked. Anytime one of the little rascals saw me shooting their way, they made a face. That group made me work for the handful of candid shots I felt were salvageable. Very rarely did the "outtakes" folder contain more than the final edits, but it did that day.

"Get one of me doing that duck face. It'll make my cheekbones look fierce." Her duck face more resembled my betta fish, but I snapped away to make her happy. And made a mental note to check who she was following on social media.

"Okay, Nana. I think we got a keeper in that bunch." I wasn't going to tell her it was the first shot I took.

"Let me see 'em," she said. Her deluge of costume jewelry jangling as she tottered toward me. I held my camera out of her reach.

"Oh no. I have a strict policy. Clients do not peep at the back of my camera."

"I am not a client, Alexandretta Lightwood. I'm your grandmother! The matriarch of your family. The life blood of your lineage."

"All true. But today, you're also a client. So, hands off."

She crossed her arms like a petulant child again. I giggled remembering my earlier comparison to the preschoolers. Life really was a cycle.

I swear I looked down for one second to pack up my gear in anticipation of meeting the next client in her room as we'd arranged—she was going to pose by her collection of porcelain cat figurines—only to glance back up and see Nana K with her head in the well again. Both feet were suspended in the air.

"Nana K!" I shouted.

She startled, tipped precariously forward, but managed through some miracle of physics to right herself, thank goodness.

"What were you doing?" I admonished.

"I dropped my glasses down there," she said. "And I wanted to see if I could reach the pennies. We've got Bridge tonight. It would teach those card sharks a lesson if I used their own wishes to bet against them. Half of them pretend to be senile just to get away with things."

"I'm sure you've never done that," I said sarcastically.

"Who me?" She batted her eyelashes. Wait a minute, were they fake? I didn't even wear fake eyelashes.

"So, you gonna get my glasses or what? I paid two bucks for those suckers at the Dollar Store," Nana K said.

I didn't think I'd be able to reach them either. I may have three and half inches on her in height, but my arms were just as stubby. Still, it was easier to pretend to try than to argue with Nana K. I put my camera bag beside the well and peered into the darkness. It was deeper and darker than I thought. I leaned over the edge in a half-hearted effort to reach the bottom, which I couldn't see.

But Nana was hip to my game. She pulled my feet up and pushed me forward until my entire upper body was down in the well.

"Pull me back up this instant!" I shouted, trying to push against the wall of the well with my hands. The kept slipping on the damp and mossy surface. It smelled terrible in there.

"I got you. Just reach a little further. I think I almost had them before."

"I'll buy you new ones. Just pull me up."

"See if you can grab some change while you're down there too," she suggested.

Completely at her mercy, I sighed and slowly reached down toward the dark abyss. My fingers felt nothing but air. As a passing cloud revealed a bit of sun, something shone from the side of the well just opposite me.

"I think I actually see them on a little ledge. Can you push me just a smidge forward without dropping me?" I asked. I suddenly flashed to the scene at the end of *Indiana Jones and the Last Crusade* when Indy was reaching for the cup of Christ in the ravine. Luckily, Indy's dad was able to pull him back to safety.

My grandmother, on the hand, dropped me.

Chapter 2

There are not many times that being short has been to my advantage. In fact, I could probably count them on one hand: when playing hide-and-seek—I can squeeze into impossibly tight spots; when buying clothing—my size is always in stock; when flying on an airplane—I don't mind a middle seat; and when falling down—I'm closer to the ground, so it doesn't hurt as much.

I could now add "when being pitched down a well" to the list. Like a cat, I somehow managed to curl myself into a ball and land more on my hands and knees and pretty much avoid the rocky edges with my head.

"*Kurwa!*" Nana K's voice echoed down the well. I don't know a lot of Polish, but I know I got my mouth washed out with soap for saying that one when I was younger. Grampa K thought it was hilarious to teach me. I thought he should've been the one eating Ivory.

"I'm okay," I said, when I got my breath back. Marginally okay anyway. It was darker than midnight in a jungle cave and smelled just as bad. At least I landed on soft dirt and not in a pool of stank, old water. Only about an inch or so covered the bottom of the well. I could feel the years of coins digging into my knees and hands as I slowly sunk into the muck.

"I'm calling Security," Nana K said. "Just hold on."

"Tell them to hurry. We might have a quicksand kind of situation happening here," I said trying not to breathe too deeply.

I sat back on my heels, using the rocky sides of the well to help me sit up. I still felt a little dizzy from the fall—and the smell—and didn't trust myself to stand right away. How deep was I? Could I simply climb out? The fall didn't seem that long.

While I waited for the nausea to clear, I felt around for Nana's glasses. My eyes weren't adjusting to the pitch darkness, so I shoved a handful of the dirty coins in my pocket instead. Maybe that would get me an extra line in her will. Or at least an extra slice of cheesecake.

No luck on the glasses by feel alone.

"What's happening, Nana?" I called up the well.

"They're on their way. They gotta find a ladder that fits down there. They didn't think the bucket would hold you."

And now I was conjuring images from *Silence of the Lambs*. Great.

My nausea and dizziness had abated some, so I took the risk to stand. Reaching up as far as I could, I was still about a foot away from the top edge of the well. Being stuck in the well was absolutely *not* on the plus side of being short.

I kept moving my feet around to make sure they didn't get sucked too far down into the muck. It was like when you stand in the sand at the beach and let the waves crash over you. Little by little the sand underneath is carried out to sea and more sand is deposited over until your feet are buried. Sometimes you could even see little sand crabs rolling up and down with the ebb and flow of the waves.

Thinking of sand crabs made me wonder what critters could be lurking in the undisturbed depths of this void. I didn't want to think about it, but I had to know. Against my better judgment, I reached into the back pocket of my jeans for my phone.

The pocket was empty.

Well, poo. Had it fallen out? If it landed in this mess on the bottom that probably meant I needed a new one. The smell alone would be hard to combat. I crouched down again and started feeling around in the dirt and along the sides of the well. I'd made it almost all the way around the edge, when my hand disappeared into an opening. I caught myself against the side of the well. With my face.

Trying to wipe the grime and slime from my cheek, I slowly felt along the wall for the opening again. There was a shaft or tunnel or something at the bottom. Probably originally to fill the well from the local stream when it was still functional. I reached in and felt something solid and cold blocking the way. Too soft to be a rock; too hard to be vegetation.

I pulled my hand back immediately, hoping I wasn't patting the backside of a Jurassic-sized spider.

"Nana! Turn on your phone flashlight and shine it down here." My voice sounded high-pitched and thin. I really hated spiders.

"Okay, Peanut." A minute later the shaft was filled with a surprising amount of light. I located her stupid glasses right away and shoved them into the pocket with the coins. I glanced around once again for my phone with no luck. It had either been sucked up by the goop never to be seen again, or I'd left it in my camera bag. Please, let it be the latter.

"Did you find my glasses?" Nana K asked.

I rolled my eyes. "Yes, Nana. I have them."

"Oh goodie." She moved the light away from the well.

"Hey! I'd rather not be stuck in the dark down here!" The light reappeared.

Taking a few deep breaths, I worked up the courage to peer into the small opening at the base of the well.

Please, don't let it be a spider. Please, don't let it be a spider.

When I finally saw what it was, I would have gladly used all those ill-gotten coins in my pocket to wish it were a spider.

I recoiled immediately and swallowed a scream.

"Nana, call the cops," I screeched. If I thought my voice sounded scared before, this was full on panic mode.

Still, my grandmother needed an explanation. "Why?" she asked. "Security can handle a ladder. If I called anyone else, it would be the fire department. If they can get cats out of trees, they can get a Peanut out of a well."

"No, Nana. Call the cops." I took a deep breath and pressed myself as far as I could away from the opening. "There is a dead woman down here."

To Be Continued in *One Click in the Grave*
Book 2 of the
Alex Lightwood Cozy Mystery Series

To keep up with all Alex's adventures, be sure to subscribe to Kari Ganske's Cozy Mystery Newsletter or bookmark her website (kariganske.com)
Get a FREE novella for subscribing to the newsletter!
She promises not to spam you!

Author's Note

TL;DR - I'd love it if you could <u>leave a review on Amazon</u>. Good, bad, or great I genuinely care about what readers think. I'd love to say I write for myself, but really, I want to reach readers like so many authors have reached me. I read every single one of the reviews and take any feedback with me when writing and editing the next book.

Thank you so much for reading one of my books! This was so much fun to write. The Alex Lightwood series is the first series of books I've written and published in the cozy mystery genre, so it has a special place in my heart. Although the idea of a mystery series has been marinating for a while—and by a while, I mean *years*—the COVID-19 pandemic gifted me the time and opportunity to really bring my musings to fruition. If nothing else good came out of lock-down, for me this series was it!

I've been an avid reader of mysteries since I learned the ABCs. Cozy mysteries especially really speak to my true crime loving soul. As though maybe one day *I* could become an amateur sleuth and solve a real-life mystery. While I love true crime, the process of solving the mystery is really what intrigues me. Which is another reason why the cozy genre was a perfect fit.

My kids (two daughters who also love to read and write) are finally old enough to entertain themselves—praise be—so I had some extra hours to spend in the world of Piney Ridge, Maryland. I hope you enjoyed being immersed in it as much as I did! Although I took some inspiration from my real small-town hometown, most of Piney Ridge is an amalgamation of everywhere I've lived and many of my own experiences growing up in small town Maryland.

Since my husband and I have a second chance love story, I knew I wanted to include that trope in this book too. We dated in high school—after having met in marching band—but then lost touch after we graduated. Teasingly, he never lets me forget that I broke up with him when I was in 10th grade—an egregious error that is apparently not remedied by the fact that I did marry him and have had his children. Luckily, a decade after high school, we reconnected and have been inseparable ever since. Perhaps Linc and Alex can find a happily ever after as well...

Although, like many of you, I read voraciously and in all genres, my favorite genre is actually romantic suspense. Give me some crime, some murder, some adventure, an alpha male, an equally strong female, and a death threat and I'm all in. Since I'm also a true crime junkie/murderino, I have a lot of plots and characters swimming around in my brain, so there will be many more Alex Lightwood adventures to come.

Why photography? Because I was always told to write what I know. And I'm a hobbyist photographer as well. You can follow my photography (mostly pictures of my kids and farm) on Instagram (@kariganskephotograpy) http://www.instagram.com/kariganskephotography if you are interested in photography. I'd love to connect with other photographers—both hobbyist and professional!

As a new author, and a teacher trying to overcome the "those who can't do, teach" cliché, I'd love to hear your thoughts on this first series. What did you love? What was your favorite part? What left you wanting more? What photography questions do you have?

One way to connect is through the Amazon reviews. Good, bad, or great I genuinely care about what readers think. I'd love to say I write for myself, but really, I want to reach readers like so many authors have reached me. I read every single one of the reviews and take any feedback with me when writing and editing the next book. Plus, they let Amazon know that you have read my stuff and they'll put it in even more reader's suggested book lists. And that means that I can supplement my paltry public school teacher's salary and keep writing.

Thanks again for reading! I look forward to hearing from you.

About the Author
Kari Ganske

Kari Ganske, pronounced Gan-ski, is a wife, mother, reader, writer, photographer, fountain soda addict, and true crime aficionado. She married her high school sweetheart and has been a hopeful romantic ever since. She lives with her husband, two daughters, and a menagerie of animals on a small farm in rural Maryland. When she isn't writing, you can find her binging true crime shows or stalking her kiddos with her camera.

She has a dual B.A. in English—Secondary Education and Psychology. Kari's Master's Degree in Liberal Arts included classes in ceramics, grammar/linguistics, the madness in genius, and juggling among other things. She still practices juggling with oranges in her kitchen much to the delight of her children and horror of her husband.

Check out Kari's official website for Giveaways, blog entries, and more. Follow her on the socials for updates. Or join her mailing list to help make decisions about future novels! She loves connecting with her readers about reading and photography.

Newsletter (FREE book):
https://dl.bookfunnel.com/ssn3i8nmeh
Email: kariganskeauthor@gmail.com
Instagram: @kariganskephotography
Amazon Author Page: https://www.amazon.com/Kari-Ganske/e/B093HHB4TL
Goodreads:
https://www.goodreads.com/author/show/21452303.Kari_Ganske
Bookbub: https://www.bookbub.com/profile/kari-ganske
Website: https://www.kariganske.com/

SCAN ME to go to Kari's Website

269